T]

TOMBSTONE MAKER'S DAUGHTER

THE
TOMBSTONE MAKER'S DAUGHTER

AMANDA TAYLOR

Published by West End Publications

WE
WEST END
PUBLICATIONS

A CIP catalogue record for this book is available from the British Library.

ISBN 978-1-0687998-0-8

Book layout and cover design by Clare Brayshaw

Prepared and printed by:

York Publishing Services Ltd
64 Hallfield Road
Layerthorpe
York YO31 7ZQ

Tel: 01904 431213

Website: www.yps-publishing.co.uk

Narcissus was a handsome Greek youth who rejected the desperate advances of the nymph Echo. As punishment he was doomed to fall in love with his own reflection in a pool of water. Unable to consummate his love, Narcissus lay gazing enraptured into the pool, hour after hour, and finally pined away, changing into the flower that bears his name.

CHAPTER ONE

It had been all of eighteen years or more. The ending had come in autumn, a suitable season for endings.

He had never known anyone who thought like her, expressed herself like she did. He had grown to love her deeply, yet she had given him so much more pain than kindness and love.

He stood by his horse, high on the cliff, watching her. He was partially concealed in sand dunes and the grey-green tufts of marram grass. He never thought he would see this beach and sea again. He never thought he would live to see her again. Today he desperately wanted to see her without being seen. He traced his fingertips down the raised scar that ran from the corner of his left eye to his mouth. Not like this – never like this.

That last time she had been wearing a Puritan dress. On his return to England, he had noticed that the female dresses of his homeland had become far brighter and cleaner than those of continental women. Since his years of exile in France, he had to admit he was more than familiar with women's plain gowns and petticoats, and regrettably what lay beneath them. Such pleasures were fleeting, never lasting, failed to fulfil him. The love of flesh alone, wasn't love at all.

He felt ashamed of those memories. He would never have acted the same with a fellow countrywoman. Although he remembered he had come close, as near as dammit, to full intimacy with the girl, now a woman, shimmering on the beach below. Within their community to act in such a way always led to commitment, a commitment he would have been willing to rush into with her despite knowing he was at risk. With her he always felt like a male garden spider about to be devoured by its mate. Maybe things would have turned out differently if she had become pregnant. Either way she consumed him.

Gone was the svelte twenty year old, a wild romping girl who acted like a spirited boy, a tomboy in the true sense of the word. She had grown fuller with the years, a woman approaching her middle years. If anything she was more beautiful than his memory of her.

She tossed her head. Her flaxen hair had the suspicion of copper in it. It reminded him of festuca that burst into the colour of a sunrise on Bodmin Moor in June. He felt his heart bursting out of his chest wall with want.

In contrast the sea rolled in calm in mood, an empty peaceful blue expanse. There wasn't even a bark sail to be seen out there on the horizon. Old Noll's troops had driven him and his kind from their native land, pursued them across the water. Not a quiet water like the one now but a cruel violent sea to match the emotional upheaval of leaving all he knew behind.

Why had her father and her eldest brother chosen to follow Cromwell, when a fine hall and deep love was promised to their kinswoman? Why had they banned him from their house, their lives, because he chose to follow the King? So many lives ruined for the same.

All was lost to them now with an avenging Charles II back on the throne of England. All was lost to him and the woman a long time ago. Still that flutter in his chest like a caged bird at the sight of her.

He held the reins of his horse, and again with his free hand nervously fingered the scar. The blade had struck him out of nowhere, the edge so sharp at first he hadn't felt it.

No, now was not the time to reintroduce himself to the tombstone maker's daughter. Thomas Huck reluctantly mounted his horse and turned for home and his estate.

* * *

Someone had been watching her. Whether or not the woman was aware, sensed it … She sat on a rush mat on the beach examining and separating stones. Her cream petticoat and green overdress billowing about her like an exotic nest.

With Cromwell dead, it was a relief to have some colour back in her life. Gone were the drab greys and browns of the Puritan age. She speculated that the wearing of colour was the English reaction to the austerity they had just endured. Gone were the high necklines hiding her credentials for an improbable motherhood at thirty-eight, gone now was her desire to reproduce herself.

She jingled the pebbles together – orange, pink, red and blues. No rare gems to be had here. Nothing of value amid the white veined quartz invading slate, quartz that would eventually be released like a pale prisoner to look up glinting into the sun. Disappointed, she threw them all back onto the sand. That is when she saw it. Reaching out she stretched forward, too lazy to get to her feet.

She examined the hag stone carefully. A lucky fairy stone, a small perfect hole bored through the middle. She could do with some luck. Her village could do with a little luck at this moment in time. The whole of England could do with some luck going into the future. She rolled the stone in the palm of her hand and prayed silently that it would protect her against curses and pestilence.

Folk believed hag stones were formed by Druid magic. She did not believe this. She believed them to be the remains of molluscs which had once penetrated soft rock, died and dissolved, leaving only an empty space as to their existence.

'Ghostly fossils that is what they are,' her father once told her.

She could understand this. Knew her father to be a fine mason, practical though uneducated. Knew he was knowledgeable to the ways of nature, to the fish in the sea, to the beasts on land, to the birds in the sky, if not to her. But, as she rolled the stone over in her hand, something primitive inside her wished it to have magical powers, powers that could help her situation.

Her whole life seemed to be made up of stones, stones on the beach, the tombstones her father erected and carved while she played as a child in the graveyard. She looked to the stone again in her practical hands, big artisan hands like her father's, and wished her spirit was at peace like the folk resting in the graveyard under the trees.

England had suffered years of turmoil – those loyal to the Crown and those loyal to Cromwell. Iben's own family had been divided by their allegiances. Many good men had died including an uncle on the Cavaliers' side at Naseby. Her eldest brother, Raph, had been spared but still bore emotional scars. Both he and their father had fought for Parliament and later in Cromwell's newly formed Model Army, an army known to their enemies as 'ironsides' because of their intransigence in battle.

A returning Parliamentarian soldier, who had joined up with Cromwell from their village alongside her father and brother, told her that her favourite uncle had been unlucky to fall victim when the Cavaliers were first routed. The soldier regarded her unnervingly with one eye. The other had been gouged out by an enemy sword during the heat of battle, the lid roughly sewn over the empty socket soon afterwards by a barber surgeon attending the field, he explained.

Were such tragedies a matter of bad luck, she wondered, or had God himself brought this division upon them. If so, why? She glanced to the sky and then back across the water. There was no God, only the eternal motion out there, she was sure of it now.

As she watched the waves curling in and gently slipping back, with her free hand she pushed strands of escaping hair out of her eyes. Often she had her hair plaited neatly down her back but not today, today was a day of freedom. This sea had moulded her like the pebble she held. Her moods even fluctuated like the sea, sometimes she wished it was otherwise, but that was the way it was.

She pushed her little finger through the hole of the hag stone. Some believed the stone to have fertility properties. She knew lovers who had gifted them to each other as a pledge or romantic invitation, the biggest stones often taking pride of place in their homes. An old grandfather, on a neighbouring farm, had told her that the hag stone represented the sacred vagina of the fertility goddess and could create powerful love spells and potency. She wasn't sure if the old man was gaining lewd pleasure from telling her these things or if he really believed them. Couples, he told her, would insert a stone or stick to fit exactly into the hole, make a love request, and throw the connected pair into the sea. What better way to bind lovers for eternity.

Thinking of the old fellow's rotting teeth and lascivious mouth as he formed the words, she flung the hag stone with disgust into the approaching waves. She no longer had a wish to be burdened by a child or a man's love. She had loved deeply once and that had come to naught. She had no inclination to try again.

Strangely though when she had suffered from louse-borne typhus many moons ago, her one thought was that it was a tragedy that she would die without a family of her own and many children. Sensing the disease was upon her, she had taken herself to the river. Washed naked and dressed in fresh clothing, burning her original garments at great cost. Next she had taken to her bed with a potion of honey and crushed garlic. There she had remained for two weeks in isolation from the rest of the family. Bread and meat broth were left outside her door once her health began to improve. The contents of her chamber pot were flung out of the window. It took her another two months before she regained her full strength.

Desire was left far behind these days, survival alone was difficult enough. Despite having a mother, she played mother to the family. She cooked and cleaned for an apathetic matriarch, her disengaged father, her malevolent eldest brother and simple younger brother Walter. Though he was witless, Walter was the nearest thing she knew to love. She loved him because he was helpless, solely dependent on her and demanded nothing more than a cuddle from time to time. Above all she loved him because he wasn't judgemental. She could not take criticism. She could not take rejection either as she had had to cope with maternal rejection from an early age. Then there had been the rejection, or more accurately indifference, by someone she loved very much. Thereafter Iben would spurn first rather than be abandoned later.

* * *

Iben, Iben Hartmann – a name handed down through the generations from her Norse forebears. Men and women who had settled and farmed northern lands some eight hundred years before.

Josh Haymaker rather fancied himself as an irresistible Viking warrior carrying off a fair maiden, or more precisely maidens in the plural. Iben was a little special though. Huck wasn't the only one to have once been connected to her. Haymaker had returned from his post-war travels earlier than Thomas. During and since the war he had done his fair share of whoring at home and abroad, but, unlike Thomas, he had no shame about seeking pleasure wherever he could get it. Josh was adaptable, a lad of the land. He had known Iben since childhood. He had never deceived himself into thinking their relationship was anything other than physical desire, certainly not a romantic one. Josh didn't do romance. In truth he barely thought of Iben nowadays. He had found her a funny creature, spiritual in many ways. He had to admit she wasn't like the usual women he coupled with. Maybe he liked her more than he was willing to admit. Though their relationship was years old, the memory of her body for him had remained young and pure in comparison with those creatures of the night.

Once he had withdrawn from her, they lay wrapped together in silence. One time she had whispered breaking the spell, 'I love you more than life itself.' Josh had not known what to make of this, had been annoyed by it at first. How can anyone love anyone more than life itself? But standing there on the battlefield about to die, it was Iben's compliment rather than all the lustful acts he had indulged in with other women that came to mind.

He had quite enjoyed being part of Cromwell's Model Army. A pikeman, he felt dapper in his red woollen uniform, the uniform was a great pull for women. Josh was a rather inadequate man who needed a regular supply of puffing chest approval and lots of it.

He was aware of Iben's liaison with Thomas Huck but that was just one of those things. Huck could give Iben so much more materially than he ever could. He accepted that. However if he had ever come across Huck in the field, Josh had vowed he would spear him in the back like a fish.

* * *

He was in a wooden crate with only his head exposed to the sky through a small square hole. He was being swept in this wooden coffin down one of the great rivers of the New World – rivers that explorers of the previous century described as angry foaming waters falling from a great height. Trapped, nailed down and helpless, he knew he was doomed.

Thomas woke up in a sweat. His dream had been so vivid. What could it mean? He knew it must have something to do with Iben Hartmann. Before the Great Rebellion altered everything, before this war divided kinsfolk and friends alike, he and she would have generally been acknowledged by the community as a couple about to be betrothed. But privately Iben had always given him mixed signals. She would be sweet one minute and then harsh the next. It was as if she were two people. *She loves me, she loves me not*, became everyday for him. Often she would treat him with offhanded indifference then occasional affection. Thomas wondered if the problem was that she felt pressured into a match with him – a beneficial marriage, beneficial for the whole Hartmann family. Was she playing hard to get or impossible to get? For him Iben was light and shade. He felt there was always something she was holding back from him.

Then the war came for him and changed all that. One day he found her poor peasant family and his rich Royalist family were firmly on opposing sides. He wrote to her before he went off to war. He had taught her to read a little. She was a fast and easy learner. However she did not reply to his letter. He tried to visit her on the day he was going away, but John Hartmann senior, her father, barred him from their cottage, banned him from seeing his daughter ever again. Strange, in any other circumstance, this behaviour would have been expected from his family rather than hers. Though he was only a second son, Thomas knew his father would have disapproved of the match had he lived. But Sir William had been killed along with Thomas' elder brother, Robert, at Lostwithiel early on in the conflict, only thirty miles or so east of where he was standing at present. Well before taking up arms, Sir William had betrothed his second son to a gentlewoman near St Clether. Thomas was fourteen, the girl twelve, when the deal had been fixed by their fathers. No papers were actually signed just a loose understanding between gentlemen.

With both fathers dead in battle the promise was lost in the mire of war. Thomas was now the sole inheritor of Rockfoot Hall and the vast Cornish family estate that went with it. He could do and marry as he pleased.

The Hartmanns' cottage was situated on a neighbouring estate whose landowner embraced the Parliamentarian cause. A further cause for hostility, turmoil and embarrassment between neighbours.

Although pressed for space, Iben had her own bedchamber in the cottage which she guarded jealously from other family members. Thomas had been allowed in that chamber only once and he was surprised to find Artemisia Gentileschi's *Mary Magdalene as Melancholy* in such humble surroundings. Some student of Gentileschi must have copied her masterpiece, or maybe an English artist visiting Italy, or an artist meeting Artemisia while she worked with her father for Charles I. Iben told him the picture had been given to her by a better-off uncle who owned land with a tin mine near Camborne. Iben revered that painting by the female artist. There was something that seemed to speak to her directly, some heaviness of mood that she identified with but as a man he could never lessen or reach. Perhaps it was too much time spent playing among the graves as her silent father erected those tombstones, perhaps there were difficult relationships within that poor confined dwelling, perhaps, perhaps many things.

Sighing Thomas drew back one side of the heavy drapes surrounding his poster bed. He felt reluctant to start his day. He was troubled by his dream. Hadn't Iben always put him in a box, away from any greater intimacy with those close to her? Didn't she always compartmentalise everything? Of course that was the meaning of his dream. Pulling up his breeches, he was content to start his day with this interpretation. However, for all that, he was less than happy to realise that he still loved her, had always loved her. He also knew that now with his disfigurement he had little or no chance of winning her back – if he had ever won her at all. This was his dilemma with Iben. She could say the most romantic things to him, things no one else had ever said, and at other times she would be cold and unresponsive. Always mixed messages – *she loves me, she loves me not …*

During their initial courtship he had been so troubled by Iben's erratic behaviour that he contacted a soothsayer. The old crone lived in a hovel on the edge of his estate. She had an ugly parchment face in a curtain of long white hair. Her hair was tinged yellow from the clay pipe she habitually smoked, and from the open hearth that burned peat night and day in the middle of the floor of her cottage.

'Love for you will never be straightforward,' she croaked. 'Partly through your own doing as you always desire perfection.'

His visits to the old woman became more regular. Bewildered by Iben's frequent, casual offhand attitude, he sought more reassurances. Finally even the soothsayer began to weary. She pointed out that there must be problems with the relationship or Thomas would not need to consult her so often.

'Leave her be. She is only a poor maid whereas a fine young gentleman like yourself could have the pick of the cornfield rather than the chaff come harvest time. Without the need of troths and rings,' she added.

Thomas never visited her again. He did not want the pick of the cornfield, he wanted Iben. Perhaps there was one of the reasons for his obsession – for once he couldn't have something he wanted.

He next resorted to flipping a coin. The result as topsy turvy as Iben's changing nature. *She loves me, she loves me not.* If the coin fell with the face of the hedonistic Charles I upright then Iben loved him. He did not of course believe in luck or fate, he just wished it to be so. He did not believe in fantasy but what else had he to fall back on.

With war all that had come to an end. There was no time for the spinning coin.

And yet, and yet, what had kept him going through those long hours of fear, hunger and bloody battles, followed by exile in a foreign land, had been the memory of Iben's face, the sound of her climaxing through his stroking fingers. That was as close as she would allow him to full intimacy. The memory of Iben was something he shared with Josh Haymaker, an enemy soldier, something that saw them both through the most distressful life-and-death experiences of their young lives.

CHAPTER TWO

'Well, well, so you are finally back. And where are you bound for?'

'The Five Weeks Fair at Truro.' Thomas decided to give a civilised exchange a chance at first.

'Aye, the one at High Cross. What are you after there?' asked the countryman, pausing in his hay hauling and adjusting one shoulder beneath his cloak as he looked up at the horseman.

'A tenant of mine wishes to buy a flock of Longwool sheep.'

'Longwools? Would have to be in these parts. Thems shall cost thee a shilling or twain,' said the man. Thomas merely nodded not rising to the bait. 'But then I expect money is no problem to the likes of thee. So who's the lucky tenant?'

'Jowan Carter, if it is any business of yours.'

'Oh, Jowan. Jowan Carter over at Beechfield?'

'Too many questions, Raph,' said Thomas, his patience finally snapping above the head of Iben's brother. 'I would have thought you were at the church assisting your father with the stones.'

'Not enough work for the two of us,' replied Hartmann. 'And particularly as we've set on another skilled mason who will need paying.'

'If the plague spreads here from London, you'll find plenty of employment.'

'God save us from that.' Hartmann surprisingly crossed himself in the old manner despite fighting in the Puritan army.

'So how did your war go?' he asked Thomas, abruptly changing the subject from plague to the Wars of the Three Kingdoms.

Thomas made no answer. The temperature between the two men cooling further.

'We won at great cost but …' continued Hartmann before stopping mid-sentence on closer scrutiny of Thomas' scarred face. 'I see we have marked thee for the cowardly scum that you are.'

'And that said from a traitor.'

'A traitor is it?' lisped Hartmann, raising his pitchfork threateningly towards Thomas' face. 'The only traitor was your man, Charles I, a traitor to his hard working subjects. We've succeeded in getting rid of him at least.'

'But not his son.' Thomas' horse shuffled impatiently beneath him.

'Aye, his son.' Hartmann spat on the ground.

'You ought to be glad that you are not tenants on the Rockfoot Estate, because in my father's time he had to raise a small army for the King, an army in which you and your father would have been forced to serve.'

Scowling Hartmann responded with an obscene gesture.

Although there was something mean and spiteful in Hartmann's manner, there was something else, something skulking, cowering and not quite masculine there too. 'The King is raising taxes on all the noble families hereabouts who embraced Parliament's cause. Which falls on a doubling of rents for us their tenants, society's riffraff.'

'Be glad you were not hanged, drawn and quartered when his son took the throne. There is something to be said for being riffraff.'

'Maybe, but we are being slowly starved to death instead.'

'Regards to your sister.' Thomas raised his tall-crown hat with a sarcastic smile.

'There's lots you don't know about her either,' shouted Raph, after the wide retreating backside of Thomas' stallion. 'Lots best not knowing.'

'I knew enough.'

'Stay away from her. Do you hear me? Stay away from our Iben.' Raph's words became thinned in the wind until they were lost completely.

* * *

Truro was heaving with folk coming to buy and sell. Drunks tumbled out of the tavern doors fighting fit, looking for a brawl. Yelping dogs attacked each other, fur flying across the cobbles. The cockpit was filling up with betting men eager to witness the Welsh Main. Sixteen cocks with only the last standing taking the prize. Soon the pit punters would add to the drunks spilling out onto the streets, adding to the mayhem as small skirmishes flared up through claims of being robbed.

The town's energy hit Thomas like a blast of heat as he entered Old Bridge Street. One time soldiers now beggars reached up to touch the hem of his riding coat as he passed between the closely pressed houses. Many of these men had lost arms, legs and mutilations of their favoured hands – all their fingers cut off. Added insurance that they would never wield a sword again. Cruelty in war has no boundaries. Thomas realised that not so long ago some of these men would have been his enemies in Cromwell's army, some perhaps had been allies, some might have been his patients on the battlefield.

War, as it had for so many others, had interfered with Thomas' education. Just as he had begun a medical course at

Edinburgh, he had been seconded into Charles I army as a military physician. They must have judged two years of study sufficient enough to take the needle and knife into the field of battle, then again both sides were desperate for doctors and even the less respected barber surgeons to deal with terrible battlefield wounds.

Yes, some of these poor maimed souls he might have done his best to stitch up or operate on. Outside St Mary's Church he decided to reward them, and then wished he hadn't as he watched them scrabbling over each other to scratch in the dirt for the odd copper coin.

Once he had procured a bed for himself for the night and stabling for Russel at The Bear, Thomas set off on foot for the sheep pens.

He was amused watching the townswomen of Truro trying to negotiate the horseshit and rotting fruit in their long skirts. Despite leering men, lifting seemed the preferred method for avoiding the filth. He was grateful that he wasn't so encumbered.

He elbowed his way to the Devon Longwool pens. The farmers stuck out proud chests as if they too were for sale. They appeared to see him coming. From his manner of dress they could sense a few guineas might be heading their way.

Thomas moved from one pen to another assessing the livestock. He always found the Devons particularly appealing with their fulsome curly forelocks and fleeces. And perhaps more to his liking was that their meat was sweet and much valued.

'Sir Thomas, a good morning to you,' shouted a farmer from across the street. 'How goes it with thee?'

'Well. I am well on the whole,' replied Thomas. 'One of my

tenants is looking to build up his flock. I've decided to gift him a few Devons to set him going.'

Joseph Crenshaw nodded, interested. 'I might be able to help you there.' He indicated several pens crowded with panting sheep moving like choppy disconnected waves in the limited space.

Knowing Crenshaw to be a fair man, Thomas crossed towards him.

'I like the look of those,' he told him.

'Pretty aren't they?'

'How much a pen?'

Crenshaw raised all the fingers on his right hand. 'Guineas,' he said.

'Six for both pens.'

Crenshaw's brow wrinkled offence. 'Six, sir?'

'Eight for both pens then. Any rams?' asked Thomas.

'Aye, one or two behind there.'

Thomas stared into the white faces of three small rams. They looked sturdy with good fleeces.

'How much?' he asked again.

'How much are you willing to give?' asked a more circumspect Crenshaw.

'Ten for the three.'

'Ten?' Crenshaw shook his head, feigning outrage. 'These are three of the finest Devon rams.'

'Fifteen then,' offered Thomas hopefully.

The farmer took his outstretched hand reluctantly, muttering that it was the end of the day.

'Will you be able to deliver them to Jowan Carter at Beechfield Farm on the Rockfoot Estate?' asked Thomas.

'The day after the morrow,' agreed Crenshaw.

Through the throng of people and livestock, Thomas spotted Agnes Hartmann's small stall. She stood behind a sparse selection of homemade rushlights and eggs.

'How's business, Aggie?'

'Fine, fine and yourself, sir?' she asked out of the side of her mouth. Aggie's face was deeply wrinkled, her body wizened and, like the soothsayer of old, her teeth stained yellow from the small clay pipe that was invariably in her mouth. Her teeth clamped onto the pipe like an infant onto its mother's teat. Thomas had often wondered how a creature like Aggie could have given birth to a beauty like Iben. He could never imagine Aggie being anything other than ugly. However his reception from her was far better than that from her eldest son.

'Passed the time of day with your Raph on my way over here,' he told her.

''Im,' sniffed Agnes. 'Shouldn't have bothered with 'im. Was he shirking as usual?'

'He seemed to be lifting straw for winter feed.'

'I've no time for any of the men in my house,' sniffed Aggie. 'A lazy lot made worse with drink after the war.'

'And Iben?'

'Oh, our Iben is a good enough lass. She's a hard worker. Still carry a little flame for her, do you sir?'

'Many flames have come and gone since I was acquainted with Iben.' Thomas flushed up.

'But none that have kept burning?'

'Alas, no.'

'Would you like me to speak to Iben on your behalf? Though she be a funny mowes and her heart's difficult to fathom.'

'As the Greek, Heraclitus, said, "No man ever steps in the same river twice, for it's not the same river and he's not the same man."'

'I am only a simple woman, sir, and know nothing of clever Greeks. But I do not agree with that. It might not be the same water but it is the same river and man. Folk do not change that easily.'

'Perhaps you are right, Mother Hartmann, though we evolve we are basically the same person.'

'I don't follow all thy fancy words, sir, but would you like me to pay your respects to our Iben?'

'Thank you, Mother, but I think that it is better that you do not.' Thomas raised his capotain to take his leave.

'But I think you still have love for my daughter.'

'Do *you* have love for your daughter?' Thomas dared to enquire.

'A strange question that to ask a mother.'

Thomas smiled, knowing it was the most pertinent question he had asked in a long time. If there was one thing he had learnt about Iben, it was that she felt both used and unloved by her mother. Her mother was forever telling her she hadn't wanted children, certainly not a daughter, a sense of rejection had come early for Iben. Thomas suspected this maternal rebuff had created an emotional void for any of Iben's developing relationships. But then, although they had been somewhat physically intimate, he was aware that emotionally he knew so little of Iben. Secret Iben was an enigma.

'She's good with our poor Walter, I'll give her that,' Agnes Hartmann shouted after him.

From High Cross, Thomas decided to explore Truro. His boots were growing heavy with animal and human filth. He was walking in a daze after his encounter with Aggie. What a terrible woman, he thought.

Agnes from St Agnes. He wondered if Aggie's given name had been inspired by the place name. It couldn't be so. Hadn't

Aggie come from away? The village and parish had got its name from the local legend of Bolster. Bolster was a mighty giant who terrified the villagers and was alleged to eat small children, but he fell in love with a young woman called Agnes and wanted to marry her. Seeing a way to free the community from his tyranny, Agnes asked Bolster to prove his love for her by filling a hole in the rocks by Chapel Porth with his blood. What he didn't realise was that the hole ran right down through the cliffs and opened into the sea, and so the more blood Bolster let bleed into the hole, the more ran out of the bottom and the hole never filled. Having rid the parish of Bolster, Agnes was proclaimed a heroine. Thomas imagined such a cunning trick wouldn't be beyond Aggie, her current namesake. And this the mother of a fascinating beautiful daughter like Iben. The Iben he remembered was all of that. Intriguing, her mind was intriguing, you never knew which direction it would take her in. Indeed he suspected she never knew herself.

Still lost in thought he was approaching The Red Lion, at the corner of Calenick Street and Victoria Square, when a young lass standing on the pavement outside suddenly stepped forward blocking his route. She had a fiddle in hand. She could not have been more than fourteen or fifteen. There was an open cap with a few coins in it by her right foot.

'Would you like me to play something for you, sir? she asked, lifting the instrument to her shoulder.

Thomas shook his head, eager now for supper and a good bottle of red wine.

'Something slow or lively?' Her lilting accent wasn't local or English.

'Where are you from child?' he asked.

'From across the water.'

'Where?'

'Ireland, sir.'

'And your name?'

She hesitated. 'Ayla, sir. Ayla Nolan.'

'So how does Ayla Nolan finish up in Truro?'

'The land failed. Land that had to support me and my fifteen brothers and sisters.'

Thomas winced, he knew that Cromwell's army had committed summary executions, slashed and burnt swathes of land to subjugate the Irish – the Irish Catholics.

'Then the pestilence …' mumbled Ayla.

'Of what persuasion are you Ayla?'

Ayla frowned, her mouth clamped.

A question too far, recognised Thomas.

'How old are you, Ayla?'

'Eighteen, sir.'

'Eighteen?' It could be so though Ayla looked barely out of swaddling clothes.

'If music isn't to your taste.' She lifted her skirt a little, instrumentalist turned to coquette in an instant. 'Would you like to take your pleasure with me in the inn's back yard, sir?'

'Another time perhaps,' replied Thomas, throwing a farthing or two into the hat.

'A shilling for a minute or two by the stable,' she persisted; her voice high in accordance with just being out of the crib.

He shooed her away. He had no desire to take his comfort by a stable with a child, not with his stomach growling with hunger and his head fresh with thoughts of Iben. Although pathetically thin, walking away back along Boscawen Street, he had to admit the girl was pleasing enough with her long flowing titian locks. Her grubby face concealed fine features.

* * *

'Saw Thomas Huck at Five Weeks Fair around noontime,' Agnes told her daughter that evening. The older woman regarded Iben intensely. Raph and his father pricked up their ears. Walter kept singing nonsense and smiling at Iben inanely.

'What's that to me?' snapped Iben.

'Just that he was your intended at one time.'

'I wasn't his first choice and that was a long time ago,' she replied sulkily. 'He left for war without so much as a goodbye.'

'That might be so but I think he still carries a torch for you. He isn't spoken for yet either,' insisted Agnes.

'Some maid will be after his fortune soon enough. That maid will certainly not be me.'

'He's Sir Thomas Huck now.' Agnes' shrewd eyes narrowed.

'By hook or by crook,' sneered her husband.

'By hook or by crook, by hook or by crook,' sang Walter.

'Sole owner of Rockfoot,' emphasised Agnes, undaunted by her family's usual pandemonium.

'Our lass has no time for anybody but herself,' scoffed her husband.

'Then she takes after you, ye old goat,' snapped Agnes.

Raph and his father fell quiet. Iben knew nothing of the ban they had imposed on Thomas, or how they had watched gloating over his passionate letter of farewell to her burning in their hearth. But she did not miss the curious look that passed between father and son. Cromwell's New Model Army – a time for the poor man's revenge on his rich masters.

'Our lass always preferred Josh Sheep Shagging Haymaker.' Raph cleared his throat. 'Isn't that so, sister?' he asked. Iben blushed anger. 'But he wasn't as good an option as Huck for any bairns she might fall on with. Isn't that the way of it, sister?'

'That's enough,' said Old Hartmann.

'Haymaker, love maker, jumping Josh, that's what I've heard about the village. He met his match with our Iben, only my sister could play two or three fellas at once,' continued Raph.

'Enough, I said,' grunted his father, turning to Iben. 'A hundred years ago you would be walled up in a cell, never to see the light of day.'

'You mean as an anchoress? I would have had to be a lady for that.'

'That you certainly are not,' squawked her mother. 'Though you could be married to Sir Thomas Huck.'

'Not that again,' groaned Iben.

* * *

Tucking into a rare beef fillet, Thomas began to question the coins he had tossed away that afternoon. He had been charitable because he could afford to be. With so much poverty around him was that truly magnanimous or solely an exoneration on his part – an action purely to make him feel better. Next his thoughts turned to Iben and then to the street girl. Maybe he had been too precipitate not to indulge in carnality for a shilling. On the other hand, by a miracle, he had escaped the French disease so far. He had no wish to chance his luck further. He had done his best to treat the genital sores of other men in the field, without he feared much success. Many had obtained these lesions from camp followers, women who followed the baggage wagons for trade. As a student in Edinburgh, Thomas had seen the terrible effects of syphilis in the latter stages.

That night he dreamt he was lying naked next to Iben. She had her back to him and he was locked around her, holding her in an embrace. The dream was more comforting and loving than erotic. Iben twisted round but to his shock and horror the face looking back at him had become Aggie's. In his dream he went desperately in search of Iben asking her friends if they had seen her. But on waking the dream made sense: there was always something out of reach about Iben. She appeared to be in a deep well of unhappiness and try as he might he could not haul her out of it.

The ostler at The Bear had looked after Russel well and the horse looked rested and eager to go.

'Fed her some dried nettles along with oats. She seemed happy with that,' the ostler explained.

He rewarded the man with a few extra coins, again he was playing the big benefactor, but this time it was expected of him. The man grunted his appreciation beneath a mop of red hair.

Making his way out of town, Thomas looked about Calenick Street and Victoria Square to where Ayla had stood on the corner outside The Red Lion. She was not there. Obviously too early for musical entertainment or carnal appetites.

* * *

Iben did her best to avoid Raph for the next few days. She often sought solace in the privacy of her bedchamber. She hated her brother and was afraid of him at the same time. Now she hated him more because he was right: Josh Haymaker's goodbye had been perfunctory at best before going off to war but, for her, it had been worse than receiving no goodbye from Thomas Huck. With Thomas she had avoided a full physical connection, she had played him for better things to come, with Josh her attraction had been electric from a young age, she found it difficult to refuse him. She hated her body for being so weak and accommodating to Josh's needs. She was under no delusion that Josh loved her, Josh loved only himself. That she could understand. She suspected his indifference was part of his attraction – a challenge.

However there had been a miscalculation. Josh had been too pushy one warm summer evening and failed to withdraw in time. She spent weeks fearing she was pregnant again. Since that time Iben had been more cautious regarding her cycle. Much to Josh's chagrin she would refuse him two weeks before she menstruated. She was as regular as the phases of the moon, so the calculation was not hard to make.

Back then she reassured herself that before passion became too intense there was always lime skins and lemon juice. She could not stop herself loving both the fear and danger of Josh. She could not stop herself … maybe the war coming had been a blessing. She could not stop herself so, in many ways, she was glad he had been out of sight, if not out of mind, maybe even dead during all those years of conflict.

However there had been replacements with Haymaker and Huck away at the war. Once broken in by Haymaker to a fulfilling bodily congress, her young fecund body had its needs. She was no angel. For her own enjoyment, she had flirted and allowed one or two village lads to take liberties with her. Some she should have said 'no thank you to' others 'thank you very much for that' but mainly their ejaculations were premature – none of them had the staying power of Josh – usually resulting in a dissatisfying experience for her. Love never cluttered these involvements for Iben. They were merely new adventures, new stimuli, fulfilment of her natural urges. Basically she knew that she lacked warmth and passion deep within, some emotion was missing and dead where it should have been. She knew it but could not change it. Pure lust had some compensations particularly when she began to realise she could not conceive. This left her the freedom to copulate like a man when and where ever she wished.

CHAPTER THREE

The sheep never arrived at Beechfield. On leaving the Parish of Kenwyn where the lane narrowed through a wooded area, the two young shepherds guiding them were leaped upon and badly beaten up with cudgels by three masked men.

'Shitten shepherds,' mocked their assailants, as the two boys watched on semi-conscious, helpless and prone in mud and sheep crap as the flock scattered and were stolen away.

Luckily a pedlar was walking down that green leafed lane a little while later. He dropped his buttons and bows in shock coming across the unfortunate victims, left his colourful merchandise scattered beneath the trees, before running away to summon help from a nearby cottage. The constable was sent for. One of the shepherd boys was severely injured. He had head injuries caused by a final kicking from a heavy boot. The other boy suffered only minor injuries and was soon arrested and accused of collusion with the thieves. After a few days he was released from gaol through lack of evidence.

''Tis a capital offence to purloin one sheep let alone a serious attack on two young lads. Any idea who could be responsible locally, Sir Thomas?' asked Constable Fox.

Thomas hesitated, thought carefully before giving a positive 'no'.

'You'll let me know if you hear talk.'

'Of course. What I don't understand is how can a flock of two dozen sheep simply disappear?'

'You would be surprised,' shrugged the constable. 'They could be butchered and stowed in someone's larder right now.'

Thomas initially did not have any confidence in the constable hired by the community. Although one of the questions Fox asked came to haunt him.

'Who knew you had ordered sheep from the Five Weeks Fair at Truro to be delivered to Jowan Carter's farm?' he had asked. Thomas could only think of the animals' previous owner, farmer Crenshaw, then there was Raph Hartmann and his father. He did not want to think of them, think that they might be culpable, think they might bear him such hatred. Anyway he had no solid proof for that being the case.

* * *

Thomas made his way to Beechfield and Jowan Carter. He had decided to recompense his tenant for the loss of sheep.

Beechfield was a rundown farm just on the far edge of the Rockfoot Estate. There were deep cart ruts on the path leading to the property; holes in the barn big enough for a man to climb through; the gate was hanging open with only a bit of cord to secure it. Jowan was pumping water into an oaken pail out in the yard. He hadn't a wife to help him even with that womanly task. Though it dismayed Thomas to see such neglect in one of his farms, he rationalised that Jowan was single-handed as his sole family – his parents – had died a few years before. That was the problem with a family run farm, if the family died off leaving only one. Thomas rode up and greeted him cheerily. Jowan remained his usual sullen resentful self. He wasn't unusual in this attitude to his landlord. Thomas had got attuned to it. Dismounting he shrugged off the hostile atmosphere.

'I've decided to replace those sheep that were stolen a few weeks back. I expect you have already heard, one of the two lads shepherding them was seriously injured.'

'No, no I haven't heard a thing.' Carter looked genuinely surprised.

'The constable asked me if I have any notion as to who might be responsible for the theft and the assaults. Have you any thoughts on the matter?'

'Not really. Though there were Scottish drovers in the district at the time. They could have easily added my sheep to their flock bound for a local fair.'

'So you don't think it could have been anybody local then?'

'No.'

'Someone who got wind that sheep were on the move?'

'No.' Carter shook his head in bewilderment. ''Twill be the drovers. A low thieving band of men as ever I've seen.'

'Ah, the drovers. The Scottish drovers are always to blame,' replied Thomas, thinking cynically that foreigners are always too easy to blame. 'And a while or so back it was the wolves that got the blame.'

'Aye my grandfather used to tell me that a wolf lived in the forests of Ludgvan, near Penzance,' replied Carter, missing the point. 'The last of his race he was a gigantic specimen, and terrible was the havoc made by him on the flocks. Grandfather said eventually he carried off a child into the greenwoods. This could not be endured, so the peasantry all turned out, and this famous wolf was captured and killed at a farm near Rospeith.'

'I know Rospeith Farm,' said Thomas.

'Everyone knows that farm.' Carter was dismissive.

'I'd best be on my way,' said Thomas, sensing he had outstayed his welcome.

As if eager to see the back of him, Carter helped put Thomas' foot in the stirrup.

'I'll see you have replacement sheep by spring,' Thomas promised him once mounted. 'By the way we are having a Twelfth Night party at Rockfoot Hall. You are more than welcome to attend, Jowan.'

'Not my sort of thing, Sir Thomas.' Carter gave one of those secret smiles of his that conveyed nothing.

* * *

Early next morning there was heavy knocking on Rockfoot's oak door. Breakfasting at the parlour table, Thomas could hear the shuffle of his manservant, Josiah Bentham, making his way to answer the caller. Josiah's boots beat irregular notes as they scraped and dragged across the flagstone floor. Thomas' late father's old retainer was beginning to fail. He hadn't the heart to put the old fellow out to grass just yet.

'It's our Mary,' he heard a male voice calling out to Josiah. A male voice made lighter with anxiety and close to hysteria. 'She's been taken real poorly. Her mother and I are at our wits end. Do you think Sir Thomas might take a look at her? We could think of no one else with medical skills here or hereabouts.'

'I'm not sure ...' The manservant began to explain.

'I am begging you,' pleaded the father. 'Please allow me a word with Sir Thomas.'

'William Wood.' Thomas joined Josiah on the threshold. 'What is this all about?'

'It's our little Mary, she's been taken badly.'

'I am sorry to hear this,' commiserated Thomas. He knew Mary, had seen her many times rolling her hoop down High

Street. She was a beautiful child, doll-like with golden ringlets that jiggled as she moved. 'And how has the illness taken her exactly?'

'Fever, headaches, shivering all the time. We found swellings under her arms and on her neck.'

Thomas' face fell. 'I'll come immediately. Josiah, my medical bag and have my horse made ready.'

'No need for that, sir,' said Wood. 'I have come in my cart. I'll take you and bring you back.'

The door was flung open by a white-faced Mistress Wood on their arrival at the half-timbered thatched farmhouse. Her hair was standing on end like an inmate of the madhouse, three naked unwashed bairns clinging to her skirts and an old woman pushed to the side wall.

'Thank goodness you both have come for she is taken much worse,' she told Thomas and her husband.

'Let me take a look.' Thomas brushed past the mother and children.

Little Mary lay in the one living room. Her face was indistinguishable from the pillow beneath her head. Thomas felt under her armpits and examined the three tumours there, then the one on her neck. They were a mixture of blue, purple and black coloured sores.

'The botch of Egypt', he muttered to himself.

'What's that? What did you say?' asked Mistress Wood.

'These protuberances are made up of corrupt humours and plague poison accumulated under the skin and trying to escape.'

'Plague?' screamed Mistress Wood.

'Plague?' screeched grandma crossing herself.

'I'm afraid so. The location of buboes on the body are taken as an indication of which organ the disease had taken root in.

Under the arms, the heart had been attacked, while the groin is a sign that the liver is harbouring the pest.'

'Are you sure 'tis the Black Death?' asked Wood.

'All the outward signs are there – blains, botches, carbuncles, and buboes. These are the key indicators that your daughter is suffering plague rather than another disease. I fear 'tis the plague,' he emphasised to the collective gathering of father, mother, grandmother and siblings. 'The first thing to do is isolate her from them.' He pointed to the other three children, two young boys and a girl. 'Send them as far away as you can.'

Mistress Wood began to cry. Thomas ignored her.

'This room is cold. We need plenty of heat and smoke to cleanse the impure air. I must give thought to any further treatment.' He nodded towards William Wood to make his exit. Turning back from the door he told Mistress Wood, 'Have no fear I will be back tomorrow.'

That night there was a hammering on the door. There was an urgency to the knocking. Thomas did not wait for Josiah to answer it.

'Mary is much worse, sir. We fear she is slipping,' said Wood.

'I will come with you shortly in your cart. Allow me to put on my boots and day clothes.'

Mistress Wood and grandma in the corner were weeping. The one candle cast an eerie light on Mary's bloodless face which was if anything more devoid of colour than before. He noticed the slight discolouration of her nose and fingers. Lifting her nightshirt he began to examine the inert prostrate body. There was a protuberance beginning to form in the little girl's groin area. Mary's petite toes were turning black too. Her breathing was laboured. Thomas put his ear to her chest, her heart beat sounded weak and stressed.

He felt the worst feeling a medical man can experience – impotence. He shook his head. More crying from the gathering.

'It cannot be long,' he told the family. And it wasn't. He stayed with little Mary until the end. The end came as dawn began to flicker into life on the horizon. This was a day that six year old Mary Wood would no longer be running beside her spinning hoop.

'Once I've set you down, best I call on the village carpenter,' muttered Wood, on their way back pulled by the clopping horse. 'I'd like a proper coffin for our sweet Mary rather than a winding cloth.'

'Here,' said Thomas, reaching into his coat pocket. 'A guinea towards a fine oak coffin.'

Wood shook his head. 'I couldn't sir. This is far too much.'

'Yes, you can for little Mary.'

'But your fee, sir?'

Thomas waved him away. 'Nay, I could not save your child.'

'I must get one of the local women to wash and lay her out afore she's put to rest in the ground.'

Thomas scowled at this. 'My advice is to keep this task within the family. Mary's death is the first I know of from the plague hereabouts. If news gets out that plague is in the district, there will be widespread panic.'

'Aye, I get your meaning,' agreed Wood. 'We'll say not a word and have a private affair.'

Thomas gently patted the bereaved father on the back and the man finally gave way to tears.

'I cannot bear to think of leaving her laid in the ground on the cold side of the church with all the other poor folk,' he sobbed.

'Such a small grave, taking up such a small space. I will have a word with the priest,' Thomas reassured him. 'And you must arrange for a tombstone to remember Mary by. I've heard tell that *John Hartmann and Son* are looking for work.'

'Aye, I know John's work well.'

'There you are then.'

'Get up!' Satisfied, emotionally embarrassed and red-faced Wood chivvied his horse to greater effort. The cart bounced, his passenger rocked next to him.

* * *

The day of little Mary's funeral came in with a sea fret. It could not have been more eerie and dramatic. The whole village appeared to have turned out. The vague term 'ague' was given as the cause of the child's death. Thomas saw Iben standing opposite him. The emptiness of little Mary's grave stood between them as they waited. The lumbering image of Josh Haymaker seemed to hang over, dominate, put Iben in shadow. Thomas watched carefully. Whether or not she had seen the farm labourer, was aware of him standing directly behind her, Thomas could not tell for sure.

Tears streamed down the normally composed Iben's cheeks. She ran her fingers through her hair in distress. Indeed she seemed as affected as the child's mother – close to collapse in her mourning. Perhaps it was a preventative measure that Haymaker stood so close behind Iben, fearful that she might fall into the gaping hole before Mary was interred.

'I am the resurrection and the life saith the Lord.' The priest met the coffin at the gate to the churchyard before leading the official burial procession to the graveside. A tiny spray of Christmas roses shuddered on the coffin top. 'He that believeth in me, though he were dead, yet shall liveth: and whosoever liveth and believeth in me shall never die.'

How cruel a separation was this for Harriet Wood, reflected Iben. She would be left with the sensation of sweet smelling softness – unlike the pain of giving birth – no, that memory of softness would last with her for years.

'O spare me a little, that I might recover my strength: before I go hence, and be no more seen.'

Little Mary was carefully lowered into the earth.

'For as much as it hath pleased Almighty God of his great mercy to take unto himself the soul of our dear sister here departed, we therefore commit her body to the ground; earth to earth, ashes to ashes, dust to dust, in sure and certain hope of the resurrection to eternal life, through our Lord Jesus Christ.'

Soil pitter-pattered on the wooden coffin as if rain drops. All that was left was the tombstone to be engraved with a simple message by *John Hartmann and Son*. Iben wondered what wording the Woods would want inscribed to express their loss. But that would come much later.

* * *

Thomas seemed to be the only one in his parish to be fully aware of the threat from the east that was engulfing the island of Great Britain once again like a tidal wave. He wasn't surprised to be called to another dwelling, a few days later, by villagers who knew he had been an army doctor. These good people had not seen their neighbour, a farmer, for a week. Lucan Beadall lived alone and they had become concerned.

Arriving in Beadall's yard, they found his hens hungry and running amuck. With the help of Thomas, another fellow and a discarded beam found by a derelict outhouse, they broke down the farmhouse door.

The sickly sweet smell of sweat and death permeated the entire building. Thomas feared the worst. The expression on the face of the man with him exhibited the same. They crept through the house with trepidation until they reached an upper chamber.

Lucan Beadall lay there in his own vomit and shit.

'Is he alive?' asked Thomas' companion, Henry Winter, beginning to retch.

'Barely but he is breathing. Be good enough to get me cloths and a pail of water from the well in the yard, Henry. I cannot examine the man properly in this condition.'

Beadall moaned as they turned him. Thomas gently mopped away at years of dirt encrusted skin together with more recent embellishments. When they had finished they wetted the sick man's lips with minuscule drips of fresh water.

'Not too much,' instructed Thomas.

On examination Beadall's condition was far more advanced than little Mary's. His tongue was swollen and two buboes in his groin had begun to suppurate and bleed.

'What's wrong with him?' asked Winter.

'I'm not sure yet,' lied Thomas, but he was.

On his way from Beadall's, later that afternoon, he accidentally encountered Iben sat beneath the cross set outside their village. Which Iben would it be for he had come to realise all those years ago that she was two characters wrapped up in one. The flippant non-caring, sometimes cruel Iben or the sweet charming version.

She was stroking a feral cat in her lap that had obviously taken to her. Cats, like Walter, made no emotional demands on her, asked for little, and they seemed to sense they were safe with her. Thomas remembered other cherished cats in Iben's life. Otherwise he feared Iben was unable to love in an adult sense.

'Isn't he lovely?' she asked him.

'A fine creature,' he agreed.

'Creatures don't judge us, not like folk. Give me a cat any day to a man.'

'That is because you are not normal.'

'What is normal?' she replied.

Normal. Was Iben normal? Definitely not. That was part of her attraction. In thought and speech she was so different to any woman, or man, he had ever come across. He had also learnt from the past that delving into Iben's mind only led to greater divisions between them.

Thomas imagined he could smell the remnants of bitter vinegar still in the basin of carved stone by her clog. The plague tradesmen would leave food for the villagers during outbreaks. After picking up payment, the tradesmen would wash their hands in the stone bowl of vinegar. Between 1348 and 1665 there were periodic surges of plague even in Cornwall, thankfully in the last two years only the occasional outbreaks to be contained.

'How's Walter?' he asked, feeling this was safe ground. She continued stroking the cat. He watched as her strong practical fingers moved sensually through the grey brown fur. The cat purred satisfaction. He began to feel jealous of the damn creature.

'Walter is Walter,' she giggled. Walter her favourite brother. There was something innocent about Walter. Iben and Walter went about more like friends than brother and sister. They were close, very close, they shared some sort of understanding. Thomas often wondered about the nature of their relationship but he could not find it in his manly heart to be jealous of Walter.

He had heard Iben had something of a reputation with herbs as a neighbourhood healer.

'What do you know about pestilence?' he asked.

'I am not sure that I know very much. Some believe a posy of roses prevents the spread.'

'Do you know of any remedies other than sneezing into a posy of flowers?'

'Such as, Thomas?'

'Such as the ingredients for London treacle.'

'London treacle is made up of many mixtures. Too many compounds for me to be confident of obtaining here in St Agnes.'

'Have you heard of Water Germander locally?'

'Aye, I believe some are growing in Locken Pond down the lane there.'

'I have a patient gravely ill with the pestilence. Lucan Beadall.'

'Lucan? I'm so sorry.'

'Maybe we could work together. At least help alleviate some of his suffering.'

'Work together?' Her smile was both intense and flirtatious.

God! He loved her. But he could not risk going there again.

'Yes, please join me. I will be at Beadall's Farm tomorrow morning before the church clock strikes eight. Say nothing to no one. Secrecy is the essence.'

It was as he rode away that he realised she had made no comment about his disfigurement. She must have seen the scar running the length of his cheek. But that was Iben and to be expected, she was unpredictable.

Iben remained seated with the cat on her lap beneath the cross. She began to reflect on her relationship with Thomas Huck. She was glad it wasn't Haymaker that had chanced upon her. She wasn't sure how she would feel or react if it had been. It was fine here in the village with other folks around but to be on her own with Josh would have been another matter. Though Thomas was way above her social station, she always felt comfortable with him, in control. Far more in control with him than with either her mercurial mother or the indifferent Haymaker.

Iben avoided examining people too closely. It was better not to feel too deeply – that way you couldn't be hurt. Working with Thomas healing the sick rather appealed to her. She could use her skills with the herbs and become better thought of and respected in the community. She knew some of the lads that had taken their pleasure with her would have boasted about it in the taverns. She knew that would be so. Nevertheless, she had let it happen. She had allowed her reputation to be tarnished among the working people. Somewhere deep inside herself, she knew she had let herself seriously down too.

In so many ways Iben respected Thomas Huck and yet she was extremely jealous of him at the same time. He had always been so much more privileged than she was: educated, wealthy, with a man's freedom to travel, and he was kind as well. Kindness was a quality she had no need to resent in the selfish Haymaker. Kindness was something she couldn't afford to allow herself.

Anyway, Iben shrugged, she was only a second choice. Thomas had been promised to another before her. Despite the other being a girl of twelve, in her vanity Iben always regarded this as a slight. Had the old baron lived he would never have approved a marriage between her and his son, either son.

Iben was so self-absorbed with her own position in these betrothal matters that she disregarded the horrors that both Thomas and Haymaker had recently confronted in the war. She considered that there was something gallant about that from which her sex was excluded, more honourable than being second choice in a wedding proposal.

Deep down she resented Thomas Huck for somehow always making her feel inferior.

CHAPTER FOUR

Thomas was surprised to find Lucan Beadall a little improved the next morning. Lucan had found his voice though faint. He requested water and a crust of bread.

Just as Thomas was concluding his examination, he heard the downstairs door click and climbing footsteps.

'I found a few of these at Locken Pond.' Iben handed Thomas a spray of small pink purple flowers lost in a mass of dirty green woolly foliage. 'Water Germander,' she announced triumphantly.

Businesslike, Thomas appeared to be unimpressed. 'They must be ground down into a paste and used as a poultice on these sores,' he told her.

'I know, I know,' she replied brusquely. Unabashed she gazed down on Lucan's exposed groin. He obviously found the bedding unbearable rubbing against his suppurating buboes. 'I'll get on with it forthwith.'

'Lucan has requested a cup of water and a crust of bread,' added Thomas. 'We should be thankful for small mercies, unlike town water the water here should be pure.'

'I'll see what I can find.'

Thomas could not help noticing the sway of hips under her floral dress as she walked away through the doorway. She soon returned with a pewter drinking cup containing fresh water pumped from the yard.

'There was only bread with mould left. Still I'll see what I can do with some flour I found.'

Thomas gently lifted the sick man's head for the occasional sip of water.

The two men talked for a while until Iben reappeared. 'Luckily I found some yeast as well in Lucan's pantry.'

Thomas excused himself for an hour or two to check on other tenants, leaving Iben with her bread making. When he returned he was greeted with a wonderful comforting smell, a smell that wafted through the entire house and up the stairs.

'I think you are in for a treat,' he told Lucan.

His visitors were amazed and a little alarmed at the way their patient gobbled down the slice of freshly baked bread.

'He is hungry,' whispered Iben.

'Maybe he hasn't eaten in a week,' suggested Thomas.

'Maybe,' agreed Iben.

'Steady on, old man,' Thomas warned Lucan. 'We don't want you vomiting again.' But there was no need for apprehension, Lucan devoured the slice and it stayed down. Then he dozed off again.

'Have you looked into theriac or London treacle yet?' Thomas whispered to Iben.

'As I told you I've heard of it but have no idea what it is made up of,' she whispered back.

Thomas lifted up his medical bag and took out a leather backed notebook. 'Opium, Myrrh, Agaric, Saffron, Cinnamon, Spikenard, Frankincense, Castor, Pepper, Gentian. It is accounted a cordial, Opiate, Sudorific and Alexipharmic.'

'But how can we hope to have these ingredients available in our little corner of the world?'

'We cannot exactly. It was at one time viewed to be more effective against poisons than Venice treacle. We will have to improvise. Later versions of the antidote incorporated dried blood or the dried flesh of lizards of vipers. Now we do have a few of those around.'

'If you know where to look,' pointed out Iben.

'I am sure if anyone knows where to look, it is you Iben.'

Iben shrugged as Lucan opened his eyes.

'How are you feeling?' Thomas asked him.

'My head still hurts. I feel as if I have great heat within me while my extremities feel cold. I have pricking and shooting throughout my body. Difficulty catching my breath, feel sleepy and yet fitfulness all the time. And I am sweating like a cow in labour. The strange thing is I am seeing things all in one colour. You and she are all grizzled.'

Thomas felt for Lucan's pulse. 'A little swift,' he confirmed.

'Me mouth tastes bitter and dry, me arms and legs feel weak.'

'Would you like the chamber pot?'

'No need. I feel I want to piss but cannot,' admitted Lucan.

Iben murmured to Thomas that she would return in the morning with a dressing for Lucan's sores. 'I think I will be able to procure binding honey, wine and a little cinnamon. Water Germander I have already as you have seen. As for viper flesh we will have to wait and see,' she shrugged. 'Unfortunately this concoction will have to ferment over night.'

'Alas time isn't our friend,' replied Thomas, frowning as he looked down on the ailing Lucan.

* * *

Thomas knew that in 1665 the Great Plague of London broke out and Charles II turned to the Royal College of Physicians for advice. It was eventually published as: 'Advice set down by the College of Physicians (at the King's Command) containing certain necessary directions for the cure of the plague and preventing infection. The streets are to be kept clean and flushed with water in order to purify the air, fires are to be lit in streets and houses, and the burning of certain aromatic materials such as resin, tar, turpentine, juniper, cedar and brimstone is enjoined. The use of perfumes on the person is recommended.' Special physicians attended by apothecaries and surgeons were appointed to carry this out. Regrettably these measures were not available to his desultory Cornish subjects, two years on, with few cases to show so far. In short, Thomas was aware that the Hartmanns' cottage lacked the cleanliness and privacy of the apothecary's shop never mind the court. Still, he was sure Iben would do her best.

She did, making do with the kitchen table. As she worked the pestle and mortar she thought about Thomas Huck. If anything, she had to admit, his scar had made his face more interesting and, yes, him altogether more agreeable if that were possible. She pounded the seeds harder as she felt desire for him – a desire she had always resisted – rising in her loins. Her feelings for Thomas had always been complex and hesitant. She now began to realise it was because she had always felt he was too good for her in so many respects both morally and socially. A woman of low self-worth, with a veneer of self-assuredness, this only served to add to her inner sense of inferiority.

'What's that you're doing?' Her mother's voice cut across her lascivious thoughts.

'A poultice mixture.'

'Poultice? Why a poultice and who for?'

Iben had to think quickly. She had finally obtained her viper flesh early that morning under an upturned milk churn discarded by the quarry. 'For a snake bite which has gone wrong.'

'Who has a snake bite gone wrong?'

Iben could hear the suspicion growing in her mother's voice. 'A country chap from Perranzabuloe or thereabouts,' she lied.

Raph, while drinking a pot of small beer with his boots up on a stool by the fireside, had been quietly listening to their women's talk. 'She's making up that preparation for her one time lover mark my words,' he piped up.

'Which one?' cackled his father.

'The rich one. The one that didn't put her in the family way.'

An ugly silence fell over the small parlour.

'Wash your mouth out,' growled Agnes.

'You thought I didn't know,' sneered Raph. Iben blushing to her roots, hung her head. 'Well, Sheep Shagging, Sister Shagging Haymaker couldn't resist boasting about his accomplishment to any one with an ear to listen, that is until he went to war.'

'And you believed him of course,' snapped back Iben.

'Stop it both of you. It doesn't help no one going about repeating it,' barked their father. 'And you …' he turned to Iben. 'Might as well forget about yon softling Cavalier friend, once he hears about yer's goings on.'

'If he hasn't already,' put in Raph maliciously.

'Spoilt goods! He'll play with you like a toy for fun,' added her father, usually a man of graveyard silence.

'Like all the others,' muttered Raph.

Is that all she had become, a toy for men's pleasure? The tears began to roll. She made for the sanctuary of her room.

'You have only yourself to blame,' her mother screamed after her.

* * *

Luckily the distance between Iben's cottage and Lucan Beadall's farmstead was only a mile. She arrived in the early morning. Her flat-soled mules clip-clopped her arrival on the wooden staircase.

Nevertheless it was a drowsy patient that received the cup of water and slice of yesterday's bread smeared with a knob of butter brought from her home.

She held the back of his head allowing him to drink, asking 'How are you Lucan?'

Lucan attempted a smile. 'Could have felt better,' he wheezed.

'These blister plasters will help those nasty sores heal.' She began to coat the buboes. 'I am sure Doctor Huck will call in later to take a look at you.' She failed to add that she had no wish of running into Thomas herself, not after the scene in her home. Though her present confidence was at its lowest point, she had no intention either of being regarded as 'a toy for men's pleasure' – certainly not Huck's.

'Stay awhile,' pleaded Lucan as if he had read her mind.

'No, I'd best be on my way.'

'Just a little while. Talk to me.' He reached for her hand.

And so she did.

Iben felt virtuous in her new role. Appreciated for once in her life for the good she could do rather than just her body.

Another half hour gone and she was on her way, not before she heard horse's hooves on the cobbled yard.

'Mistress Hartmann.' Thomas raised his hat. 'How goes our patient?'

Always high up, high above her, so smug and superior there on his horse.

'He does well enough. I have applied the first poultices.'

'I am sure he does well with such a lovely maid in support.'

Always so assured, self-satisfied – that comes with money. Always so well turned out and bloody good looking despite the scar – that comes with good food and breeding.

'Are you not going to bleed him?' she asked, placing factual management of the patient above Thomas' flirtation.

'No, I am going to incise the buboes directly, allowing them to drain naturally. I've little time for leeches, bleeding and suchlike.'

'Do you wish me to reapply the poultices this evening?' she asked him coldly.

He mistook her coldness for efficiency. 'That's very kind.'

'Think nothing of it. Lucan is a good man and one of us.'

'And I am not, I suppose.' Finally he detected her hostility, her hostility of old. An attitude that he had struggled to understand and come to terms with in the past.

Iben made no answer but turned her back on him and flounced away.

Back to her old ways, observed Thomas dismounting. The cold shoulder one minute, flirtation the next. She was the most frustrating person he had ever had to deal with. That hard knot of historical anger and hurt restored itself within his soul. She had not wished him well as he went off to war. She had failed to respond to his final letter. How unpleasant was that.

Thomas skilfully hid the scalpel from Lucan's eyes before he drew the blade across one of the buboes in the sick man's groin. Lucan winced slightly as Thomas scored the second.

'Sorry if that hurt.'

'Not at all, doctor,' Lucan lied.

It wasn't for a day or two before Thomas called at the farm again. He found Lucan's buboes had started to emit pus rather than blood.

'Much of the pain has gone,' Lucan told him.

'That is because the pressure in the sores is beginning to be released.' Thomas, mopped away the pus with a clean kerchief. 'Looks like the incision and poultices are working.'

'That lass has been visiting three times a day.'

'Three times?'

'Yes, she's a good 'un. Doesn't say much but she cares.'

'She does,' said Thomas thoughtfully. Lucan wasn't sure if this was said rhetorically or as a question. In truth neither did Thomas.

'She is very beautiful,' announced Lucan instead.

'Is she?' asked Thomas.

'Surely you have eyes to see.'

Once outside, he looked up to a window of cold blue sky between billowing clouds. That same sky that had been always there – there before Iben – and despite Lucan's appreciative words he sensed he was breaking free of her spell.

* * *

'Have you been visiting Lucan Beadall's place?'

'What if I have?' Iben watched as her father chiselled out the words:

HERE LYETH THE BODY
OF MARY WOOD

Old Hartmann worked fast in the peace of his yard. She hoped his spelling was up to scratch, it wasn't always, so many tombstone makers were not literate.

'Why are you visiting Beadall?' he asked.

'He is unwell.'

'In what way is he unwell?' Iben did not answer her father. 'Folk are saying Beadall might have plague.'

'And what of little Mary?' she asked pointing down to the tombstone, deflecting the subject.

'Aye, her too.'

There were other malignant forces abroad. Whispers began to circulate around the village. Iben had heard them all but shrugged them off. She would not be diverted from her task. 'You risk us all,' pointed out her father.

'We are at risk anyway,' replied Iben. 'And I remember you rubbing your hands together on hearing of the London epidemic, saying should it come west it will only serve to further our business.'

John Hartmann looked up from his work. He tended to let Iben say whatever she pleased and go her own way. It was in compensation for his wife's indifference and what he felt to be Agnes' lack of affection for their daughter.

'You are such a skeptic,' he told Iben. Frowning he watched as undeterred she strutted off in the direction of Beadall's Farm.

Iben had done her best to avoid her visits coinciding with Thomas Huck's. Not today. His stallion was already tied to the post and pawing the ground irritably.

'Good day.' She announced her presence as she mounted the staircase to Lucan's bedchamber.

'There she is, my angel,' said Lucan. His smile so big.

'And how are you today, Farmer Beadall?' She smiled back. A cursory nod to Thomas.

'All the better for seeing you, Mistress Hartmann.'

'The patient's buboes have begun to dry up,' cut in Thomas. 'He feels as if he is almost ready to quit the bed.'

'Good, good,' said Iben, gently examining Lucan's groin.

'Amazing recovery,' Thomas told her once they were out in the yard.

'Yes, amazing,' replied Iben quietly. She looked away, any way but at him. Did she still have feelings for this man? This man for whom she was always second choice, an inferior choice.

'I always loved you.' It was as if Thomas had read her mind.

'Only after your father died.'

'I always loved you,' repeated Thomas.

'For as long as it suited you. You were promised to another.'

'She was a child. I never laid sight on her.'

'And never laid with her as you did with me.' Iben's words were full of recriminations.

'Nor that.'

'You can leave all thoughts of that happening again far behind.' Her mouth clamped down meanly on the words, clamped into a straight line, before the edges curved down into deeper bitterness.

Thomas was reminded of Iben's favourite painting, *Mary Magdalene as Melancholy*. Although the Gentileschi's model in that portrait had a fuller mouth, a mouth sad for all that. It suddenly struck him that melancholia could be at the root of all Iben's problems.

'Can I? Can *you* let all thoughts of us go?' he asked her.

Without answering she turned for the farm gate. Without turning back she lifted her skirts above the mud. He watched her undo the latch, he watched her disappearing into a backcloth of fields and pastures. He watched her all the way, thinking how close were the feelings of love and hate. All those beautiful words she had once spoken – how she played him – but then that had been another time.

At first Thomas had been captivated by Iben's sweet thoughtful nature. A quiet nature no doubt inherited from her father, certainly not from the brash Agnes Hartmann with her no-nonsense harsh northern accent. But then Iben would have an occasional outburst, a cruel whiplash temper, now that was all Agnes. That was what she had just exhibited today.

Unknown to Thomas, or to Iben herself, somebody had begun stalking her on these regular visits to Lucan's farm. Someone returned from away. Someone who, in his absence, had learnt his trade travelling enemy lines in the recent war. Someone who had learnt to blend in, move with stealth.

Josh Haymaker had also followed her to the quarry and watched her looking under stones for sleeping snakes. Was she into some sort of sorcery? It would not have surprised him. He was like a dog sniffing around a bitch and the thought of being bewitched was no deterrent. He didn't particularly hold Iben in high esteem either but there wasn't any other strumpet locally that took his fancy. And, yes, he remembered that there had been a few merry times with Iben.

He became curious about these visits of Iben's to Lucan Beadall's. Had she sunk so low as to be whoring herself out to old Beadall. Then again, seeing Thomas Huck there, had the Beadall farm become a convenient meeting place for an assignation between the two of them, or maybe even a bawdy house?

Maybe Iben was short of a penny or two. Maybe she was taking both men on at once, he smirked. But soon smirk changed to jealous glower. Could it be that he was missing out on something here?

CHAPTER FIVE

Iben had reminded Thomas of his betrothal to the child over St Clether way. Many years had passed since then. Mary Ansell would be an adult woman now, no doubt married herself, or a confirmed spinster, or in a nunnery somewhere. Maybe he should have looked into it earlier because Iben seemed to have no interest in him anymore. Maybe it still wasn't too late, but deep within himself he knew he wasn't ready to open his heart to another.

Thinking back, Iben had spoken beautiful words, beautiful words after their love making, but she had never actually said she loved him. How he had wished she would have spoken the words, sealed some commitment. Though deep within himself he suspected she did love him, something stopped her expressing it. He had asked her about it many times. Her answer was she was of Viking stock and Vikings did not say much. He had asked her so many questions always to be greeted with vague retorts or flippant dismissals. When he had expressed his own sincere love for her, her reply was 'you are right and I am not wrong'. What on earth did that mean? She was a conundrum. A never-to-be-answered conundrum and he was tired.

The 7th December 1667, Christmas was on its way. Letting go of all thoughts of Iben seemed to galvanise Thomas. He decided he could not wait until spring to replenish Jowan Carter's flock. He would make his way back to Truro and visit Fortnight's Fair held the next day.

About the same time Raph was telling his sister in the Hartmann kitchen that Josh Haymaker had been seen in the area asking after her.

'Our lass knows how to amuse herself with men right enough,' sniggered Raph.

Old Hartmann raised an eyebrow in another habitual warning to his son.

'You'll have nothing to do with that scoundrel either or it is to me you will answer,' Old Hartmann warned his daughter.

For Iben, Josh Haymaker rapidly became more appealing.

* * *

The lanes to Truro were thick with mud and almost impassable in places. Thomas wondered if he had made the right decision. Nevertheless, Russel did his best to plough through all obstacles.

Mid-winter Truro was a very different place to a month back, very much colder. A weak sun did its best to wink through the clouds.

Again Thomas secured stabling for his horse, a night's sleep for himself at The Bear, before making off to the sheep pens. Again he was lucky enough to make contact with Joseph Crenshaw.

'Sorry to hear that Jowan Carter's sheep never reached home,' commiserated Crenshaw straight away.

'How did you hear about that?' asked Thomas.

'Constable from your parish came sniffing round asking questions.'

'And?'

'And I knew nothing. I had told no one anything.'

'Well, I need twenty-four Devon ewes and three rams to replace them. And I would appreciate your confidentiality regarding the transaction once again.'

'Say no more, sir, mums the word.' Crenshaw pressed a finger to his lips. 'We've just the job for you over in those pens.' He pointed to a maze of hurdle cages. Warm clouds of breath from the animals hit cold December air. 'Longwool ewes in the finest of condition. And over there a few frisky young chaps eager for action. Good getters everyone of 'em.'

'How much?'

'Same as afore. Eight guineas for the ewes. Fifteen for the three rams.'

Thomas immediately nodded agreement.

'Better luck this time with the delivery,' said Crenshaw, once Thomas had passed over the jinking gold coins and made his purchases. 'I'll make sure adult armed men accompany the sheep this time to guarantee their safe passage.' Thomas gave him the cross-finger sign. Crenshaw made the sign of the cross over his chest, no doubt, like Raph, unintentional conditioning from the old religion. Only a few years before, in Old Noll's time, signing the cross was regarded as superstitious and idolatrous.

Thomas made his way to Calenick Street and Victoria Square to where Ayla had once stood on the corner outside The Red Lion. She was not there. He could not say why he was drawn there but he was. Some natural urge perhaps. He shrugged his shoulders, surely not. Just when he had given up hope with a small amount of relief – she was there. Appearing from the back yard, pulling down her skirts, an old punter in her trail.

Thomas felt sick to the bottom of his stomach. She did not see him as she sat on a step muffled in a woollen shawl, her small nose red with the cold.

The punter nodded a goodbye. Ayla ignored him. Business completed. It was simply a business transaction like the one

Thomas had just concluded with Crenshaw over the sheep. Indeed if anything it wasn't as warm as his connection with Crenshaw.

'Ayla,' Thomas called out. 'Ayla, you are still here.'

Sitting on a stone step, blinded by the sun, the slight Irish waif lifted her hand across her eyes. 'You, sir.'

'You remember me.'

'I do indeed. It is not often that a gentleman is not interested in business.'

Thomas hesitated, uncertain how to proceed. 'I'm sorry if I offended you.'

'No offence taken, sir. Indeed far from it.'

'Are you hungry, Ayla?'

'I am always hungry. We Irish have learnt to live with hunger, poverty and famine. My mother told me of her struggle to feed me as a bairn in fifty-three. Her milk was so poor that I barely thrived. Then plague, brought in by Cromwell's men, finished Ireland off. Finished her and most of my kinfolk off. And here I am, sir, seated on a cold orphan throne before you.'

'Would you like to take supper with me at The Bear tonight?'

Ayla's starved gaze looked doubtful. 'Are you sure, sir?'

'Yes, I am sure. Seven of the clock, the church clock.'

The landlord asked if he was ready to order his supper yet. Thomas shook his head and said he was waiting for a lady friend. The landlord gave him a discreet knowing wink. However, discretion turned to blatant disapproval on Ayla's arrival. The landlord's gauping mouth was wide enough to accommodate a carriage and horses. He was not alone. Some of the male diners paused their cutlery over plates as if they were uncomfortable concertmasters waiting to begin a discordant symphony. Their wives looked uneasy and wrinkled their noses in displeasure.

'I see one or two of my gentlemen in here,' whispered Ayla. Thomas had forgotten how beautiful her lilting Irish accent was.

'Gentlemen? Is that what you call them? I have worked out that you cannot be anything above fourteen years of age. You are still a child.'

'A child who has to eat,' justified Ayla.

'That being the case what is your choice?'

'I am not sure, sir. Maybe you could make a suggestion for me.'

'I can recommend the fillet of beef. Then I have heard they do an excellent game pie.'

'Game pie is fine by me.' Ayla tried to sound nonchalant as her stomach growled at the mere mention of food, nourishing food at that.

'I think a good claret would benefit the dish.'

'Whatever you think is best, sir.'

From a room of listening ears, murmuring voices began to lift and knives and spoons resumed clattering on tin.

'What will you be having?' The landlord asked Thomas, his voice edgy.

'A game pie to share. And a bottle of your finest claret.'

By the time the pie arrived, Ayla looked ready to eat her tatty dress so great was her mouth-watering anticipation.

Along with the rest of the room, he had never seen anyone eat in such a way, save a wolf. The way she devoured that game pie, most of the game pie as Thomas did not have the heart to deprive her of the majority of his share, and she such a scrawny lass.

'Enjoy that, did you?' The landlord asked her sarcastically as he removed her licked clean plate.

'Could have done with a few more Munster tatties,' she replied cheekily. He turned his back on her impudence. 'Not been down Calenick Street of late have you, mister?' she shouted after him.

The landlord hesitated in his tracks, his back to her. Thought about it, thought about countering the accusation, before deciding his best course of action was the security of the kitchen.

Thomas glared at Ayla. Ayla defiantly met his eyes, unsure how he had received her boldness.

'You know that man?' asked Thomas.

'I know a lot of men. That man as you call him is a friend of the Red Lion landlord. He has misused me badly like many in here.'

Thomas shrugged at the hypocrisy around them and gave the room the middle finger.

'Not so much an angel after all,' commented Ayla with a wry smile.

The female diners gasped outrage while their escorts looked abashed but reticent about getting involved. Thomas and Ayla began to laugh. They both laughed until their sides ached.

'Where are you sleeping tonight?' Thomas asked Ayla. Ayla's mouth turned down in dismay. 'No, no, I didn't mean …' began Thomas.

'It is not for me to know what you meant, sir, but as always the straw in the Red Lion stable suits me fine.'

'Forgive me for asking but are you not afraid of being with child from all these associations?'

'I have my methods.' She flushed up in indignation.

'I am a medical man. I am curious about these matters.'

'Really.'

'Yes, really.'

'I use a rag coated with honey and vinegar if you must know.'

'And it has worked so far?'

'Some believe in a sprig of mint stuffed high up there too. I am not so sure about that.'

He did not pursue the subject further but believed her infecund state might be due to starvation rather than a barrier rag. An uncomfortable silence dropped between them like a curtain.

'All these questions. Do you want to sleep with me tonight, sir?'

'No, I would like to offer you employment as a maid at Rockfoot Hall.'

To Thomas' surprise Ayla did not jump at the offer. She frowned instead. 'As your mistress?' she asked.

'No, as I said, employment as a maid.'

'I hope you don't regard me as merely a project to be saved. Because I will let you down.'

Again Thomas was taken aback. He did not quite understand what she meant by let him down.

'No. Rockfoot Hall needs a maid and you are too good for life on the streets.'

'But surely …'

'No the Hall is short of staff since the war. Since my father and brother were killed, and I was away in the army, we only kept a butler and cook.'

'I hope you don't intend to entertain this lady here in your room.' The landlord was suddenly hovering over them. There was no doubting his sarcasm in reference to 'this lady.'

'Certainly not,' replied Thomas. 'Neither I nor this lady will be enjoying your hospitality tonight if it is any of your business.' Offhandedly he threw some coins on the table for the landlord to collect. 'Please be good enough to have my horse made ready for departure immediately.'

'Well … well, I never,' glared the landlord in amazement.

Thomas quickly collected his luggage from the bedchamber. A stable boy stood waiting with Russel already saddled up out in the yard. The landlord waited outside with Ayla, leering and attempting to paw her. Ayla was doing her best to rebuff his attentions.

'That's enough,' Thomas told him.

''Tis the straw for you in the Red Lion stable then. But then you'll not go cold with a whore for company,' sneered the landlord. 'You such a gentleman.'

'Unlike yourself.' Without further ado Thomas sunk his fist into the landlord's plentiful gut. The man crumpled back into the wall of the inn. The stable boy looked on in stunned silence. 'Come,' he told Ayla. 'Come right now.' He hauled the agile girl up next to his luggage in the saddle in front of him.

They could hear the landlord's curses drifting and then fading into the distance behind them.

'Where will you sleep?' asked Ayla, bemused as they trotted down Old Bridge Street.

'We will not sleep. We will collect your belongings and ride through the night to Rockfoot Hall.'

A confused but joyous Ayla soon reappeared from the stable. Her entire wealth bundled into a shawl.

Back on the muddy lanes out of Truro. With Ayla being so light Russel was able to absorb the extra weight with ease as he drove on, the wind and the rain lashing into their faces.

'We must stop a moment for I need to piss, sir,' Ayla shouted into the wind.

She managed to find a hedge and shallow ditch. Thomas averted his gaze as she struggled with her petticoats.

Hours later and soaked to the skin, he was screaming for Josiah, his old manservant, to quit the warmth of his coverlet and make up a bed for Ayla in the attic.

'Please get any hot coals left. Both beds must have warming pans or I swear the young lady and I will die of the winter fever.'

'What on earth possessed you to travel on a night like this?' muttered the old man.

'Let us say pressing circumstances forced it upon us.' Thomas winked across at shuddering Ayla.

'Quick man, the coals for the warming pans.'

* * *

The entire household of Rockfoot Hall was enjoying a late morning in bed following the events of the previous night. As so often happens something came to interrupt those daylight dreams. Thomas could hear the persistent hammering on the front door but felt his arms and legs paralysed to move. He swore he had never slept so deeply.

'Constable Fox is here and insistent on speaking to you, Sir Thomas.' Josiah's hand shook Thomas' shoulder as Thomas kept his eyes firmly shut. Once fully wakened he must remember to reprimand the old reprobate. 'He says it is urgent.'

'Be good enough to get my gown.' Thomas finally succumbed to the inevitable. 'Show the constable into the withdrawing room.'

The constable looked a little perplexed by Sir Thomas' state of undress, still in his night attire. 'Sorry to bother you, sir, but I have some rather disturbing news.'

'Go on then.' Thomas could not hide his irritation at being disturbed.

'Remember those two lads from Truro way, beaten up for shepherding your sheep?'

'Oh, no, it hasn't happened again.'

'No, sir, although the lad that was beaten most ill but seemed to be recovering from his head injuries …' Fox hesitated and sucked in air. 'Well, that lad died early this morning.'

'In Truro? I was only there yesterday.'

'Yes, he started vomiting and fell into a coma.'

'According to a local medical man, like yerself, he must have sustained some injury to his brain.'

'Causing a delayed death even weeks later,' frowned Thomas. 'I've seen the like occasionally happen with soldiers who have been bludgeoned by maces in battle.'

'Well, the whole of Truro is up in arms and calling for retribution. It seems he was a popular lad and his father prominent in their gaming society. Fearing a riot the magistrate has signed a warrant for the immediate arrest of the perpetrators and for them to be brought to account.'

'Good, good.'

'I know I have asked this before but you still have no idea if anyone over this way might be involved.'

'No, no, nobody springs to mind. Not with any certainty,' added Thomas.

'With any certainty,' pondered the constable.

'That's right,' said Thomas quickly. 'So how can I help?'

'We wondered … ' The constable cleared his throat. 'For the cohesion of our two communities we thought a reward for information would not go amiss.'

'And you thought I might contribute?'

The constable nodded. 'If you could see your way, sir.'

'I will write a note to my goldsmith for one hundred pounds. Will that see you right?' The constable was astonished. 'Now if it pleases you I must get dressed,' said Thomas.

'Thank you, thank you, sir.' The constable backed out of the room as if Thomas was some grand eastern potentate. Grovelling downplayed his standing but that was the power of position and wealth in post-Cromwellian England. The man undoubtedly feared for his livelihood if he didn't get a favourable outcome and apprehend the murderer or murderers.

A little while later as Thomas breakfasted there was a second knock on the door. Josiah answered and called an irritated Thomas to attend.

Iben stood there in a turquoise dress. The dress enhanced the colour of her eyes. Thomas took a deep breath. 'Iben?'

'I've just called to tell you Lucan Beadall is much improved and will no longer require my ministrations,' she told him coldly. Was there accusation in her voice?

'Good, good. I'm sorry I have been unable to visit but I've been away in Truro on business for the last day or two.'

Ayla emerged peeping over his shoulder and apologising for being so late abed and not answering the door.

'Business,' huffed Iben. 'I see.'

'No, no, you are mistaken,' began Thomas. Just as quickly as Iben had appeared she was gone.

'Is that your lady?' asked Ayla.

'No.'

'Would you like her to be?'

'I'm not sure.'

'She obviously would like to be.'

'We were close at one time before the war came.'

Thomas wasn't sure why but Iben's visit troubled him so greatly as he munched into his cold beef and tore at his saffron bread.

Conscience, he decided. It was *conscience.* For all their animosity to him the Hartmann father and brother were kin to Iben. With his lucrative reward offered for information, there would be many in the county willing to point the finger. He also recognised Constable Fox's renewed enthusiasm for apprehending the culprits. If the Hartmanns were responsible they would hang. They could both be hanged for the sheep alone, but because the murdered lad's father was significant in Truro the need for a result had gained impetus.

* * *

'What are you doing in our yard?' asked Old Hartmann.

'Yes, don't recall the likes of you being invited here again,' pealed in Raph as hostile as ever.

'I came to advise you that a reward of one hundred pounds has been put forward to arrest the men who stole my sheep.'

'One hundred pounds?' Raph gawped in disbelief.

'And for the murder of one of the drovers,' Thomas added.

'Murder, you say? We don't know nought about sheep or murder, do we Raph? You're not suggesting me and my lad might be involved,' snarled Old Hartmann.

'You're not accusing us of such wickedness, Sir Thomas?' Raph looked uncomfortable.

'No, I just came to inform you of the situation,' Thomas told them.

'Or to see what the situation is with our lass, more like,' sneered Raph.

'No, that is not why I came.'

'You weren't man enough for her. She got plenty of what you couldn't give her. Fellas lining up to fill the gap as it were.' Raph's laugh was lascivious. 'I heard tell even your brother, Robert, wasn't indifferent to our lass's charms.'

'Shut up!' snarled Old Hartmann. 'You's got a mouth as wide as a whore's queynte.'

Thomas shuddered at the old man's coarseness. It was amazing that his daughter had grown up with any delicacy at all. But could it be true that Robert had been interested in Iben, he was so much older.

Thomas remained in the saddle, towering above the two men. He leaned so far off Russel, he nearly fell on top of Iben's brother. Raph took a step back. Thomas was used to soldiers' talk but never about someone he had loved. But then wasn't Raph merely telling him something he already knew. Iben didn't seem to want his love, any love, she wanted something more primitive. And maybe he recognised some hypocrisy on his part, that was what he found so attractive about her, he wanted some of that animal magnetism too, some of her too.

Angrily he pulled Russel away. Anger at his own weakness and desire – be it specific, certainly more specific than it seemed Iben's was.

'I did hear some sheep were driven up to Launceston for slaughter,' Old Hartmann shouted up at him as he turned.

'Too late, old man. I came to give you neighbourly warning as I did not want to see you both hanging in Truro gibbet cages on Comprigney field.'

'For the sheep or the lad?' sneered Raph.

'Either. Both. It seems the dead lad's father is bent on revenge.'

* * *

Iben watched Thomas Huck ride away from the farm from her bedchamber window. From their body language she deduced that there had been some form of confrontation between the three men. If there was one thing she was fearful of, more than her dubious sexual reputation, it was that Raph would tell Huck of her secret. She felt no commitment anymore to Thomas but dreaded his reaction. During their loose betrothal she had been duplicitous with him at best.

She flung herself on the canvas mattress. Why should she care what Thomas Huck felt and thought after the experiences she had endured? Apart from war, menfolk had it easy, and even war was of their own making. But giving birth at a tender age was on an entirely different scale. She was only thirteen going on fourteen. When the birthing began she had wanted to die. The birth itself had been like passing a huge rock through her untested birth canal. Iben had been sent away to have the child in secret. Sent away to a female relative, a cordwainer's wife from far away. The relative had been calm and kind enough and, with the help of another woman from the nearby village, did her best to help her through the agonising process with reassuring words and cordial. She hated men for putting this thing inside her. She hated all men. She vowed she would make them pay in the future.

Then something amazing happened. She heard a squall and sensed she was rid of her burden. And looking across a minute or two later at the ruckled red faced infant, wrapped in a towel in the neighbour's arms by the window and lit up in a beam of light, she felt such love. She felt a love she had never known, not even for Walter, this funny little creature was part of her.

She had called her baby daughter Ulli – gem of the sea – another family first name handed down from the old language.

She had formed a bond with her daughter, breast feeding her for those few weeks.

She and her daughter became closer and closer. Although Iben suffered a fever following the birth, in a state of stupefaction she continued to suckle Ulli until she grew into a healthy specimen. On waking one morning there was none of the usual gurgling from the crib. Alarmed, still in a febrile state, she struggled across to her baby. The crib was empty. She crawled on her hands and knees beneath it like a mad woman. Alerted by the commotion, the female relative arrived. Iben screamed and sobbed for her to tell her where her child was. The woman eventually confessed that she had taken Ulli away in the night to order as Iben slept.

'You have taken part of me away,' sobbed Iben.

'The child has gone to a good home to be adopted by a childless yeoman farmer and his wife.'

The woman did her best to reassure her.

When pressed the relative maintained she knew nothing of Ulli's present whereabouts or final destination. Only when she had sworn on the Bible, that that was the case, would Iben be calmed.

She determined, there and then in her young mind, if she could not live for her daughter then she would live only for herself. She had nothing else but herself now. That did not stop her wondering. What had Ulli grown up to be like? Or, God forbid, was she in a small cold grave now like little Mary Wood?

CHAPTER SIX

Thomas decided to improve his standing in a community where many, like the Hartmanns, had fought for or been sympathetic to the Cromwellian cause. He pulled in many of the estate workers to prepare Rockfoot Hall for a Twelfth Night party of reconciliation. However, Thomas had not thought fit to invite Hartmann father and son. He knew they would despise his invitation. Everyone else in the village was welcome to attend.

Following a month of fasting, when villagers avoided over indulging in rich foods, they were more than ready to drink and gorge for the twelve days of Christmas climaxing on that final evening.

Thomas watched them come through the door, watched their mouths open with surprise and delight at the colourful scene greeting them. The banqueting room was illuminated by hundreds of candles and a dozen flaming torches. The glossy dark green leaves and red holly berries displayed about the room shimmered the decorative season. Two tables met to form an L shape. They were covered in spotless white linen tablecloths something unknown to the envious cottage wives.

Agnes Hartmann half curtsied to her host.

Iben did not follow suit, saying instead, 'I cannot see Lucan Beadall here.'

'No, although he is much improved as you noticed yourself, he did not feel quite well enough to attend tonight.' Thomas hesitated, 'And perhaps it is for the best.'

'Perhaps so,' Iben agreed.

'Jowan Carter chose not to attend as well.' Thomas scrutinised the room. 'But apart from Lucan and Jowan everyone else seems to be here.'

'What a feast you have provided, Sir Thomas,' Agnes Hartmann cooed. She obviously hadn't given up on the possibility of a match between himself and her daughter.

As the two women walked away – Iben with defiant head held high – Thomas felt that any future match with her was more unlikely than ever after all that had happened between them.

Thomas was loath to call the fare he had provided a banquet but it was. What a lavish meal awaited everyone in the great hall. The smell of cooking alone stimulated appetites. There was a suckling pig and a carcase of wild bull roasting on spits over the open fire at one end of the room near the kitchen. The centre piece, where the L shaped tables met, was a pig's head surrounded by mutton pies, cold chicken and fresh bread loaves. Almost any bird that took to the wing, and those that preferred scrabbling nearer the ground, were roasting or boiling in large cooking pots alongside local fruits of the sea of course. To follow, for those with room to spare, were custards, jellies, cherry pottage, rose puddings, sweet almonds and gingerbreads.

Ayla was responsible for replenishing the tables, with a few other trusted village women, under the scrutiny of the old resident cook. Thomas had added one or two more permanent kitchen staff recently, along with a lad to attend to Russel's needs and the outside stables. Josiah was promoted to a supervisory role for the evening, which involved him standing around in his smart new uniform complete with leggings and creaking leather boots and waving his arms about in a pretence of supreme command. He was further instructed to make sure none of the young farmers got too inebriated and troublesome.

'And what can the likes of me do about it if they do? Me suffering from the gout,' he complained.

'There will be others to help,' Thomas attempted to mollify him.

'What others? 'Tis my experience that others fall away when needed,' grumbled the old man.

'There will be the King of Misrule presiding over the evening for example.'

'And who might that be?'

'We don't know yet.'

The guests were all presented with pieces of cake to start with. Somewhere in the cake was a surprise hidden for someone. A trinket representing Christ would be found in the King of Misrule's slice. Suddenly a tussle broke out at the far end of one of the tables. At first Thomas put it down to youthful high spirits.

'Here he is! Here is the King of Misrule for the night.' Josh Haymaker's mates lifted his arm. Haymaker held the trinket aloft in his hand.

Iben knew most of them. They were part of Haymaker's old brigand clan. She scowled as Haymaker took up his makeshift throne. It would be him, she acknowledged angrily. And if he hadn't found the trinket in his piece of cake, his mates would make sure he did and no one would dare to oppose them.

Thomas could hardly eat following Haymaker's enthronement. The enjoyment of watching the red-faced farmers stuffing out their cheeks soon evaporated – their faces a match for the holly berries. His face matched the berries too as he was forced to serve Haymaker a trencher holding slices of mutton.

'Thank you indeed kind sir,' parodied Haymaker.

'Don't take advantage of this,' Thomas warned him. 'I'll only go along with the tradition so far.'

'But you are to serve all my wishes, Sir Thomas, this night. An additional chicken leg would be pleasing,' said Haymaker, mocking Thomas' fine manner of speech.

Thomas beckoned Ayla to bring Haymaker a chicken leg.

'You've to choose a queen, Josh,' shouted one of the lads from down the table.

'Here she is.' Haymaker pulled Ayla onto his knee, his coarse hand stroking her intimately. Ayla's natural pallor blanched even more.

'Let her be,' warned Thomas.

Haymaker just laughed at him.

Thomas reached for a large carving knife from the table. 'Let her be or I swear I will run you through with this here and now.'

'Ah, I see this little lass is already spoken for,' mocked Haymaker, allowing Ayla to slither to the ground. 'Then I will take her over there standing next to Agnes Hartmann.'

Iben shook her head. 'Never,' she shouted back at him.

'You will have to be without a queen this night,' Thomas told him jubilantly.

'So why only two Hartmanns present for these festivities?' Haymaker hadn't finished yet.

'I felt John and Raph were best left in their yard with the stones.'

'Bet you did.'

'I see you've got your hooks well into him,' hissed Iben to the escaping Ayla.

'Into him?' Ayla froze.

'Into Sir Thomas of course.'

'I am not his harlot if that's what you are suggesting. I am nobody's harlot. I am a maid,' said Ayla with as much pride as she could muster.

'Is that how you style yourself nowadays? I've heard you had a reputation in Truro for giving pleasure to any man with a need.'

'Unlike yourself, I suppose,' sneered Ayla contemptuously. 'You are without honour.'

'That's good coming from a whore.'

'My association with gentlemen was strictly business and they knew it. I didn't lead decent men into thinking it was anything else. While you blatantly deceived Thomas Huck into believing it was a serious relationship.'

'I never told him I loved him.'

'No, though you do.'

Iben was speechless, staring at this slip of a girl in disbelief. It was disconcerting: so brazen and worldly for her years.

'So you assume that I am in love with Thomas?' she grunted sarcastically.

'As far as you are capable of loving anybody. I came across damaged girls like you working the streets everyday. Any tender affection had been knocked out of them long ago. They had little room left for love other than for themselves. It was called survival.'

'Now ladies,' intervened Josiah, suddenly aware of raised voices.

Aggie stepped in, pulling Iben away, telling her to stop humiliating herself.

Though there were wine bottles on the table most villagers chose the locally brewed beer, even the women, or spicy wassail wine. The party was well behaved and orderly, apart from the tensions created by Haymaker's occasional lewd comments made towards one or two shy unmarried maidens. He studiously ignored their fathers' red-faced anger. To Thomas' relief the irritation in certain areas of the room lowered as the supply of alcohol subsided and most folk fell into a quiet stupefaction. But not Haymaker, a flagon never far from his lips, whatever else Thomas had to allow the farm labourer had stamina and could take his drink.

The candles began to struggle and flicker in seas of tallow – the fish oil torches dimmed on the walls as they burnt down – signals for the mummers' arrival. Rockfoot Hall was to be their starting point before setting out to entertain outlying farms and villages. Mouths stuffed with figgy pudding, the guests waited and watched on.

So tumbled in the troupe. No women, only men in dresses.

'I could see you garbed so, Sir Thomas,' shouted out gloating Haymaker. 'I see this must appeal to one of your bent.'

It was Haymaker's turn to be ignored. His words were drowned out by the comical rhyming introductions of the horse, the ram and the horned goat. Their identities hidden behind masks made of flax, willow and straw. Despite an old law passed in 1418 forbidding actors in mumming plays to wear feigned beards, painted visors, deformed or coloured visages upon pain of imprisonment – the Rockfoot troupe remained obdurate.

The tables laughed, screamed and welcomed them with delighted clapping hands. Finally came in a creeping figure in a leather mask with a long bird's beak.

''Tis the plague doctor.' A shocked murmur travelled the tables. The gathering fell quiet.

'Yes I am Doctor Quack, ye can be sure of that. I am less bird more bat, sucking your blood until I'm fat.'

No one laughed as they had done with the other introductions.

'Plague here, plague there, soon plague will be everywhere,' concluded the actor playing Doctor Quack.

A worried conspiratorial look passed between Iben and Thomas which wasn't lost on Haymaker.

'It's you. It's you he's representing.' Haymaker pointed at Thomas. Then he began to laugh so much he nearly fell off his throne. He was joined by one or two congenial sniggers down the table. Otherwise the room remained in an uncomfortable silence.

'I think you have had one too many beers already, young man,' Josiah told Haymaker, stepping forward to save the day. 'Best you leave now.'

'But I am King of Misrule,' objected Haymaker.

'Not anymore, you're not.' Josiah moved behind him and held his shoulders firmly.

'You are joking old man,' snarled Haymaker, twisting round.

The village smith, who had already been mortified by Haymaker's vulgar comments to his daughter, rose to his full six foot three. His arms were as thick as most men's thighs. 'I have just about had enough of you,' he told Haymaker. 'If you wish to take on Josiah here, then you must get past me first.'

Once faced up to, like most bullies, Josh crawled away without a bleat. Alas he missed the concluding mummers' performance of Little Johnny Jack. Johnny was played by a local man-boy who wasn't as young as he appeared to be. His wife and family were represented by dolls in a model house carried on his back. First he asked for food and then more urgently for money.

''Tis like the church offering on Sunday,' complained a bushy-bearded farmer. Nevertheless, shamed by the little man-boy's serious expression, he furnished him generously with a groat or two.

'Josh would have missed out on giving,' Iben muttered sarcastically to her mother.

'He gave you something though, didn't he? Something for you to think about.' There was no compassion in Agnes Hartmann's words. How Iben despised her mother.

After the mummers' performance ended, the guests began to slowly drift away. In the distance the church bell rang out midnight.

Josiah Bentham considered the wreckage from the party and decided that the clearing and cleaning would have to wait until the morrow. The rest of the household had already retired.

Thomas still in a state of exhilaration could not sleep at first. He lifted his bedchamber window to breathe in the night air and see the starry sky above. He felt the party had been a success on the whole. Sucking the cool night breeze deep into his lungs, he saw an expanding glow on the horizon. Was that smoke in the air he could smell or was he imagining it? He sniffed more greedily – hound-like – no, that was definitely smoke.

Calling for Josiah, he pulled on his breeches and topcoat.

'Whatever is the matter, Master?' Josiah arrived, confused in his nightshirt.

'There's smoke above the trees. Awaken the stable lad and have him saddle Russel.'

'What at this hour?'

Thomas did not trouble to answer. Josiah quickly concluded there really was some sort of serious emergency afoot and further enquiry would be pointless.

By the time Thomas galloped into Lucan Beadall's yard the thatch had gone, and roof beams were snapping and exploding with the heat.

Good neighbour Henry Winter was again on hand organising a human chain of men and women passing pails of water from the pump to the burning property. But it was a hopeless task apart from making the farming folk feel better about doing something.

'Lucan?' Was Thomas' first question to Winter.

'I fear lost.'

'Lost?' repeated Thomas in disbelief.

Winter shook his head explaining that the mummers were first to arrive to see the place going up in flames. ''Twas them that raised the alarm. They'd just visited my farm and then on to here. They knocked on Lucan's door. No answer. Then this …'

'So where are they now?'

'They fled. Afraid they would be blamed, I expect. Forgive me, Sir Thomas, I must get back to the pump.'

'I fear it is already a lost cause, Winter,' Thomas told him as another beam crashed through the roof, a top floor and down to ground level. The floor of the farm house began to glitter with several separate fires. It was only a matter of time before they joined into one conflagration. 'A lost cause,' emphasised Thomas. 'We don't want any further loss of life.'

'Move back lads and lasses, 'tis too late,' empowered Winter yelled across to the men and women.

Thomas walked before an agitated Russel, reins tightly in hand. The rest of the helpers, with soot blackened faces, followed on to watch the final destruction of Lucan's farmhouse safely from beyond the yard fence.

'Mummers you say alerted you all to this tragedy?' Thomas asked Winter.

'Indeed.'

'They had played at Rockfoot Hall earlier in the evening. I wonder if it was the same troupe.'

'I seem to remember a horse, a ram and a goat, a few fellas in dresses and someone was wearing a plague doctor's mask,' said Winter.

'Can you remember anything else?'

'Come to think of it there were two stags. One seemed slightly adrift from the rest of the troupe. But then he would be as he was there to stamp out evil.'

'Two you say?'

'Yes, it was very unusual. Some in the company of players, of a more superstitious mind, feared it was a bad omen.'

'Did the stags leave with the rest of the mummers?' asked Thomas, curious. He racked his brains to remember one stag mask at Rockfoot Hall let alone two.

'I cannot tell you for certain but I think after seeing a stag was already there, the second stag to arrive was first to leave.'

Thomas' eyes began to sting and Winter began to cough from smoke inhalation. Russel's eyes rolled back white as tongues of flames lashed through the farm cottage walls.

'Best be on my way. 'Tis almost dawn. There is nothing more to be done this day,' Thomas told Winter. 'I will inform the constable at first light.'

The stable lad was asleep on a bale of oats but hearing his master's arrival jumped to attention to unsaddle Russel. Josiah opened the door to the Hall still in his nightshirt.

'What's afoot, Master?' Josiah's fearful wide eyes reminded Thomas of Russel's rolling whites as the flames burnt through Lucan's farmhouse.

'Lucan Beadall's house has been burnt to the ground,' explained Thomas, flinging his coat off in helpless disgust.

'Evil spirits are abroad, sir. Look at them stolen sheep of yours and now this.'

'Evil spirits? Evil people, is more the way of it.'

Thomas was sure that Lucan had been the victim of plague hysteria. But how had word got out into the community at large about Lucan's illness? And who was responsible for such savagery? Just when Lucan was on the mend.

All these questions must be addressed to Constable Fox tomorrow. Meanwhile Thomas wrestled with possible culprits, tying himself up in bedsheets. Surely not Iben's family, or Henry Winter, or someone else holding a historic grudge. Sleep finally came but not before a stag had trampled across his half dreams.

* * *

Constable Fox arrived at Rockfoot Hall in late afternoon darkness. Thomas soon realised he wasn't a priority.

'We finally located Lucan. From the broken and twisted aspect of his body, we think he must have fallen from his bed down through a floor into what was once the parlour. He was blackened and burnt like charcoal beyond recognition.' Fox rubbed his nose across his sleeve. 'There was considerable damage to what was left of his skull from falling from such a height. We suspect foul play was involved in starting the fire.'

'But why? Why should anyone do such a wicked thing?'

'Fear of Black Death contagion of course.'

'But hardly anyone knew about that,' objected Thomas.

'I understand you were attending to him along with Iben Hartmann.'

'I was.'

'Nearly the whole village knew about poor Lucan, Sir Thomas,' scoffed Fox.

Unlike Iben, Thomas had been totally unaware of the local gossip and Iben's own father's suspicions that his tombstone business was about to thrive.

'I did my best not to spread news of his illness to avoiding panic among his neighbours.'

'Is the plague as highly contagious as they say and how is it spread?'

'Yes, it is very infectious though it is uncertain how it is transmitted. Some folk still believe it is a punishment from God, some believe that foreigners or those who follow a different religion have poisoned the wells, some think that bad air is responsible, some think the position of the planets is the cause.'

'But what do you think, Sir Thomas?'

'I would go for person to person contagion myself. However for some reason, despite attending Lucan Beadall at close quarters, Mistress Hartmann and I have been spared so far.'

'Hmm.' Thomas smiled as Fox surreptitiously stepped back.

'Then again in some people the plague has changed its nature, become even more deadly and affected victim's lungs. So that would suggest an airborne transmittance.'

'Hmm, airborne you say.' Fox took a further step back.

'Have you spoken to Henry Winter?' Thomas changed the subject.

'I have indeed.'

'Did he mention that the mummers were first on the scene at Lucan's farmhouse?'

'Yes, he was very helpful.'

'He is. He is a tenant of mine with a toft close to Beadall's Farm. He manages his holding extremely well with the help of two young sons.'

'Seems a capable fella.'

'Are you going to question the troupe?'

'I am. Though it will be difficult to know who is whom with them all in disguise that night.'

'Winter mentioned to me seeing two stag mummers at the fire though I cannot remember one playing here at the Hall.'

'Perhaps they joined the troupe later,' suggested Fox.

'Perhaps.'

'Are you not convinced?'

'I truly don't know. I don't suppose Lucan's murder has anything to do with the shepherd boy killed herding my sheep.'

'A little far fetched.'

'Not so far fetched. Both incidents happened within a few miles radius of St. Agnes.'

'I will look into it, Sir Thomas.'

'Do you not think it strange that there can be two such serious incidents in such a small parish when for years we have had none?'

'Remember only two decades ago, the majority of men were far from here away at war.'

'I am hardly likely to forget, Constable. I served King

Charles for many years myself before being exiled for many more.'

'A word of warning about that Hartmann lass, Sir Thomas. How can I put this delicately? She has something of a reputation hereabouts.'

Yet another innuendo about Iben. Thomas said nothing.

CHAPTER SEVEN

There was a cottage down the lane from the Hartmanns'. Unlike their neglected property the path was weeded, the garden immaculate. A widow in her mid-seventies lived there. Ann Collette was everything Agnes Hartmann was not. Ann was Iben's escape, her loadstone, her plateau. Far more important to her than any passing dalliances with village boys. Sometimes she took that other love in her life, Walter, to see Widow Collette. Her brother Walter loved Ann almost as much as Iben did. She made delicious honey cake.

Though Ann did her best with arthritic hands to keep the inside of her property in good order, Iben enjoyed cleaning and dusting for her. She got satisfaction from this charitable act, felt better about herself, hoped others would judge her in a better light.

'Is it true that you and Sir Thomas were treating Lucan Beadall for the Black Death?' the old lady dared to ask.

'I'd rather not say.'

'Forgive me child but when you reach my age only a valid explanation is satisfactory.'

'So I gather,' replied Iben a little sulkily.

'Have you heard some rogues burnt poor Lucan's house to the ground? Him inside it.'

Iben hung her head and said nothing before finally admitting that, yes, she had heard about the fire.

'You might think I am here cut off from the world but when you are old and wise the world comes to you.'

All the while Walter was yelling and riding Ann Collette's hobby horse wildly about the parlour.

'Walter be quiet for a moment. I cannot hear myself think,' Iben told him.

'I heard tell that the visiting mummers might have been responsible.'

'No, I cannot believe that.'

'Well they would hardly admit it, now would they, my sweeting?'

'They were all so nice when they visited the Hall.'

Walter started up again, astride the stick pressed high into his crotch, bouncing forward and up and down.

'Is that wild buck of yours still with the troupe?'

'Josh Haymaker? No they expelled him years ago.'

'Why?'

'Demanding more of the takings than was his due.'

'I heard a whisper that Haymaker was mainly responsible for the fire at Lucan's farm.'

'I can hardly believe he is that bad.'

'I never took to that lad, never saw what you could see in him. You are too good for the likes of him.'

Iben shook her head. How could she tell an old lady that it was solely Josh's sexual potency that took her by storm?

'Now Thomas Huck he was a far more likely swain for you.'

'Whatever you say Grandma Collette.'

'I do say.'

'You and my mother,' scowled Iben, beginning to dust energetically.

'So that is why you never took to Sir Thomas because Agnes pushed the match.'

'No, no, I…' Iben started on a vehement denial.

'Know ye, child, much of thy troubles comes from differences with Aggie.'

'But I've got you.' Iben kissed the old lady's cheek.

'I am not blood,' pointed out Ann emphatically. 'I truly wish I was but I am not, sweeting.'

* * *

Iben debated who she should tell about Ann's accusation about Josh Haymaker. She had to tell someone, the weight of the charge was too great for her to carry it alone. Her spirits fell as she realised there was only one person she could trust, one person significant enough to know how to deal with this information. She braced herself and strode out for Rockfoot Hall. Strode, that was the way Iben always walked. Her stride was more male than female – the walk of a young man – with purpose and today with even more motivation than usual.

Josiah opened to three firm knocks. He scowled on seeing it was Iben. Masters who think servants don't have a feel for situations are wrong. Iben glowered back at the old man.

'Sir Thomas,' she demanded.

'I'll enquire if he is at home,' Josiah sniffed.

'Do and don't be long about.'

Finally Thomas appeared. 'Come in, come in,' he told her, with far more enthusiasm than Josiah had been able to muster or liked to hear from his master. Behind Thomas' shoulder, Josiah frowned disapproval.

'I don't have long,' said Iben brusquely, sensitive to the atmosphere.

She stood warming herself at the glowing open fire in the parlour. There was a chasm of awkward silence between her and Thomas born of their uncomfortable history.

'So.' Thomas was first to speak. 'What can I do for you?'

'I have come across some rather disturbing news, Sir Thomas.' Iben decided to keep their conversation formal.

'News? Indeed.'

'Yes, news of a very delicate nature. It has been suggested to me that Josh Haymaker might be responsible for the fire at Beadall's Farm.'

'Haymaker? Well, that wouldn't surprise me. But why, why would Haymaker start the fire?'

'Plague,' whispered Iben. 'Gossip has been rife in the village for days that the Black Death is already amongst us.'

'Yes, so I have heard and we were so careful to keep it quiet. I was at least.'

'So was I,' she retorted edgily, making him feel guilty at his lack of trust. Then again he had never fully trusted her on anything.

'But tell me what did Haymaker achieve personally by committing such a vile act? I cannot imagine Joshua doing anything unless it was of direct benefit to himself.'

Iben pondered this statement. She was aware she had this in common with Haymaker. She never did anything unless it was of some direct advantage. Maybe, perversely, this shared personality trait was why she found Haymaker so attractive.

'He enjoys wickedness. He would look good in the community, a leader, a man of action against the disease,' she finally explained.

'You seem to understand this man's disposition well.' Thomas' irony was not lost on her either. She blushed. 'I will see that this allegation against Joshua Haymaker reaches the correct official body,' he concluded abruptly.

'Thank you.' She nodded.

'No, thank you,' he replied. 'Thank you for coming.'

As she was leaving Thomas hooked his arm through hers walking her to the door. She untangled and jerked her arm away from his – yet again breaking the chain of any possible intimacy. He shrugged and turned back into the Hall.

Thomas tried to gather his thoughts. He was well aware that Haymaker had once featured in Iben's life. How much, how little, he wasn't sure but he did not want to appear to be acting out of spite. However it was his duty to help solve such a heinous crime as the burning alive of Lucan Beadall, his tenant.

Summoned by Thomas' stable lad, the correct official body arrived in the corpulent form of Constable Fox soon after Iben had left. Thomas rapidly realised that Constable Fox was already cognisant of the allegation against Haymaker.

'Can I ask you, Sir Thomas, did you happen to notice if Haymaker stayed all evening at the Twelfth Night party?'

'Unfortunately it was hard to miss the fella as he was made King of Misrule for the night. However his behaviour became so offensive and outrageous we asked him to leave before the entertainment concluded.'

'What time would that have been?'

'Well the mummers hadn't quite finished their performance and the church bell hadn't struck midnight.'

'I did speak to Henry Winter about the stag mummers he said he had seen at the fire, or at least one stag as the other had vacated the scene shortly after his arrival. Interesting because we found a discarded straw stag mask in the Haymaker's family barn. His father and two brothers denied all knowledge of the thing at first. Although Haymaker senior eventually admitted to being a mummer at one time, said the battered old straw mask with its horn appendages could have been his, although he'd not seen it in years.'

'Of course, I had almost forgotten, the stag at the fire.'

'Well, in fairness, we don't know if the stag was responsible for the fire but it certainly looks as if the younger Haymaker was there in disguise.'

'Indeed.' Thomas began to rank Constable Fox a little more highly.

'There is a history to all this. There are two bands of young brigands, one in Perranzabuloe and the other in this parish. They hate each other. Mainly because Josh Haymaker fell out with the leader in Perranzabuloe to form his own band over here. Either of the bands is usually at the bottom of any thieving or trouble in our district.'

'Could they be responsible for stealing my sheep and killing that innocent lad as well as poor Beadall?'

'It is too early to say, Sir Thomas. We have to have proof rather than suspicion. However I am bearing everything in mind.'

Thomas was relieved to let his suspicions of the Hartmanns go for the time being, now with more viable culprits in the picture.

* * *

Jowan Carter's farm, Beechfield, was just within the boundary of the Rockfoot Estate. Whereas Beadall's Farm had been well within the estate's perimeter. Thomas decided to ride out to Beechfield and see how the new flock was faring. On his way he passed the smouldering embers of Lucan's farm. His heart went into his mouth – such a sad sight to see.

'Surprised to see you here, sir, today. What with Lucan's farm and all,' said Jowan Carter.

'Life has to go on. Where there is life that is.'

'Aye, you are right enough about that, Sir Thomas.'

'So are you pleased with the new Longwools that finally reached you?'

'They are doing well enough,' admitted Carter cagily.

'Have you heard anything about who might have been responsible for stealing those original sheep?'

'No, sir, nothing. Although I have my own unsubstantiated opinions on the matter.'

'And what may they be?'

'Did you know that there are two gangs of felons between this parish and Perranzabuloe? The Perranzabuloe gang is led by a Roger Martin, the leader of the gang in our parish is Josh Haymaker.'

Haymaker again, Thomas sighed quietly to himself. 'Constable Garren Fox was acquainting me with this situation only an hour or two back.'

'What did he say?'

'Very much the same sort of thing as you are telling me.'

'If there is any thieving, violence, assaults on womenfolk look no further than those men. They are as bad as they come.'

'So what would your guess be as to who was responsible for stealing the sheep and murdering one of the young chaps herding them.'

Carter looked perplexed at being put on the spot. He stroked his chin thoughtfully for a full half minute. 'Josh Haymaker,' he finally came up with. 'Though I've no proof,' he reiterated.

* * *

'How's Ayla settling in?' Thomas asked Josiah after she had cleared away his breakfast plates and swayed from the table towards the kitchen. She was seductive without intending to be.

'The little lass is trying hard,' replied Josiah. 'At least she is warm hearted unlike that other.'

'That other?'

'Aye, Iben Hartmann.'

Thomas sighed, there had never been any love lost between Josiah and Iben. Josiah had never been married and considered all women to be a threat. As far as Thomas could remember in the Rockfoot Hall family he had always been regarded with amusement, famed for his misogamy. Judging from his views on Iben they were correct.

'How does Ayla get on with the rest of the staff?'

'Keeps herself to herself but not without difficulty.'

'How do you mean? In what way?'

'Some of the scullions tried to waylay the young lass. I have already had to intervene, not once but twice. They cornered her in the buttery.'

'Which scullions?' Thomas felt a surge of anger.

'Two young lads you recently set on for kitchen duties.'

'Send them to me now.'

Josiah brought in the two young whelps as if he was arresting them. His hands balled up the shoulders of their shirts tightly revealing their flat bellies. Both were skinny and could have been little more than eighteen. Eighteen with bulging breeches and erotic potential, Thomas could see that straight away. Again the surge of anger or was it jealousy, he didn't care which but he wanted to beat them to pulp.

'Here they are, sir, Yates and Cuthbert,' announced Josiah. 'The two young gentlemen with no respect for womenfolk.'

'So what do you have to say for yourselves about molesting Ayla Nolan.'

''Twas just meant as fun,' piped up one of them.

'Fun?' asked Thomas in disbelief.

'No harm was done, Master,' said Yates, the self-appointed spokesman.

'No harm was done because Josiah got to you first.'

'True enough,' pealed in Josiah. 'Poor wee Ayla.'

'Poor wee Ayla was a whore back in Truro so Josh Haymaker told us.'

Not Haymaker yet again, sighed Thomas. 'So that made you both feel free to take liberties with her.' He struggled to collect himself.

'Just a little fun,' repeated Yates. 'She was game for it.'

'Was she really,' snapped Thomas.

'Yes, she loved us touching her, didn't she Cuthbert? Touching her all over. But he barged in and spoilt it all.' Yates pointed vindictively to Josiah. Cuthbert's cherubic lips seemed unable to form any agreement, any word. He looked frightened to death.

'She had a pair on her like I've never seen before, sir.' Yates formed the shape of breasts.

The fact that Yates thought Thomas would fall in with his smutty remarks increased Thomas' fury. He was used to soldiers' talk about camp followers, used to keeping his feelings under wraps, but this in his own home and about Ayla.

He suddenly grabbed Yates by his neckcloth. The boy looked surprised, then alarmed, then the eyes in his reddening face began to bulge.

'Sir Thomas you are strangling the life out of him,' warned Josiah, bringing Thomas back to his senses.

He pushed the shaking Yates away in disgust. 'Dismissed!' he snarled at both lads. They turned for the door to escape, perhaps thinking they had got away with it lightly. 'Dismissed and never return to Rockfoot Hall again,' Thomas screamed after them.

'We …' began Cuthbert, shocked. Younger and babyfaced, he began to cry in the doorway. Jobs were not easy to get in this part of Cornwall.

'I've no more time for this.' Thomas swotted them and any further lame excuses away.

'But Master …' pleaded Cuthbert. 'I've young siblings to support.'

'Get out before I take my fists to you.' They soon saw there was no mercy to be had in those blazing eyes.

Josiah smiled as he escorted the pair out.

'Jealous old bastard,' Yates spat back at him. 'Too old for any action yourself. And all this over an Irish scullery maid and whore.'

Thomas kicked over a chair, still incandescent with rage.

Later, after noon, he had Josiah make up a January fire in the parlour. He loved the cosy intimacy of the parlour. Only then did he begin to question the reasons for his extreme reaction against Yates and Cuthbert. Was it merely that Ayla was his personal project that her molestation was so abhorrent to him? He slid his leather marker from the pages of *Paradise Lost* and sat back to read. *The mind is its own place, and in itself can make a heaven of hell, a hell of heaven.* Milton's words played out as he stared into the flickering flames. He struggled to understand it. Is that what he was doing? Was he becoming as helpless as Milton's Adam in the Garden of Eden? Was he falling in love? But who with? Iben, who wanted nothing to do with him, or Ayla, still a child though an experienced provocative one?

CHAPTER EIGHT

Following the New Year festivities, the leap year came in more with a creep than a leap. In accordance with the Julian calendar, legally in England the year did not start until 25th March. But only legal men took much notice of that. Farming folk went by the seasons: brown leaf autumn moved into bare tree winter into burgeoning spring into plentiful summer.

Thomas stood in his bedchamber staring out of the mullioned window. He thought he saw one or two small brown birds fluttering across the grounds but soon realised they were blown leftover leaves, remnants of a harsh season. The moorland and fields beyond looked as if all life had been sucked out of the grasses and heather. Thomas felt a little like that himself, all life had been sucked out of him.

He wasn't often subjected to melancholia but a black cloud had descended from a far off horizon – he needed a project. Spring would soon travel in on the back of winter. There and then Thomas decided he had to rebuild Lucan Beadall's farm.

'You might have difficulty getting another tenant for that place,' Josiah warned him.

'Why, in God's name?'

'Nothing to do with God, Master. The farm has been doubly cursed, once with plague and then arson.'

'Superstitious hogwash and twattle,' Thomas told him.

Horse hooves could be heard scraping on the cobblestone yard outside. Thomas had a visitor to stay that February night. He was a staunch Royalist friend down from York and, following the war, was an occasional visitor to Rockfoot Hall. Under Charles II, Seymour Glover had become a Parliament man. Over wine and a beef dinner, he told Thomas of his concern that England might be thrown into a civil war again.

'Some in Parliament and the bishops are seeking to suppress the new Thomas Hobbes' treatise *Leviathan* in Latin,' he informed his host frowning. 'The chambers are buzzing with rumours.'

'*Leviathan,* I am not very familiar with the work,' Thomas admitted.

'It promotes the King as absolute ruler.'

'But Charles II *is* absolute ruler.'

'No, not quite as much as his father had been. It is stirring up old animosities once more. The question of how much power should parliamentarians and bishops have to that of the King in running the country.'

Ayla next appeared with apple cake. Seymour hadn't noticed her at first. He did now as she bent over him offering an accompaniment of fresh cream from the dairy. He ran his eyes up and down her smock, petticoat, tight corset emphasising her extraordinarily narrow waist.

'You're a shady cove, Thomas, still surrounding yourself with lovely things I see.'

'I am not alone in that,' chuckled Thomas.

'Expect you've not had word out here yet of the duel between the Duke of Buckingham and my Lord of Shrewsbury. London is full of it.' Seymour loved to gossip. 'It was all over that whore Lady Shrewsbury, whore to Buckingham.'

Why is it, wondered Thomas, if a woman is involved in an adulterous affair she is called a whore. Whereas a man …

'The two men met in a close near Barne Elmes to sort out their differences. Buckingham's main men were Holmes and one Jenkins. My Lord Shrewsbury's seconds were Sir John Talbot and Bernard Howard. Shrewsbury was run through from the right breast to the shoulder, Sir John Talbot slashed all along one of his arms and Jenkins killed upon that place. Buckingham escaped unharmed. The rest of his men were just slightly wounded. How foolish are we men to fight over a whore?'

'Passion,' suggested Thomas.

'Passion, that's it. Speaking of passion how's that lass that you were forever talking about?'

'Not sure who you mean.'

'You attempted to draw a likeness of her once.'

'Oh, Iben.'

'Iben, that was it. An unusual name.'

'I believe it was an old family name retained from her Norse ancestors.'

'Must say you depicted her as something of a valkyrie or shield-maiden, a skjoldjomfru. A very strong looking young woman, if my memory serves me right.'

'She is that all right but no longer young.'

'None of us are anymore. So, did you ever propose?'

'No, I am certain she would have refused me if I had.'

'Come on, man, the clock is ticking.'

'I know but the match is hopeless.' Thomas avoided Seymour's searching look.

'Sorry.' His friend reached his hand across the table to briefly touch Thomas' arm. Thomas noticed for the first time that his older friend was beginning to go bald.

'Anyway, what about you?'

'Betrothed at last at the age of forty-four.'

'Come Seymour you are still in your prime. We both are. Who is the lucky lady?'

'Matilda March from Suffolk, Lady Matilda March. And to cap it off we thought it would be jolly to marry next month in March,' chuckled Seymour. 'That is why I am here, Thomas, to invite you to the wedding.'

'Well ... I.' Thomas hesitated, he had the rebuilding of Beadall's Farm to oversee.'

'I would like you to be a groomsman.'

'Then how can I refuse,' Thomas smiled.

'The wedding is to be on Saturday 21st March at two of the clock in All Hallows-by-the-Tower.'

'The Tower?'

'The same.' The irony was not lost on Seymour.

'Then if I am not detained there by our King, I shall make a London week of it,' laughed Thomas.

'Matilda, my intended, was once wife to Sir Henry March, a brave officer of the Northern Horse killed at Marston Moor,' explained Seymour, suddenly serious.

'Too many good men on both sides have perished so,' agreed Thomas.

'She was married to him at twelve years of age. So she still might be of age to conceive my child.'

Thomas wondered if the same applied to Iben. If they were to marry would she still be able to give him an heir. He quickly discounted the possibility. She didn't even like him and he wasn't too sure of his feelings for her anymore. Both men supped deeply into their cups and memories.

In his bed that night, Thomas reflected that a visit to London could prove timely. He tossed about in confusion. He needed to break the toxic bond between himself and Iben and his growing unhealthy attraction to Ayla.

* * *

Thomas decided he would design the new farm himself. He wanted something special. He asked around the estate if anyone could recommend a good builder who would be sympathetic to his vision of buildings in a contemporary style.

'Heard about poor Beadall's misfortune,' commiserated Theodore Gillingham, an old friend and local tin mine owner.

'Aye, it was terrible. I plan to build an up-to-date farm in its place. I will draw the designs myself but I need a builder with an impeccable reputation. No expense spared.'

'Albert Spear of Bodmin is your man. None better for a quality job,' said Gillingham confidently. 'But do you feel experienced enough to play architect?'

'I have seen enough properties built on our estate since childhood to have a good idea.'

Thomas' design began with the farmhouse's foundations or strip footings. These consisted of a continuous level strip of lime mortar as a base for a linear construction such as a wall or row of wooden joists. A three-course layer of bricks would then be laid on top of the strip below floor level. The house would be timber framed with brick panels in the modern style. However it was the bank barn that captivated him as much as the house. Built across a slope the barn would have two levels – a combination barn of two storeys. Through constructing the barn against a bank, both floors can be entered from ground level. There would be a threshing floor and storage bays, a granary and hayloft, sited above cattle housing, stables and other functions such as cart sheds. He intended for Rockfoot

New Farm to have a separate dovecote, a dairy and even possibly a brew house.

Iben called as he was formulating his designs. She was becoming a regular visitor. A rather worrying visitor. A sulky Josiah showed her in.

'Just called to see if there is any further news about Josh Haymaker's possible involvement in the fire at Lucan Beadall's farm.'

'You are very concerned.'

'Not at all. Just concerned for a friend's welfare.'

'So you can warn him,' sighed Thomas.

'If I was going to warn him, I wouldn't have told you about that piece of local tattle in the first place.'

'True enough,' he agreed. 'Would you like to see my new plans for Beadall's place?' An appeasement gesture.

Iben turned up her nose unenthusiastically as he explained his plans in detail.

'You don't like them?'

She said nothing.

'See, an ash house for fertiliser could go there.'

'Lucan would have loved to live in this.'

'I regard it as a monument to the man.'

'Is that how you see it?' she sneered.

'What about you? Could you live in a place like this?'

'Me?' She stared at him in disbelief.

'Yes, you, but you would have to find a husband first.'

'Chance would be a fine thing,' she shrugged.

The irony of her comment 'Lucan would have loved to live in this' hadn't passed him by either. What did he expect? – Iben never showed any approval for the projects he was involved in. And he wasn't so sure her disapproval was simply based on money and class.

In the quick forge and working house of thought,
How London doth pour out her citizens.

The Mayor and all his brethren in best sort, Like to
the senators of th' antique Rome.

Shakespeare must have found London bewildering at first as it was a culture shock for a country boy. It housed 350,000 inhabitants, dwarfing most other cities in Europe. Was he risking his life coming here if not from violent thugs then from disease? The Great Plague had recently cost 69,000 Londoners their lives. In contrast only a few people lost their lives in the Great Fire, started in Pudding Lane in September 1666, however London was a place of desperation. The fire consumed 13,200 houses, 87 parish churches, St. Paul's Cathedral, and most of the buildings in the city authorities. With thousands left homeless, theft and other crimes swept what was left of the city, as well as sickness and disease. Temporary buildings and camps were made to shelter people through the winter of 1666/67 as the city slowly began to rebuild.

After arduous days of dusty travel the first thing to hit Thomas, standing on the bank of the Thames, was the stench. Everything was thrown into the water: excrement, decaying food, dead animals, even dead people occasionally. Londoners believed all this filth would eventually flow into the sea, unfortunately what they didn't realise was how strong the river tides could be and what went downstream soon floated back upstream.

Despite that, despite plague and fire, the streets buzzed with commerce. Nonetheless, Seymour had warned him that many buildings were made from such cheap materials –

crumbling bricks and knotty timber – that it was not unusual for them to collapse. Heavy, pendulous shop signs projected out from storefronts on large iron bars. The signs, regularly whipped by the wind, could create such force that the entire facade of a building would come crashing down with them. This sometimes happened on top of unsuspecting passers-by. So, though exciting, daily life was hazardous in the capital because of quick and shoddy workmanship. Thomas could see how houses and tenements had been thrown together in a slapdash manner following the fire, with little attention to plans or codes. Buildings were patched up, subdivided, and subdivided again to cram as many people into as little square footage as possible, which left a jumble of narrow, unlit passageways between residences and shops. He decided not to walk through any of these stinking airless alleyways – particularly after dark – judging them to be dangerous, since the convoluted pattern of streets provided excellent cover for lurking criminals. This lack of attention to design and function only served to make him more determined that Rockfoot New Farm would not follow suit.

London was filled with the smell of wet horses and the waste materials associated with them. Sanitation was unheard of. Beware, he had been warned, beware of opening bedchamber windows as you strolled below. It was common place for residents to empty their chamber pots out of their windows on the heads of passers-by, or leave slippery garbage out in the street to trip you into a broken leg. He could see an amazing variety of rotting filth slopping down the cobblestone streets. Along with dirt, dust and animal manure, there was the ever-falling London rain to add to the mess. Cesspools of human waste collected in puddles everywhere. Dead animals such as dogs, cats, rodents, even horses were left to decay in the streets. Seymour had told him he had once come across the corpse of an old man abandoned in a dark alleyway.

Seymour had donned a fashionable silver peruke, gathered at the back with a green ribbon, for his wedding. It was a long affair with curls at the side, perfect for concealing his approaching baldness. Matilda March was lined but still a comely enough woman in her late thirties. The wedding was a more modest affair than Thomas had envisaged. There were some of Seymour's army pals invited to act as groomsmen as well. Thomas could not restrain a smile in the knowledge that groomsmen were in Biblical times nothing more than bride snatchers. A bride-to-be was required to receive her family's permission to marry. If this did not occur, the bride was often forcibly removed from her home by the groom and a troop of 'bride-knights' in a practice known as 'marriage by capture.' So during a large portion of the history of groomsmen, these men served as the groom's army, fighting the bride's relatives so that the groom could abscond with the bride. Thomas was glad his role would not involve kidnapping and combat.

The best man back in history was the best fighter. Looking at Seymour's choice for this role, the man conformed in every way, particularly in appearance, to that canon. Jeff Challenger had the flat nose of a pugilist, indeed his whole face appeared to be scarred and flattened. Such a contrast to the beautiful bridesmaids in their Italian pastel shaded dresses.

Soon the formalities were over and the happy couple married. The rest of the wedding party decided to retire to The League of Seven Stars tavern in Carey Street. Challenger told them it was named to attract Dutch seamen, reminding them of the seven provinces of the Netherlands.

Challenger, it seemed, was a familiar of this particular drinking den. The fare was excellent and the mutton pie went some way to settling Thomas' rumbling stomach. It even went as far as to distract him from Challenger's overt flirtations with the bridesmaids.

'Interested in a little fun this night?' asked a woman, lifting her skirts and cavorting her wares in a hovel doorway as Thomas made his way to his rooms. He shook his head. How different this strumpet to Ayla. A little fun and a lifetime of the pox, he thought.

However thoughts of a lustful encounter did nothing to prevent the return of his stomach churning on reaching his rooms in Rosemary Lane. Indeed perhaps they exacerbated it. Nothing makes a more detestable sight than the end-of-the-day butchers' stalls, especially in that neighbourhood. The guts and other refuse are all thrown on the street and set up an unbearable stink. In addition, if you failed to tread with care, you risked slipping on slimy offal and falling flat on your face. Not the best entrance to make to your lodgings, bloodied and looking like Ingram Frizer escaping the murder of poor Marlowe.

However his landlady, Damaris Page, was a fat heavy woman who looked capable of looking after herself in any circumstance. Initially one would have thought her to be an open soul, however there was something secretive behind all that cheerfulness. Her rooms had been recommended to him by Seymour. She greeted him with 'Good evening, Master Huck. I hope you had an enjoyable day and that Master Seymour's wedding went well.'

'Indeed, Mistress Page, all went off well,' he informed her, amused at her discreet use of 'Master' as a form of address, before scuttling off to his room.

The next day, Sunday, saw Thomas in church. Though he was away from home and a tacit non believer, he was conditioned to attend, to be seen attending in metropolitan society. Sunday was a peaceful day in the city – the quiet before the storm – before all hell broke out.

Monday, and London was about to be in ferment. The only oasis of calm would be the Globe Theatre across the river in Southwark. A great fan of the late William Shakespeare, Thomas had hired a wherryman to row him across to the south bank that morning. He wished to pay homage to the bard's genius if only by seeing where his plays were performed. On his return he saw small groups of young men, hanging about the streets and kicking their heels, with seemingly nothing to do. Many of these idlers looked to be no more than apprentices. He thought little of it. It was Easter Monday when all was said and done. Thomas called in at the George Inn near London Bridge, where he was told Shakespeare had been a regular, and that afternoon first learned from the frosty looking landlady of trouble in Poplar.

'The levellers are at it again,' she moaned. 'I thought the war would put an end to all this once and for all.'

'Not with a licentious king on the throne. A king who will allow young men to visit the bawdy houses but not have them retain their Puritan belief and hold church services,' retorted one stiff looking fellow.

'A weak excuse for burning and looting if you ask me,' said the landlady.

'No one is asking your opinion,' snarled a miserable looking individual wearing a spotted neckerchief in the French fashion.

'No, there is a general dissatisfaction with the common man's lot,' said another customer with blackened teeth.

'Better keep your private opinions to yourself, Will. There are eyes and ears everywhere in London at present,' warned the landlady.

'None of them can worry me,' growled back Will. 'Not after Naseby.'

The landlady turned to Thomas. 'And of what persuasion are you, sir?'

'As you said there are eyes and ears everywhere.' Thomas deflected the question, focusing down on his beer.

'I think we can guess from the bows on yer shoes and the lace at yer wrists.' Will flashed a smile through those blackened pegs – that wasn't really a smile but something far more hostile in nature.

Thomas began to feel uncomfortable. The war had been over for some eight years but still emotions were running high in certain quarters. He left his drink untouched and made for the door.

'Filthy Royalist.' He heard Will spit on the inn's floor behind him.

'You shouldn't always judge a man by the cut of his cloth,' Thomas shouted back at him as he made his escape.

So far he had resisted visiting the gruesome sight of Oliver Cromwell's, John Bradshaw's and Henry Ireton's heads held aloft on poles above Westminster Hall. But stirred up by his altercation in the George Inn, he needed convincing that the war was really over.

Oliver Cromwell, Lord Protector and ruler of the English Commonwealth died on 3rd September 1658 of natural causes. He was given a public funeral at Westminster Abbey equal to those of the monarchs who came before him. His position passed to his son Richard, who was overthrown shortly afterwards, leading to the re-establishment of the monarchy.

King Charles II returned from exile in 1660, his heart full of vengeance. A year later his new parliament ordered a January disinterment of the elder Cromwell's body from Westminster Abbey for a posthumous execution at Tyburn, as well as those of his son-in-law, Henry Ireton, and John Bradshaw the judge who sentenced Charles I to death, The men's bodies were drawn on hurdles from Holborn to Tyburn and there hanged on the common gallows. They were left hanging from morning till four in the afternoon before being cut down and beheaded. The heads were then placed on 20-foot poles and displayed on the roof of Westminster Hall, which had been the venue for the trial of Charles' father.

Thomas looked up to the Banqueting House of Westminster Hall and fixed on the first skeletal head of what he took to be Cromwell. Being on the opposing side, he had never had any dealings with the great man though he had seen one or two likenesses. However he could not help thinking this grisly exercise and display was unfitting for a civilised country – then he had seen enough to know civilised behaviour could soon break down – this was one man's act of revenge, one king's revenge on another. Thomas walked away in disgust at the barbarity of his own countrymen.

He needed a drink. He made his way back to London Bridge as Seymour had recommended the Bear at the bridge-foot. Seymour had assured him it was a *suttling* where like-minded people drank. As he crossed the bridge cold air rose up from the river chilling the very core of him.

'Warming punch, if you please,' he ordered from the barmaid. The Bear was a place of creaking antiquity with a glowing fire in the hearth.

''Tis cold out there this night, sir,' said the girl, dipping a ladle into the huge steaming punchbowl.

'The river makes it cold,' said Thomas.

'It has been known to freeze right over, sir, so much so that folk could walk from Southwark into the city. My mother talks of going to a Frost Fair held on the Thames for weeks when she was a child.'

'The river is what makes this city great,' pointed out Thomas, his spirits reviving with the punch.

In contrast the girl's expression clouded. 'It took the life of the mistress here just over a year ago.'

'How so?'

'She flung herself into the water. A tragedy, sir.'

A little more subdued Thomas took a seat by the fireside. Looking round at the other customers, he immediately saw and heard that the Bear was more Cavalier than Roundhead.

''Tis a cold evening. Might I join you?' asked a big robust individual in the uniform of a captain.

'Be my guest.'

The Captain took a seat; his long soft leather boots squeaking as they rubbed together. 'Where are you from?' he asked. 'Not from London from your accent.'

'The West Country.'

'The West Country, thought so' pondered the Captain. 'Where in the West Country?'

'Cornwall.'

'Really. That's a coincidence, I myself came from Blisland, know it?'

Thomas nodded, wondering where this was going.

'Cornwall never gets as cold as London,' said the Captain.

'Indeed,' agreed Thomas. There was something familiar about the Captain but for the life of him Thomas could not determine where he had seen him before. He had fine features somewhat lost in a full moon face, no doubt swollen by years of heavy drinking and fine fare.

'I have been a wanderer most of my life, an army wanderer. I am here under Lord Craven to put down the threat of insurrection by the prentices.'

'I was in the army too,' admitted Thomas.

'Where did you fight?'

'Worcester, under Major William Careless.'

'At the end then.'

'Yes, I was exiled with Careless.'

'Is it true he hid with the King in oak trees to avoid capture?'

'So the story goes,' said Thomas.

'What is your name, sir?'

'Huck, Thomas Huck.'

'And yours, sir?'

'Nolan, Richard Nolan at your service.'

Nolan, Thomas wracked his brain. 'Have I met you before?'

'Not that I am aware.'

'Have you ever served in Ireland?' he asked.

'To my deep regret that I have.'

'Under Cromwell?'

'Unfortunately that too.'

'So, you have changed allegiances?'

'I am a professional soldier. Professional soldiers go where they are needed.'

'And where they are paid.'

'And where they are paid,' agreed the Captain; his belly shaking with laughter.

'But you weren't a soldier for the whole time you were in Ireland?'

Richard Nolan regarded Thomas with sudden suspicion. 'What if I wasn't?'

'Were you given a farm to run?'

'What if I was?'

'Then one of the children you abandoned works for me.'

'Abandoned?' Nolan's face turned a deeper puce. 'I was driven out by a family who didn't want me there. My wife had no real affection for me, and her father hated me. It was better that I left than bring my bairns up in that atmosphere.'

'Ayla, Ayla is her name.'

'Ah, Ayla.'

'Would you like to be reunited with your daughter?'

Nolan shook his head. 'Best not after all this time.'

'She is a lovely girl.'

'Can I get you another drink?' said Nolan, deflecting any more questions on the subject – a subject he seemed to find very painful.

* * *

Thomas would have to decide if he should tell Ayla of this meeting. That decision could come later.

Meanwhile things were getting worse in the capital. The next day, Tuesday, hundreds of men began to gather. It was apparent they were all bent on trouble. In and among them were the green aprons of prentices. Thomas was curious and decided to follow on.

Among the rallying cries of the mob were 'down with the Red Coats! Reformation and reducement! We have been servants, but we will be masters now!' They threatened both 'that if the King did not give them liberty of conscience, that May Day must be a bloody day, and that erelong they would come and pull Whitehall down.'

Thomas feared this atmosphere amounted to a spirit of revolution and that King Charles would have to put it down speedily by forceful means.

'Tear down the Great Bawdy House at Westminster,' a loutish looking lad shouted. They organised into regiments, with their own captains, and proceeded to first besiege brothels in East Smithfield and Moorfields.

It wasn't long before a troop of soldiers and militia waded in and made many arrests. Thomas looked out for Ayla's father from the doorway of a coffee shop but could not see him. Luckily Nolan had forewarned him of this threat. It seems the mob ventured as far as Shoreditch but Thomas decided not to follow them that far.

Still he heard that there was trouble all day and the next day.

Mistress Page had told Thomas she owned other properties about London, including the building where he was lodging and one across the way. Even so he was amazed and terrified to see from his upstairs window, a mob had gathered outside the opposite property. They began to sack the place and assault the girls living there.

Screaming females fell out onto the street dressed in the flimsiest attire. One or two of their clients, hurriedly pulling up breeches, attempted to hide amid the women's ballooning skirts. The scene at first was almost comical before turning into complete chaos. There was no Mistress Page to be seen but there was someone else he knew. A crawling Seymour Glover emerged from the building behind the rest. He obviously had been badly beaten. As if he had not suffered enough, he was pushed to the ground by a long bearded thug who began to kick him. Thomas rushed downstairs and pulled the man off, who was still in hot and determined pursuit. Thomas kicked out at Seymour's assailant as he dragged his friend into Mistress Page's passageway.

'Thomas, you need a woman to warm your bed.' Seymour's advice was splattered into the air with blood, teeth and saliva. Thomas ducked to avoid the emission.

'A woman like you've just been with, I suppose.'

'No, like that fulsome wench back home. Iben's her name, I seem to recall.'

Thomas gave no answer as he struggled up the stairs with his injured friend back to his room.

'How come a married man wed for only four days is seen stumbling out of a bawdy house?' he asked, washing and dressing Seymour's wounds.

'I do love Matilda very much but she is … I find she has no liking for carnality.'

'But you risk the pox. You risk giving her the pox.'

'Not at all. Damaris runs the sweetest girls in town. And a man has his needs.'

'Damaris? Mistress Page? She is a bawd?' Thomas had been slow to catch on.

'Come, you didn't know?' Seymour chastised him. 'I thought if you were so inclined you might take advantage of the neighbourhood pleasures on hand. That is why I suggested you take rooms here.'

Thomas was speechless for a minute or two.

'Damaris manages the Three Tuns in Stepney for seamen and the brothel across the way for the wealthy, such as naval officers,' continued Seymour. 'She is very popular in certain quarters.'

'Is that why the mob is pulling down her house? Popularity?'

'They are conventicles dissatisfied with their lot. They despise the bawdy houses because they are not allowed to hold nonconformist services of more than five people outside the Church of England. They feel Charles condones prostitution while insisting on conformity of worship.'

'So in what quarters is Mistress Page not popular?'

'That is a little more complicated. Damaris has been suspected for some time of being involved in press ganging into the Navy some of her dock worker clientele, especially from the Three Tuns in Stepney.'

'No wonder the mob is attacking her property then,' said Thomas, looking from his window. The building opposite was flattened now, dismantled brick by brick. He was dismayed, wanton destruction always dismayed him for whatever reason. 'We didn't fight for this,' he told his friend.

A little while later, when the crowd's anger seemed to be spent and they were gone, Thomas watched Seymour shuffle away down the road professing his lifelong gratitude. Their country was in peril again walking blindly towards another civil war, and he feared his friend was limping towards destroying his marriage.

That evening a flustered Dolores arrived to tell Thomas it was still mayhem on many streets.

'Some blood hath been spilt, and a great number of houses pulled down including mine,' she wheezed and panted. 'Thankfully I have invested in other properties along Ratcliffe Highway. I have heard that the Duke of York has complained merrily that he hath lost two tenants, by their houses being pulled down, who paid him for their wine licences. One of them being me.'

To Thomas' amazement this resilient woman began to laugh out loud.

'The Duke of York?' Thomas asked his eyes agog with surprise.

'Aye, the same. The Duke is a good customer of mine. It shouldn't be long before my houses are rebuilt and my business restored. But, alas, I have heard that the mob has already freed many of their compatriots from the New Prison, Clerkenwell. Nevertheless, should you need some comfort, sir, I can send one of my best girls round to share your bed this night.'

Thomas thanked her profusely for the offer. He declined, saying that he was looking forward to returning to Cornwall the very next morning. The journey being so arduous, he was best with a good night's sleep before making it. Once upon a time, he told her, when younger he might have been tempted by one of her young delights but not anymore. According to Delores, the Duke of York's brother, the King, had said regarding the prentices' grievances against houses of pleasure, 'Why, why do they go to them then?'

'Functional mechanical fornication holds nothing for me these days,' he reaffirmed to the famous bawd of seamen, the most famous bawd in town.

She looked at him pityingly. 'Why? Why do you feel that way?' she asked. 'Maybe someone has already stolen thy heart.'

'I cannot actually say.'

CHAPTER NINE

When you have been away, even for a few days, you expect things to be irrevocably changed. Usually nothing is different and so it was for Thomas those first few days back home. No one had been charged with the shepherd boy's murder nor had a culprit been found for Lucan Beadall's fire.

He had already decided on his jolting coach journey back from London not to tell Ayla of his encounter with her father. *Ne reveillez pas le chien qui dort – Do not wake the dog that sleeps.*

He started work on perfecting his designs for Rockfoot New Farm before finally sending them off care of Albert Spear of Bodmin.

Thank God for the King's recently set up General Post Office. A service that helped Thomas keep abreast of events outside his remote little corner of the south west. While in London he arranged for the *London Gazette* to be posted to him each weekday. He learned that beyond Rockfoot Estate, affairs of state continued to be enacted. He read that Charles had recently signed an agreement with representatives of the English East India Company to lease Bombay to them for ten pounds sterling per year, with the transfer taking effect the following September.

A good deal done there by both parties, recognised Thomas privately to himself.

Several days later, Thomas had correspondence from Seymour thanking him for his kindness and solicitous attention in London. Seymour further informed him that fifteen suspected ringleaders of the uprising were arrested, and charged with high treason. Thomas later heard that four had been subsequently convicted, and then horrifically punished – castrated, drawn and quartered – a punishment usually reserved for traitors and rebels.

According to a second letter from Seymour, Henry, the Third Viscount Brouncker, a fellow medic like Thomas and Member of Parliament for New Romney, was being hunted by the Commons for expulsion. Charges were being brought against him for allowing the Dutch fleet to escape during the Battle of Lowestoft, and for ordering the sails of the English fleet to be slackened in the name of the Duke of York. This was essentially an act of treason. Such a military decision, taken without the Duke's authority, was an incident seemingly without parallel, especially as his apparent motive was simply that he was fatigued with the stress and noise of the battle.

While in Europe treaties were signed to end all wars. The Triple Alliance was signed by England, the Swedish Empire and the Dutch Republic that May. It was created in response to the occupation of the Spanish Netherlands and Franche-Comté by France. Although Spain and Emperor Leopold were not signatories, they were closely involved in the negotiations.

Another hammering on Thomas' door, another twist of fate.

'Please come, Sir Thomas.' It was Henry Winter again.

At the time these grave toing and froing deliberations were happening between nations – an old man was found dead in a ditch close to Beadall's Farm. He was found by an estate worker employed in levelling the ground before building work could begin.

'Do not attempt to touch this man,' Thomas warned his workers.

'But we can't just leave the old gent here,' objected Henry Winter.

'You can and you must for the moment,' Thomas told them all firmly. The old man's glazed eyes stared up at them from the ditch. His eyes were wide open and seemed to be asking a question. His long grey hair unkempt and matted. 'Do any of you know this man?' asked Thomas.

Much scratching of chins and shaking of heads.

'Maybe the poor soul came hoping for work with the planting,' suggested Winter.

'From London,' suggested someone else. Faces paled and fell.

'Do you think he has died of plague, sir?' Winter asked Thomas.

Thomas had already taken in the telltale buboes on the corpse's neck and the skin of his fingers and nose were blackened and dead. He nodded, there was no use pretending anymore that the Black Death hadn't invaded their snug isolation, but he had no wish to give concrete confirmation to Winter's suspicion. The terror of plague was centuries old since the first outbreak in 1348 cut the population of England by half. There had been occasional outbreaks in intervening years until the next destructive storm was to hit London less than three years ago.

'An itinerant labourer then,' he concluded. 'I shall inform Constable Fox and immediately send for Joseph May, the carpenter. Joseph will know what to do.'

Winter agreed to stay with the dead man until Joseph May arrived.

Good old Henry Winter always on hand in a time of crisis, recognised Thomas.

* * *

The next morning Constable Garren Fox arrived at Rockfoot Hall.

'The body is with carpenter Joseph May,' Thomas explained. 'I think the workers who found him thought his blackened extremities were due to natural decay. However they were not. The poor old fellow died of plague without a doubt. Do you want to see the body?'

Fox shook his head. 'No, I'll take your word for it, Sir Thomas.'

'Thank you for your confidence. I think we are better enacting containment lest we repeat yet another pandemic.'

'A terrible illness for sure. I have heard tell it is spread from rat fleas, is that so, Sir Thomas?'

'Certainly rat fleas. However I have a further theory for its rapid transmission.'

'And what might that be?'

'Human to human from the lice they carry. Though few of my colleagues would give any credence to such a notion. And now we have this new variant disease that seems to affect the lungs. As I have mentioned to you before I think it might be airborne.'

'I believe you to be a clever man. Perhaps one day you might be proved right. But how do you propose to enact containment?'

'Discourage large gatherings of folk. Maybe hold church services out in the open countryside once again.'

'That won't go down well with the priest.'

'Well, let's wait and see if there are any more cases. No good causing unnecessary panic in the community. Maybe we won't get too many folk infected here in the southwestern tip. Any news about the shepherd boy's murderer or Lucan Beadall's fire?' asked Thomas, changing the subject onto something more tangible that might be resolved sooner rather than later.

'Nothing as yet but I did find that business of the two masked stags confusing.'

'Maybe it was meant to be confusing,' suggested Thomas.

'In what way?'

'Well a masked mummer cannot be easily identified.'

'Josh Haymaker said the stag mask found in his family's barn had been originally discarded by his father. He didn't deny that he took it up and followed the mummers and went to Lucan Beadall's farm after your Twelfth Night party, but said he left as soon as he realised there was someone else in a similar mask. He insists he had nothing to do with the fire.'

'So, what was his excuse for visiting the farm?'

'Said he was angry at being ejected from the Twelfth Night celebrations at Rockfoot Hall, and therefore wanted to disrupt the night a little for your neighbours.'

'That's Haymaker all over,' sighed Thomas.

'The shepherd boy's father is pressing us hard to find the rogues who beat his son to death. He will not rest until we find those responsible. Is the reward still open?'

'Of course.'

Once Fox was shown out by Josiah, Thomas called his servant back. 'You don't like Iben very much do you?' Thomas asked him. Something had been brewing in the back of his mind, troubling him for some time. 'Why is that?'

'I just don't,' replied Josiah bluntly.

'Is there any truth that Iben might have been involved romantically with my brother?' Now it was out, now it was said.

'Romantically? I would not be knowing about that.'

'So what do you know?'

'I heard she had a bastard when she was thirteen, little more than a child herself.'

'What?' Thomas gasped.

'Aye 'tis so. That is what I heard. Agnes did her best to cover it up but word got out.'

'And who was the father?'

'Nobody knew for sure but Josh Haymaker chose to shoulder the blame. I'll give him that.'

'So he wasn't the father? Who do you think the true father was then?' Josiah fell silent. 'Josiah?' persisted Thomas.

'I cannot rightly say but there were rumours.'

'Rumours about whom?' Again silence.

'Not Robert? Not Robert in congress with someone little more than a child?' Thomas felt sick in the pit of his stomach. It was all beginning to fall into place. Iben's attitude towards him, Haymaker's hostility, Agnes' ambition to redress a wrong and to restore Iben to a pre-eminent position.

'No one knows for sure. But Robert certainly wasn't cut from the same cloth as you.'

'Was he not? I didn't really know him that well.'

'Let it be, sir. Forget about Iben Hartmann, she is ill-fated for you. You don't need any more drama, conflict and distress in your life than needs be. You have fought your war. What you need now is a cheerful home, positive folk around you and food on the table.'

'That sounds like waiting to die to me, old man. I am going out,' said Thomas abruptly.

Walking among the trees had a primeval feel to it. The leaves swishing in the wind above his head, above his swirling thoughts. He felt an innate fear in the forest, a fear passed down through generations. A fear that there might be a surprise attack from a wild animal waiting in the darkness beyond. But he was enjoying that fear as he tried to assimilate the veracity of what he now suspected was truth. No fear could be greater than his present confusion.

Iben's games and lies. Now, as she had years ago before the war, he felt her getting bored with him. He had never knowingly bored anyone in his life. Regardless of his many failings, monotony had never ever been named as one. Whatever he said or did, nothing seemed to interest Iben, nothing impressed her. Maybe she despised his ignorance of his brother's role in her blighted life. Whatever the reason she appeared to have no real empathy or affection for him. Then again, maybe those positive sentiments had always been solely reserved for herself.

Iben encouraged people to love her and yet gave little back. Her indifference wouldn't bother someone like Haymaker who was only interested in taking himself. There was a disengagement about her, despite this she always knew the right things to say to suck you in.

And yet, and yet, she often had such a sad face in repose which never failed to ping at his heart strings. She was the embodiment of Mary Magdalene as Melancholy.

Perhaps he would never know if Robert had fathered a child with Iben. Not unless Iben told him herself and he doubted very much that she would. He had never known anyone as secretive. She said so little, never told him anything.

Thomas read in the *Gazette* that Spain and France had sorted out their differences over the Spanish Netherlands. Everyone seemed to be befriending everyone if not in his personal life. He hadn't seen Iben for weeks. He was glad to be occupied with other matters rather than her. The ground for Rockfoot New Farm was ready to be built on. Albert Spear called to discuss his designs and agreed to stay the night before travelling back to Bodmin. Thomas took to him straightaway, judging him to be an honest tradesman.

'Not often am I privileged to drink a good wine like this,' said Spear. 'Complements the veal pie perfectly.'

'Enjoy,' Thomas told him. 'My aim is to put you in good spirits before I reveal a few additional thoughts for Rockfoot Farm.'

'I am sure I will be able to carry out your wishes, Sir Thomas.'

Spear was bald and rotund. He looked as if he would be physically incapable of climbing building ladders though Thomas realised this cannot have been the case.

After they had dined, they sat looking over the plans by a roaring fire in the parlour.

'Thank goodness for killas,' announced Spear.

'Killas?' Thomas looked blank.

'Yes, although Beadall's Farm was burnt to the ground, the ground thereabouts is hard sedimentary rock, good for foundations.'

'I want the building to be long and low in the traditional manner but built with the latest materials,' explained Thomas.

'I wouldn't advise anything else,' agreed Spear.

'Good, good.' A good start this, acknowledged Thomas. He felt like a grammar schoolboy facing a Latin exam.

'You haven't expressed whether you'd like the frame to be made with sweet chestnut or oak, sir.'

'Chestnut, I think.'

'And what infill panels would you like? Wattle and daub is cheaper.'

'No I decided on bricks.'

'Brick noggins it is then.'

'Rendered with Cotswold limewash,' added Thomas.

'A good choice. And you want all the buildings treated in the same manner from the farmhouse to the barn?'

'The same.'

Spear did not take notes. He appeared to commit all this information to memory.

'I like the idea of clay roof tiles rather than thatch, better wearing and less of a fire risk,' explained Thomas.

'True enough.'

'The few windows we have in the farmhouse itself I would liked glazed.'

''Tis going to be so grand I might make you an offer on the property myself,' laughed Spear.

'Then you would have to learn to be a farmer.'

Thomas lifted a decanter of port from a nearby table and poured Spear a generous glass. How different this man's enthusiasm for his building project to Iben's. But then Spear was getting paid for the work.

'To Rockfoot New Farm,' Thomas lifted his glass in a toast.

'To Rockfoot New Farm,' mimicked Spear. 'I'll set my lads onto the job come June. And what would you have me do if there are any clay roof tiles left, Sir Thomas?'

'No idea.'

'Might I suggest Beechfield's roof could do with a little restoration.'

'Jowan Carter's place? You know Jowan Carter?'

'Aye, I do just in passing. And I could not help noticing …'

'Well, of course, if there are a few tiles left over,' ceded Thomas, somewhat surprised and a little suspicious. But he had no wish to appear to be a miserly overlord.

'Good, good, we'll see how things work out then.'

'I await your estimate for this work.'

'I'll have it drawn up in a day or two, Sir Thomas.'

'You are a terrific businessman, Spear, I hope your construction skills are a match.' He replenished the builder's glass again, ignoring his refusing hand.

'Have no fear I'll do my best for you.'

'You came highly recommended after all.'

'Recommended? By whom?'

'Theodore Gillingham, the tin mine owner at Beaconcombe.'

'Ah! Gillingham.' Spear looked a little taken back. 'I supplied him with lumber for his mine props on the cheap.'

'I hope you will do your best to keep costs low for me too,' Thomas told him.

* * *

Ayla served him bacon, eggs and sausages the next morning.

'How are you Ayla?' Thomas asked the girl. 'No more trouble from the male servants, I hope.'

'No, sir.' Since her arrival at Rockfoot Hall, Ayla had become more contained and careful in her replies. Thomas had mentioned this to Josiah who retorted that maybe she knew her place.

'And pray what place might that be?' asked Thomas.

'A servant of your lower household, Master.'

'Unlike yourself.'

'Unlike me.' Josiah frowned, he did not understand sarcasm.

'In turn Thomas frowned, aware that he was becoming more sarcastic every day – a sarcasm that few grasped and many misconstrued.

Maybe it is something that comes with age, he pondered critically.

'What a lovely Irish girl she is,' commented Spear, joining him at the breakfast table.

'Ayla, tell Master Spear where you come from in Ireland.'

'Munster, sir.'

'Munster, indeed. I've never had the occasion to visit Munster.'

''Tis beautiful, Cork is a beautiful city, so it is. It has a grand wall all around and a river running through.'

'What river?' asked Spear.

'Why the Lee, sir. A long, long time ago Saint Finbar built a monastery on the local marshes.'

'Marshes, you say, now that would be a building challenge,' laughed Spear.

Thomas watched on open-mouthed. He had not heard Ayla holding forth like this since her arrival.

'Then the Norsemen came, then the Protestants, and we were driven from our homes to the edge of the city.' Ayla turned to Thomas, piercing him with sharp blue eyes and shaking her dark braids escaping the cap. 'Speaking of the Norse, Josiah told me that friend of yours, Mistress Hartmann, was one of them.'

'Did he?'

'He did.'

'Just to put matters straight, Mistress Hartmann's Norse heritage is centuries past by way of her northern farming ancestry.'

'Nonetheless, I don't have any liking for her or her for me. Forgive me for saying so, sir.'

'So your point is?' snapped Thomas.

'I saw her come here around the midnight hour, yesterday and on the previous night, staring across from the parkland to here.'

'Really?' Thomas could not ignore the missed beat of his heart. 'How could you be so sure it was Iben Hartmann?'

'The moon was full. She stood behind a tree for hours just staring.'

'Did you not think to ask her business?'

'No, sir, I was watching from a window, the night was cold, and I already knew her business.'

'And what might that have been?'

''Tis you she seeks, sir. Though she is a person who likes to watch from the outside.'

Thomas shrugged it off. Besides the dead man in the ditch there hadn't been any more plague victims recently, so the chance of connecting with Iben was dim. And how many times had he tried reaching out to her to no avail.

'Good breakfast this,' said Spear appreciatively, once Ayla had returned to the kitchen. 'Sensible girl too. A good head on her shoulders.'

'Yes,' Thomas agreed, preoccupied. He could not get over the fact that Iben had been spying on them. Him? He devised a plan for the following night.

'Good evening, Mistress Hartmann.' Thomas, on Russel, had circled behind the Hall's stables and come into the parkland through the rear gatehouse. He looked down on Iben from a great height, giving him an immediate advantage. He had taken her by surprise. She was shivering and for once looked vulnerable, whether from the cold air or being caught out he could not be sure. 'How come I find you on my land at this hour?' She had no answer.

'You are back from London I see,' she eventually found her voice.

'Indeed, and glad I am to be so.'

'And Beadall's Farm?'

'Plans are well underway. But you haven't explained why you are standing out here, Mistress Hartmann, in the cold and dark on my property.'

'Curiosity,' she said.

'Curiosity?'

'Yes, I merely wanted to know that you were safely back from London.'

'You did?'

'Why, yes.'

'I thought you didn't care if I lived or died.'

'That is not the case.'

'So why did you not answer my letter? The letter I sent you before I went off to war.'

'I received no letter. One minute you were there the next you were gone without a word. That is the story of my life with men.'

'I did write to you.' It suddenly dawned on him, dawned on them both. Could it be that his letter was intercepted?

'I got no letter,' she repeated.

'Anyone seeing you standing out here at this time of night, Mistress Hartmann, might think you were in love.'

'Love? What is love?' sneered Iben.

Thomas felt the old anger building. 'Love is something you learn from childhood. And far from being loved, Mistress Hartmann, I think you have always had a deep sense of rejection. To love, you have had to know love from childhood. It isn't a momentary coupling.'

'Are you qualified as a mind doctor now?' quipped Iben cynically.

'No, but I believe you suffer from a deep childhood wound of some sort that has never healed properly.'

'And you being the great doctor feel you can repair it.'

'I fear only you can do that.'

'How conceited you are, Thomas Huck, thinking you can assess people so easily.'

'I didn't say it was easy.'

'So superior. You doctors are always right. It is part of the mystique you build around yourselves.'

'Yes, that is so. We medical men are omnipotent,' Thomas snapped back glibly.

'I think you truly believe that,' sneered Iben.

'And you, Mistress Hartmann, cover up your inadequacies with a thin layer of false arrogance. In short you cannot risk love other than for yourself. You suck a man's love in without giving anything back. That is what you did to me.' With that Thomas angrily kicked Russel on, leaving Iben a forlorn figure alone in garden moonlight.

CHAPTER TEN

'Strumpets, harlots,' mutter, mutter, from the far end of the parlour. 'Rockfoot Hall has become nothing more than a bordello.' Josiah was disgruntled because Thomas had decided to do something that nobody in his position ever did, he had invited Ayla to share tea with him one afternoon – a Cornish cream tea – by the warm fire. 'And All Fool's Day already gone,' huffed and puffed the old man making up the hearth.

'For God's sake shut up, Josiah,' Thomas told him.

'No one ever asked me to take tea and cake in all the years I've worked here.' Josiah wouldn't be easily placated. His rant continued even after Ayla had entered the room.

Thomas smiled at Ayla with embarrassment. Ayla, in turn, looked a little concerned about the passion this change in routine had created. Josiah slapped the tray of tea and delicacies on a low table before them. Thomas tried his best to ignore the servant's rudeness. He found it hard to reprimand an old retainer who had once taken him to the privy and placed him down on the pot.

'Be so good as to leave the room, Josiah,' he told him firmly, after he had poured them each a cup of rare tea.

They could hear his complaint all the way down the passageway until it appeared to run out of energy of its own accord.

'Oh my, is this going to cause me future trouble?' asked Ayla.

'Not at all. I will personally see to it that it doesn't,' Thomas reassured her. 'Do you know what this is?' He passed her a plate with a Cornish split, strawberry jam and clotted cream topping it off.

'Never seen one of these before. We have porter cake back home. A cake made with porter beer of course, mixed fruit, spices and lemon and orange peel.'

'Sounds delicious. Now try your Cornish split.'

'The bun is light but the jam and cream is so rich. It is very good.'

'There is a lot of controversy between Cornwall and Devon as to which county created this confectionery. I understand it may have been as far back as the monks of Tavistock Abbey in Devon in the eleventh century. They fed their labourers with bread, jam and the clotted cream they had just produced. This thick cream is an essential part of the dish, made by heating cow's milk and leaving it in a shallow pan for many hours which causes the cream to come to the surface and clot.'

'I don't care who invented it. I love it.'

'There is further controversy. In Devon they put the cream on the open scone first whereas we put the strawberry jam on our lighter "split" first with the cream on top.'

'Makes more sense to me because the jam will adhere better than cream to the scone's surface,' said Ayla, her mouth full of delicious Cornish split.

That was exactly what Thomas liked about her, she did not stand on ceremony. She had known hunger and appreciated when her appetite was gratified.

Thomas poured out more tea. 'Take another Cornish split, Ayla. I had Cook make them especially for you.'

'But why, sir? Why are you giving me such treats?'

'Because I like you and want to know more about you.'

'At this rate with all these delicious buns I'll never get into my skirts.'

'Don't worry about that, plump or thin I am sure you will still be beautiful. Now tell me, I am eager to learn more about your life in Ireland under Cromwell.'

'I've already told you, sir. We were kicked off our land so the Protestants could have it.'

'Ah, the Plantations.'

'Is that what they called them? Well, it was robbery, nothing else, God forgive me. My grandpa had many children, my mother being one of them. The farm they had hardly fed all those mouths but when the English came ...'

'Must have been terrible, humiliating for them,' cut in Thomas.

'It was made even worse when my mother married the man who was gifted our farm for fighting for Cromwell.'

'Your mother married an Englishman?'

'Yes, a Parliamentary soldier, though it was forbidden by law. It was a family secret that I had to keep most of my childhood.'

'Is that why you came to England?'

'No, not really,' sighed Ayla. 'I knew nothing of my father's relatives. After he had given my mother fifteen children, four of whom were twins, he deserted us leaving us to our fate. The farm, you see, was in his name and soon confiscated back to the Protestants.'

'Your mother must have been something of a social rebel like you Ayla.'

'Not really. She wanted to keep the farm that had been in our family for years.'

'So she married your father. A practical woman then.'

'Like me, she simply didn't want to starve.'

'Nor for your grandparents to go hungry either.'

'Nor them.' Ayla's face fell at the mention of her grandparents which surprised Thomas. There was often a greater bond between grandparents and grandchildren than parents and children. Unfortunately, Thomas had never known his grandparents as both sets had died before he was born.

'Did your father return to England?' he asked.

Ayla shrugged, 'I've no idea. He just went, gone.'

'Why?'

'You do ask a lot of questions, sir.'

'As I said I would like to know more about you.'

'My pa did not get on with *seanáthair*.'

'*Seanáthair?*'

'Old father, grandfather if you like.' Ayla pulled a face. 'He was a wicked man and my pa did not get on with him.'

'In what way was he wicked?'

'He bedded my sisters and me once my pa was out of the way, and we later learnt that he had bedded my ma, his daughter, before us. Surely these are criminal acts against the cross.'

'I am not au fait with Irish law, Ayla. But from a moral standing such an act against a vulnerable child is abhorrent, and must be against God's law.'

'Yes, it must be.'

'Could your mother not shield you and your sisters?'

'The dirty old bastard misused my brothers as well.'

'And your mother did nothing?'

'My mother was raised to think that was the way things are.

It left me without sensation down here.' Ayla pointed to her crotch. Next she raised a finger to her forehead, 'And in here.'

Thomas reached out a comforting hand for her arm. She jerked her arm away. 'I share one thing with your Mistress Hartmann, sir, I cannot love. I cannot give love. I see her in me. A man, cruel men, have robbed me of all natural feeling. You are not a cruel man but I cannot give you what you need. It just isn't there to give.'

This was terrible to hear from one so young.

Thomas reddened, 'I have not asked you for anything. And Iben is not mine, never has been mine, though I thought otherwise once.'

'Why then does she stand staring outside the Hall at a late hour?'

'I cannot say. All these complications. Maybe it is wise not to love at all.'

'Maybe.' Despite what she had said, Ayla sounded less than convincing.

'Tell me, how did you finish up in Cornwall?'

Ayla shrugged. 'I needed to get away from Ireland and my *seanáthair*.'

'And your grandmother?

'*Seanmháthair*? She was as bad as he was. Turned a blind eye to all his doings for a peaceful life.'

'But why Cornwall? Why did you choose Cornwall?'

'The only place I ever heard my father mention in England was Bodmin Moor. He said there were horses on there, wild horses, like *an lucht siúil* had grazing on wasteland in Cork.'

'*An lucht siúil*?'

'Walking people.'

'Ah, Egyptians.'

'No, not quite, they are mainly Irish. Irish that lost their land through Cromwell.'

'Do you think you really came to Cornwall to find your father, Ayla?'

'Maybe, maybe not. Bodmin Moor was the only place I had ever heard of in England.'

'But what if your father had found you whoring in Truro?'

'*Mo dhaid* would only have seen a street fiddle player,' laughed Ayla, taking the final chunk of her Cornish split into her mouth with relish before getting to her feet, cream on her face. 'Now I best get back to my work or Josiah will have my guts for garters.'

She left Thomas with plenty to muse upon. His spirits fell when he thought how men misused womenkind. Ayla had said that she shared one thing with Iben, that she too couldn't give love. Thomas' skin crawled. Was that it? Had Iben suffered similar abuse. Try as he might to obliterate her from his mind, his thoughts always returned to Iben.

* * *

A miserable end to April, noted Thomas as he watched in fascination rain drops running down the Hall's glass windowpanes. The green of the lawn reflected in each translucent ball.

Thomas heard from Seymour that the Commons finally got their man. The unpopular Viscount Brouncker – who it was rumoured had a penchant for orange seller girls – was expelled from Parliament amid great commotion.

All the drama seemed to be London's whereas Thomas felt he was stagnating in the south-west.

Nothing was happening apart from pouring rain. Why is Cornwall so wet, he puzzled. He reasoned it was its proximity to the Mare Atlanticum. Why, he wondered, was that body of water named by Pliny the Roman as such. He picked out a book from his shelves and learnt it was once called the Western Ocean before Columbus.

So many different names throughout history, Thomas had an enquiring mind but he found the etymology of seas confusing.

Adding to his frustration was that the incessant rain was holding up building work on Rockfoot New Farm – his personal creation. Albert Spear did not think the weather clement enough to start work yet: wet timber frames might suffer from rot or shrinkage in the course of time.

The following day the shutters were rattling round the Hall. Curtains ballooning from cold draughts seeping through the window surrounds.

'I fear a storm is brewing,' announced Josiah as if the wrath of God was imminent.

'If so it is rather late in the year and unexpected,' said Thomas.

'Aye, some out there might be taken by surprise,' said Josiah pointing towards the sea. As if to emphasise his point, a flash of lightning bounced round the parlour walls followed by the distant roar of thunder that grew louder minute by minute.

* * *

Returning from church that Sunday morning, Iben could sense the building storm. She could see the black clouds piling up on the horizon. Her father, usually keenly attuned to the elements, ignored her begging him not to take the lugger out that late afternoon.

'We'll not be out there long. Your brother and I might bring back one or two Dover sole for the pan,' he boasted.

Raph winked at her in cunning agreement with his father.

Iben did not know it then, did not know their eagerness to sail out in a potentially dangerous sea had anything to do with the Dutch galleon anchored two miles off shore. After the recent signing of the Treaty of Breda the relationship between England and the Dutch Republic was far more amiable. Dutch vessels were not harassed so much in British waters, leaving smugglers free range to deposit their booty. So rather than bringing back Dover sole for the pan, she eventually guessed their intention was to bring back a few kegs of brandy to hide in their cellar.

Iben caught Raph glancing covetously toward the galleon confirming her growing suspicion. She shrugged. What else could she do? With her usual lack of emotion she walked away, ignoring the fact that the loss of the two family breadwinners would be catastrophic. But if they would not listen the responsibility was entirely theirs. The sea was calm when they pushed out, then the waves began to swell half a mile into their rowing. The two men saw the first zig-zag of forked lightning on the horizon like branches of a tree seeking earth rather than a diminishing sky. Raph almost jumped out of his seat at a sudden loud clap of thunder.

'Maybe our Iben was right,' Raph told his father.

Old Hartmann shook his head. 'All the arrangements have been made.'

The waves began to unsettle the small boat.

'Reef the sail,' screamed Old Hartmann. 'Point her into the wind.'

A shuddering Raph, spray in his face, could see his father's mouth moving but hear nothing for the deafening waves crashing against the hull.

Then the big wave came and there was silence, a deathly silence.

Later that night the broken up remains of the lugger were washed ashore. The next morning the sea gave up the bodies of the Hartmanns on Porthtowan beach. Both corpses of father and son were less than a yard or two from each other. It was reasoned that maybe they had attempted to swim for it.

Agnes refused to go and visit the bodies in situ. It was left to Iben to identify them.

Thomas had been alerted that wreckage of Hartmann's boat had been found the previous night, now he too went to Porthtowan to confirm their deaths.

However death was obvious, no need for a pronouncement from him.

The two men were more or less fully dressed apart from boots and coats, their faces drained of all colour. Nobody witnessing the scene could fail to be amazed by Iben's attitude. She stood watching – wooden and emotionless – as the limp bodies of her father and brother were lifted into a cart before she clambered up there with them.

She looked down on Thomas. 'I did warn them,' she said. 'They took no heed of me.'

'I'm sorry,' he said. She made no reply. He decided not follow her and her sad cargo.

Agnes greeted the Porthtowan party at the cottage door, keening as was expected of her. 'What shall we do? What shall we do?' Iben frowned, choosing not to answer her mother as she felt her histrionic grieving was counterfeit as usual.

The two bodies were carried in on ladders and placed on the parlour table. A fearful Walter ventured forward out of the shadows. He did not cry, just looked lost. Iben cuddled him in her arms.

'That's right you have comfort for 'im, a slow wit, and none for your mother,' sobbed Agnes. 'Nothing for me when I am ruined.'

'Everything is always about you,' Iben told her mother in lowered tones.

Something happened to her during this heightened moment of misfortune – something she would never be able to explain – she felt liberated.

The little room soon became crowded round the corpses on the table. Villagers whispering that it was a double tragedy, villagers giving their forlorn condolences. Iben noticed even Josh Haymaker arrived claiming friendship with her brother, which was the first she had heard of it. However, the ever vigilant Iben saw that Thomas Huck had failed to make another appearance that day.

Then one of the superstitious local seafarers made a mistake by suggesting that someone might have mentioned a hare or rabbit before the Hartmanns set sail, so dooming their voyage.

'Rubbish! Ridiculous dross,' Agnes suddenly sparked up. And slowly in stages the mourners began to drift away, knowing well Agnes' irritability and temper and fearing they might become the butt of it.

* * *

Iben both loved and hated graveyards having had to spend so much of her childhood in them as her father erected the stones. Because *John Hartmann and Son* had built such respect in the community, they had a choice spot allocated to them in the churchyard under an oak tree. It was a lovely late April day and the graveside was three deep with mourners. Agnes and Iben had debated whether or not Walter should attend the funeral. Iben believed he should, Agnes said that she could not be bothered with him on such a day.

'Father and Raph were as much kin to Walter as they were to us,' objected Iben.

Agnes pursed her lips unimpressed until Iben came up with an idea.

Struggling to the church, arthritic Widow Collette came as saviour. Though disabled, warm bosomy Ann had been assigned to look after Walter during the ceremony. Walter relished the rare experience of snuggling into motherly comfort. So much so that the burial of his father and brother passed for him too quickly.

For Iben the whole masquerade was something else. Eager to get away – once the soil was thrown – from the solemnity of it all, her mother's false tears and one or two insincerely expressed condolences, Iben wandered across to see Mary Wood's headstone was in place. The family business' new mason, Arthur Watson, followed her across the grass to the child's grave. His expression was as forlorn as any guest attending the funeral. With his new employers now gone, and he only recently set on in anticipation of more plague deaths, Watson wondered where all this left him.

'Extra hands,' her father had told her. 'We can always use extra hands.'

There was an additional piece of engraving on Mary's headstone that Iben had not seen before: two beautifully carved cherubs lifting a crown.

'Who did this work?' Iben turned to the new mason, caressing the cherubs as if they were flesh.

'Why I did naturally,' he replied.

'Well, it is exquisite. You are very gifted, Master Watson.'

'Your father did the lettering.'

'I know, I visited the yard when he was working on the words. I am sure my father and brother would never have believed they would need the same for themselves so soon.'

'Will you permit me to do that work for you?' asked Watson.

'What work?' asked Iben distractedly.

'Why, lettering and dressing their stones.'

'Of course. Of course,' laughed Iben. 'Please feel free to use our yard and premises for the time being.'

'Fashion is a strange thing, Mistress Hartmann,' said Watson, absently tracing out the name Mary Wood with his finger. 'Tombstones were once flat now we erect them vertically.'

'Why?'

'Perhaps they are easier to read. You don't have to stand over them and they don't get covered by snow in winter.'

'That wouldn't be a problem here as it hardly ever snows in Cornwall,' Iben told him.

'See, it is sleeting now.' Watson pointed up to the tree branches etched in white flakes.

'It will not lay. It is merely an early spring token.'

'In the next century we will have footstones too, marking out the grave so nobody else can encroach,' said Watson, more comfortable with the original subject.

'You are very knowledgeable, Master Watson.'

Iben and Watson were suddenly put into shadow. 'Sorry I am late, Mistress Hartmann,' apologised Thomas, on foot and dressed in a large cloak like a big black crow. He lifted his wide brimmed hat cocked to one side, black also. His left eye twitched beneath the tall crown in what Iben rightly or wrongly could have interpreted as a wink. His mouth twisted into a smile as he conveyed his condolences. 'It is snowing,' he added.

'We can see that for ourselves,' snapped Iben.

'And who might this gentleman be that you do not think it fitting to introduce us?' Thomas asked.

'This is my father's master mason,' explained Iben. 'But what it has to do with you, Sir Thomas, is baffling.'

Arthur Watson's mouth fell open. He had never heard a daughter of trade address a landowner so.

Seemingly unfazed Thomas bid them farewell with a brief nod, touch of his wide brim and was gone.

CHAPTER ELEVEN

'All but the most prestigious of buildings have basic plank doors,' explained Spear. The weather had cleared and they were onto the fine details of construction now.

'Sorry,' said Thomas, engrossed in his own thoughts.

'Basic plank doors,' repeated Spear.

'I hope you are not referring to me,' laughed Thomas.

'No, sir, but how do you feel about the doors for Rockfoot New Farm?' Spear was not a man for humour once his mind was set on a project. 'We don't want to incur greater expense than we have already.'

'How much have we incurred already?'

'We are a little over budget.'

'How much over budget?'

'A few pounds over the hundred and fifty mark.'

'Basic will do.'

The day to day business of running the estate forced Thomas to concentrate on practicalities, alas the dangerous time was the night. With the Hartmann father and son gone, gone were two malevolent forces in his life. He had been reluctant to attend their funeral but felt he had to for form's sake. He was amazed to see that he didn't seem to be the only person lacking regret for their passing. He had not seen Iben shed a tear.

If there was one thing he had always been envious of about Iben it was her ability to live for the moment. Everything that happened before didn't seem to matter and everything in the future did not exist. Alas she seemed to have little concept of what would happen to her family now without Raph and her father. It could mean starvation and penury for those left. Thomas had seen it before. Though the Hartmanns weren't his tenants, and he had no responsibility for them, could he stand by and let pauperdom happen to them. She had once promised to marry him with no true intention to do so. She cited misunderstandings, his family's disapproval of her, when it was she who was actually nonchalant about any future plans if indeed she meant them at all.

What he was unaware of was that there was a substantial reason for her indifference towards him that she could not articulate. She had been through an experience that he would never be able to understand.

Child-like, baby-like, when a baby needs something they have no empathy for the mother. If she is exhausted, if she is stressed, if she is sick, if she is in pain ... there is no sympathy from the baby, no pity from that red-faced screaming ball of self. There can't be. It is the shrieking, single-minded struggle for survival and there is no empathy in it. If their needs do not get met, they will die and there is no room for other people's pain in that equation. Iben was that baby.

He was afraid to be locked into Iben's fantasy world again, caught in an endless loop of trying to please her and hoping that one day she would finally recognise it and appreciate him.

* * *

The Hartmann's tombstone making yard was just a few yards from their cottage. Agnes called to Iben through the window. 'I heard the sound of a chisel on stone earlier. A ghostly sound and thought your father or brother had returned.'

'It would be the new man, Watson, tooling a stone,' replied Iben. Adding, 'My father's and brother's gravestone, I expect.'

'Good morning, Mistress Hartmann.' Watson greeted her as soon as she walked into the yard.

'Good morning, Arthur. It is good to see you up and on the job early.'

'It is the least I can do. I wonder what words…'

'Simple, just simple wording,' said Iben.

'Here lyeth the bodies of John Hartmann and his son Raph called too soon to God. April 26th 1668. Do you know their birthdates?' asked Watson.

'No, because both my father and Raph were born in Yorkshire. Just put aged sixty-one and forty-one respectively.'

'Are you sure?'

'No, I am not sure but it will do,' shrugged Iben. 'I don't think my father ever knew his exact age.'

'But the church records?'

'The registries were only introduced during the last century. Alas not many have been well kept by priests in our remote part of the kingdom nor I assume up in Yorkshire either. Then there was the war. My father was always complaining that much had been destroyed by fire and pillaging.'

'Indeed, many documents must have been lost.'

'Tell me Master Watson how did you find yourself in Cornwall? I can tell from your manner of speech that you are not a native of these parts.'

'London,' said Watson. Iben's face temporarily fell. 'What's wrong, Mistress?'

'Were you affected by the illness?'

'Plague you mean?' he asked. She nodded. 'It was hard not to be, it was prevalent in my neighbourhood, warning red crosses on doors everywhere. I think I had a touch of it myself with the swellings and suchlike. I was one of the lucky ones. Unless you have lived through a pandemic there is no knowing what it is like. Then the fire came and seemed to cleanse the streets.'

'That must have been terrible though.'

'We escaped the Great Plague and then the following year we had the Great Fire. Yes, you are right, two accursed things to live through. The fire started on 2nd September in the king's bakery in Pudding Lane near London Bridge. Fires were common in London but usually soon extinguished. Indeed when the Lord Mayor of London, Sir Thomas Bloodworth, was woken up to be told about the fire, he replied "Pish! A woman might piss it out."'

Iben pulled a face at this reported piece of misogyny but begged Watson to continue.

'However,' he sighed, 'that summer had been very hot and there had been no rain for weeks, so consequently the wooden houses and buildings were tinder dry. Three hundred houses quickly collapsed and the strong east wind spread the flames further, jumping from house to house. The fire swept through the warren of streets lined with houses, the upper stories of which almost touched across the narrow winding lanes. Efforts to bring the fire under control by using buckets quickly failed. Panic began to spread through the city. People tried to leave, I was one of them. We poured down to the River Thames in an attempt to escape by boat. Absolute chaos reigned, thousands of sightseers from the villages came to view the disaster as we, the citizens, struggled to leave. The King immediately ordered that all the houses in the path of the fire should be pulled down to create a firebreak. This was done with hooked poles, but to no avail as the fire outstripped the workers.'

'It must have been frightening.'

'It was. By the 4th September half of London was in flames. The King himself joined the fire fighters, passing buckets of water to them in an attempt to quell the flames, but the fire raged on.

As a last resort gunpowder was used to blow up houses that lay in its path, and so create an even bigger firebreak, but the sound of the explosions started rumours that a French invasion was taking place... even more panic. As refugees fled the city, St. Paul's Cathedral was caught in the flames. Acres of lead on the roof melted and poured gushing onto the street like a river. Soon the great cathedral collapsed.'

'We heard so little about it down here. You paint such a vivid picture, Master Watson. Tell me could you feel the heat?'

'You could indeed, if you ventured too near, and you could choke on the smoke too. Luckily the Tower of London escaped the inferno, and eventually the fire was brought under control, and by the 6th September it had been extinguished altogether. Nonetheless only one fifth of London was left standing. It was time for me to leave.'

'So what brought you to the West Country?'

'Looking for work with the stones. I heard a sad human epitaph to this story as I wandered from town to town. In the immediate aftermath of the fire a poor demented French watchmaker, called Lucky Hubert, confessed to starting it deliberately. Justice was swiftly carried out and Hubert was hanged. It was however sometime later that it was discovered that he couldn't have started the fire, as he was not in England at the time.'

'There is so much injustice in the world.'

'So much, Mistress,' agreed the master mason.

'And no allowance is made for the weak-minded,' said Iben, thinking of her brother Walter.

* * *

'A friend of yours came looking for a job,' Albert Spear told Thomas amid much hammering and builders' swearing.

'Oh and who might that be?'

'Josh Haymaker.'

'I hope you didn't oblige.'

'No, no, I want only skilled men. I know Haymaker of old.'

'So do I,' said Thomas without further elaboration.

'He used to run around with Roger Martin and the Perranzabuloe gang until they fell out over the proceeds of their wicked acts. Martin and Haymaker were like two prize bulls locked together fuelled by ego.'

'I can see that,' agreed Thomas.

'However there is a gentler side to Haymaker when he is wooing the ladies. In the past I've seen him in the company of one particular girl. Seen the same girl wandering about the village of St Altarnun when I was working on jobs there. Word went out that she was looking for her base child given away at birth. Nothing remains a secret in these parts for long.'

'What was she like this girl?'

'Lovely, I'd say. Long fair hair knotted in a braid down her back. She looked more like a foreign woman than English.'

Thomas felt his words drying on his tongue. He was sure this woman could have been none other than Iben. 'And did she find the child?' he asked, clearing his throat and finding his voice.

'I believe so, her daughter was living on a remote farm just outside St Altarnun with her adoptive parents.'

'Did the people there let her see her child?'

'Not sure about that.'

'And do you know the name of the child?'

'A funny name, I seem to remember. Alli something like that.'

'Alli short for Allison?' proposed Thomas.

'Could be. Forgive me for commenting, sir, but you seem to have a keen interest in this matter.'

'Yes, I do,' admitted Thomas. 'But I am not the father of the child if that is what you are inferring.'

'Haymaker then?'

Thomas scowled at the thought. Spear was becoming emboldened and cheeky by the minute. 'No, I don't think so,' he told the builder bluntly.

'Haymaker was certainly at pains to facilitate the young lady in her search.'

'Maybe he wasn't sure if he was the father or not,' shrugged Thomas, feigning disinterest.

'There is further talk that the girl, the daughter, is of aristocratic stock from her proud bearing as she grows older.'

'I know nothing of that either,' said Thomas walking away, sure now that Spear was on a fishing expedition. Josh Haymaker having a dalliance with Iben was bad enough but his own brother possibly fathering a child with her and abandoning her, with no Huck male heir on the horizon this could bring into question inheritance.

* * *

'If the plague itself wasn't sufficiently lethal, we noticed in London that this clever disease began to change character,' Arthur Watson told Iben, renewing his plague talk a morning or two later in the yard. She was enthralled with watching this skilled craftsman at work. And she could watch this now, in the present, where she liked to be. No empty future promises here. She could see herself working with this man in partnership.

'In what way did the plague change?' she asked.

'If anything it became more deadly, more immediate. The first signs of the illness were fever, headache, weakness, and rapidly developing shortness of breath, chest pain, cough and sometimes bloody or watery sputum. It progressed in only two to four days and blocked the lungs. Sufferers found they could no longer breathe God's own air.'

'Is it true you had beak doctors tending the sick?'

'Yes, indeed. London doctors wore beak masks stuffed with sweet smelling herbs in the hope of warding off infection and the stench of the dying.'

'Well, if their patients did not die of the illness surely to be treated by such a crow-like vision was enough to frighten them to death.' Iben laughed at her own flippancy, Arthur Watson did not. 'No, sorry, it must have been a terrible time to live through,' she said, immediately correcting herself. 'It is your and my good fortune that you are here now.'

Was she flirting with him, he wondered.

'I think we can expect to build up trade soon, Mistress,' he told her. 'Folk move around and mix much more in the summer months.'

Slowly, Iben began to wean herself off spying on Thomas and Rockfoot Hall. She could not explain even to herself why she did it. She surely was not in love with him. How could she be in love with him? – the brother of the man who had raped her and she only thirteen. The Huck family were disastrous for her. Before the war she had tried to make it right with her mother by agreeing to marry Thomas, in the vague hope that would enable her to get her daughter back. His family still had immense power and contacts in the parish. But in recent years she had rebelled. And since he had caught her prowling in the grounds of the Hall, and then she had been rude to him in front of Arthur Watson at her father's and brother's funeral, he had never called for her once, not even to attend the occasional dying patient.

Not to worry she was used to disappointments. She had immense self-control and had even stopped struggling to St Altarnun in an attempt to glimpse Ulli. Why would such a fine creature want to have anything to do with the likes of her anyway?

* * *

It was a fact that the knocks on Thomas' door had became more frequent with the new, deadly lung variant of the Black Death. It's progression was so fast and severe that there was little that Thomas' treatment could do. From the time he was first summoned to a patient's house to witness rags soiled with bloody sputum lying about the place, it usually proclaimed the onset of death. Even if he had wanted to call upon Iben's nursing and herbal remedies, it would have been too late anyway. But he didn't want to call upon her, he didn't want to see her, he was doing his best to forget her.

Even the clergy had become fearful of the disease and were holding their Sunday services outdoors in fields. Little chance of Thomas crossing paths with Iben there as he had no inclination, time or intention to attend such events.

One man's meate, is another man's poyson – with so many new customers, Iben and Watson began to make a success of the tombstone making business in their little corner of Cornwall.

Still the see-saw politics of abroad continued that spring: the Cossacks on the Left Bank rebelled against Moscow resulting in the whole of Ukraine coming under the control of Petro Doroshenko. Of course that won't be the end of the matter, wrote Seymour Glover. It never is with Ukraine. And had Thomas heard that the King had a new love interest, an actress called Nell Gwyn? Seymour concluded his correspondence saying he could recommend the marriage state.

That caused Thomas a wry smile. The memory of Seymour crawling out of Dolores Page's behind the skirts of whores and he only days newly married.

However Thomas did begin to wonder if he should be looking out for a wife himself. It could be lonely at Rockfoot Hall with nobody to share his days, days of dealing with the dying. Credulous Josiah was no good as a confidant and Ayla had her own young life to live. Indeed according to his cook, Ayla had taken to one of the replacement kitchen boys.

At least Rockfoot New Farm – more now of a complete build than a renovation – was providing some creativity in his life.

'What do you think to a stone spiral staircase replacing the old wooden steps to the upper chamber?' Albert Spear asked him.

'Yes that will go well with me.' His relationship with Spear had cooled a little. He felt Spear to be a gossip and his tittle-tattle about Iben was too close to home. However the builder was about to come up with some new information that was useful.

'Are you still in agreement for me to replace the roof on Jowan Carter's farm when I am finished here?'

'Of course, that is what we agreed.'

'Am I right in thinking that Carter had a flock of sheep stolen some little while ago?'

Thomas nodded, wondering where this was going.

'And you offered a reward of a hundred pounds?' So this was where it was going. 'Well,' said Spear, scratching his bald head, 'I have a little information for you regarding that matter.'

'Go on then.'

'You'll not like it.'

'Let me be the judge of that.'

'I heard that Carter was short on rent money. He connived with Roger Martin of the Perranzabuloe gang to steal those sheep and sell them to a farmer on Bodmin Moor.'

'But I replaced his flock.'

'All the better for him.'

'I can hardly believe this though I have heard of these rogues before,' said Thomas. 'But for Carter to be involved. Two boys were attacked, one boy died of his injuries. His father quite rightly is bent on vengeance.'

Spear shrugged. 'Sir, I am only the messenger.'

'That you are, Spear.'

'Are there others in for the reward, sir? You just said you've already heard of Martin and the Perranzabuloe gang.'

'No one has made such a detailed allegation as you, Spear. But you must take this serious information to Constable Fox in St Agnes, he is dealing with the murder inquiry.'

'And the reward?' asked Spear with what Thomas judged to be untimely haste.

'Ah, the reward again, of course. I am not sure what it stands at now. That is a matter for you to discuss with Fox not me.'

'Would you speak to the constable on my behalf, Sir Thomas?'

'About your information or the reward?'

'Both.'

'Certainly not. The information must come directly from its source, namely you, Spear.'

'I am only telling you what was told to me,' Spear was beginning to recant a little.

'Then you must tell it to the constable. And as for Carter's new roof that must be on hold for now. He'll have no need for a new roof if he is about to face the hangman's noose.'

On the ride home Thomas began to mull over all Spear had told him. He remembered that Jowan Carter had tried to implicate Josh Haymaker in the sheep thieving offence. Josh Haymaker seemed to bear the responsibility for all the ills that occurred in Cornwall.

Thomas marvelled at the duplicity of men – and women.

CHAPTER TWELVE

The breathing sickness took men and women alike. But Iben found the most heart wrenching moments were creating small stones for the babies' graves. Fortunately she found she was gifted in words for the stones regarding lives as yet not lived. Thomas had taught her words. She loved words though she did not often like to speak them. Arthur Watson would beautifully engrave angels, cherubs and smiling suns. They both did their very best to try and alleviate a little grief for the infants' parents.

Business was booming but the disease wasn't as completely overwhelming as it had been in London. Nevertheless Iben decided to take on an apprentice for Master Watson, she did not want to lose Watson from overwork after just finding him.

She set on Ann Collette's fourteen year old grandson, Dick Bishop, from the village. Dick had no previous experience as a mason but he was, according to Ann, of good character and he proved to be a willing and eager disciple.

As she had nursing Lucan Beadall, Iben felt good about herself for finding the words. She bloomed through the gratitude of relatives and parents alike. She bloomed until she needed further nourishment before the black moods came in again.

She was determined to keep away from St Altarnun because if she failed to spy Ulli it left her more bereft than ever. She was equally resolved not to prowl the grounds of Rockfoot Hall. She convinced herself that far from having any affection for

Thomas Huck, she hated him almost as much as she had hated his brother.

There was always the seashore when she needed to escape death and the tombstone maker's yard when she felt strong enough to meet it. She breathed in the salt air deeply. It helped clear her head of all the abominations that had happened to her.

Thomas felt he couldn't breathe either. Jowan Carter's possible fraudulent involvement with the sheep theft had hit him hard. He was still reeling from the news. The Carters, generations of tenants that he felt his family had always treated well, now Jowan had betrayed his trust. He rode Russel at an angry gallop down towards the coast.

Although polar opposites, he and Iben seemed to be drawn together like magnets.

He saw her straightaway in a place that had once been special to them both – a handsome lone figure on the empty expanse of sand – a clear blue sky above mimicking perfection. But nothing between them was ever perfect.

Thomas dismounted so that he was level with Iben, eye to eye.

'Twice in my life I gave you my love and support. Twice you played me like a fish on a line,' he told her.

'I have disappointed you but that is what I can do,' she said, flouncing down onto the sand.

'You gave me nothing, so there is nothing for me to miss or regret. You will not have the chance a third time.'

'It was your misfortune, Thomas Huck, to fall in love with me,' she proclaimed, staring up at him, staring him out.

'Always so trite in dismissal, rejection. Always so easy out,' sneered Thomas.

'What happened to you is nothing to all the things that have happened to me.' He watched her distractedly making circles in the sand with the pointed toe of her boot.

'Me, me, it is always about you. Whatever happened to you was of your own making. The pain you caused me and doubtlessly others wasn't of our making but yours.'

'Anyway, you've got your little maid to warm your bed nowadays I hear, or should I say harlot,' she shrugged indifference.

'There you are again such a small comment from between tight bitter lips. Are you really any better?'

'Probably not but that is not for me to say.' Another indifferent shrug.

Arrogant one moment, self-deprecating the next. Nothing is ever her fault. Nothing is consistent. She never apologises, she never considers herself to be wrong, conceded Thomas.

'Ayla might have been a harlot but she did it to eat, whereas you indulged in sexual congress for pleasure, control and ultimately to punish,' he told her. 'Though younger than you she's a woman, while you are still a mean little girl. She has a loyalty that is beyond your understanding.'

'Does she really?' sneered Iben.

'And what is all this I have been hearing about St Altarnun?' There, he had broached the subject.

She said nothing at first but regarded him with such hatred that he wanted to shrivel away. 'Who told you about that?'

'Someone who has seen you moping around there on several occasions, sometimes with Josh Haymaker.'

'That has nothing to do with you.'

'Did my brother give you a child? And was that child fostered out to farmers there?'

Iben paled. She sat up, got up and began to walk away. 'Let me be. You should have realised that damaged people are always dangerous,' she shouted at him above the roar of the waves.

'The hurt always have to hurt back,' he responded.

'If there was ever anything between us you will have to let it go, you will never get what you want.'

'Why?' he asked.

'That time has passed.'

There was no reaching her now. He saw that. His eyes filled with tears at a memory. He remembered another time on this same beach, before the war, when her entire body seemed to relax and physically open up to him.

'I loved you,' he said.

'No, you loved the image of what you wanted me to be, not who I am.'

* * *

'You will be needing a new tenant for Beechfield,' said his morning visitor.

'So Spear has called upon you?'

'Not only Spear. Another vital witness has come forward with information regarding the murder of the boy and the theft of the sheep. Carter, Martin and members of his gang are in Launceston Castle as we speak,' said Constable Fox.

Thomas remembered seeing the austere castle, built high on its motte, hanging above the town. It could have been a fairy tale castle out of the old French poem, *Lancelot, the Knight of the Cart*, but it wouldn't take Thomas long to find out this was no Camelot.

'So who is this mystery witness?' he asked Fox.

'Josh Haymaker.'

'Are you serious? Is anything that man says to be trusted?'

'In this case I would say "yes". Haymaker took me to the farm on Bodmin Moor where the sheep transaction took place.'

'When will I get my sheep back?'

'Time, in time, Sir Thomas. Be patient, we have to prove the sheep are yours through the court. And for the moment you must think who you will put in to run Carter's farm for certainly he will not be returning there.'

Fox left Thomas with a problem. Who would take on Beechfield Farm? – for Jowan Carter and those other men held in Launceston Castle would surely be heading for the gallows.

Thomas could not believe who Josiah was announcing as his next guest hot on the heels of the constable.

'Joshua Haymaker to see you, Master,' said with raised eyebrows.

Haymaker swaggered in looming large behind the stooped Josiah.

'Master Haymaker this is a surprise. What can I do for you?'

Haymaker did not miss the sarcasm in Thomas' address.

'I know you do not hold me in the highest regard, Sir Thomas.'

'You were drunk at my party.'

'I let being the King of Misrule go to my head.'

'You did indeed.'

'But I had nothing to do with burning down Lucan Beadall's place.'

So Iben must have told him of his suspicions, Thomas acknowledged, sad at a further betrayal.

'You were there though,' said Thomas.

'Where?'

'At the fire disguised as a stag.'

'Oh, yes, that I was. It was embarrassing to see two of us there amongst the mummers.'

'Tell me, did you recognise the other stag?'

'No, not even his voice as he did not speak. It was night-time see. Dark apart from when the fire started.'

'Really,' pondered Thomas.

'I heard you thought I was responsible for the fire.'

'Who told you that?'

'Just folk round and about,' said Haymaker vaguely.

'No, who?'

'Talk was all over the village. Widow Collette for one.'

'I see,' said Thomas, somewhat relieved it wasn't Iben.

'And now I might be responsible for getting your sheep back.'

'So I heard from Fox. What do you want Haymaker, my thanks?'

'No, never that.'

'What then?'

'A friend of mine is eager to be reunited with her base child.'

'Iben,' sighed Thomas.

'Yes, Iben.'

'Why me?'

'Because it was your brother who did her the great disservice of forcing his seed into her womb against her will in the first place.'

'Robert?'

Haymaker nodded. 'The same,' he said. 'I loved Iben more than any other wench afore or after. But the damage had already been done. Your brother saw to that. The Huck family owes her.'

'I do nothing under duress, Haymaker.'

'Look at it as more a matter of honour, Sir Thomas.'

'And where would this base child be found today?' Thomas tested, already conversant with the answer.

'With farming folk out at Altarnun.'

'I will think it over.'

He had often been astute in his evaluation of Iben as insincere, at the same time he had misjudged her many times. Maybe now was an occasion to make amends.

* * *

At the end of the week Thomas felt driven to take the long ride north to St Clether in search of Mary Ansell, his childhood intended. She would be a grown woman now, about the same age as Iben. He felt he was of an age no longer willing to float along on the tides of fate. He must take charge of his life. He must begin to shape it himself.

He stopped at Temple to allow Russel a little rest and nourishment: a bag of oats from an obliging bow-legged farmer and fresh water from the pump in his yard. Leaving his horse well secured with the farmer, he decided to take a look at Temple Church, built around 1120 on land owned by the Knights Templar. The Knights Templar, an exclusive and mysterious order, bent on protecting Europeans visiting the Holy Land and not averse to a little warfare when it suited. Temple Church, dedicated to St Catherine, had become famous as a religious house where marriages could take place without banns or licence.

Thomas began to fantasise about having his own wedding down the church's narrow aisle, a church that was anything but narrow. Indeed it was described as a lawless church. It was rumoured that even suicides were allowed to be buried in its consecrated ground.

But who would be Thomas' chosen bride. Now there was a question. He could conjure up the situation but not the players – not for sure.

He decided to head for St Breward where he had heard there was a good inn for the night. Russel and he passed the Trippet Stone Circle on their right. No doubt the circle, made with twenty-six granite stones, was the site where ancients worshiped the heavens. Bodmin Moor – a bleak place to feel close and find God, recognised Thomas cynically to himself. He could feel his horse growing uneasy beneath him on the rough moorland track. Russel began to shudder. They say horses cannot sense things but they can, he was sure of it.

A warmer welcome awaited him at The Old Inn with its low beamed ceilings, roaring fire and fire-flushed landlord.

Free of Bodmin Moor and its demons, Thomas was content that Russel's temperament was now more stable and he was safely watered in a stall behind the inn.

The bar was quiet that night. Over a generous chicken pie, he engaged the innkeeper in conversation. It turned out that they both shared a passion for history. The innkeeper's archival knowledge was specifically focused on the place he lived.

The chair scraped on the flagged floor as he drew it up closer to Thomas' table.

'This inn is one of the oldest in Cornwall and certainly the highest.' The innkeeper inflated his hostelry's importance and by association his own. 'The monks, who were building the church next door, used to stay here. Evidence of flints and suchlike have been found on the moor which indicates that there were even earlier settlements here thousands of years before Christ.'

'Was this an inn for the monks to partake of liquor then?' asked Thomas tongue-in-cheek.

'No, no,' laughed the innkeeper. 'It would have been some sort of hospice.'

Thomas could not rid himself of the more pleasing image of inebriate monks rolling about in ecstasy after a day's labour on the church.

'The village came along much later,' explained the innkeeper. 'Work on the original Saxon church was completed in the 11th Century. There is still evidence of the original construction even after restoration in the 15th Century. There are buildings in this village listed in the Domesday Book, there was a population of only sixty souls then.'

'Sir, you are a mine of information. Now pray tell me do you know of the Ansell family of St Clether?'

'May I ask why you want to know about the Ansells, sir?'

'My father was a friend of Sir Humphrey's.' Thomas thought it best not to go into the betrothal issue.

The innkeeper shook his head. 'I am afraid Sir Humphrey died in the war and Lady Alice followed not long after.'

'There was a daughter, was there not?' Thomas tried to keep his enquiry casual.

'Yes, Mary,' sighed the innkeeper. 'Lady Mary inherited Ansell Manor.'

'Why the sigh then?'

'I am afraid she married a good-for-nothing who gambled away most of her fortune. Sir Humphrey would never have allowed that match to happen had he lived.'

'That's terrible.'

'Gerrard Thoresby has gone and believed to be dead. Good riddance, that is what I say. Mary is left with two daughters, Joan and Isabella. Joan is married with children.'

'Mary is free then?'

'I don't know about free, I think she has forsworn all men after her experience with Thoresby.'

'And where is she living now.'

'Ansell Manor of course. She and the girls never left.'

The next morning Thomas gathered his luggage, jammed it against his stomach and ribs as he set forth back on the lane to Altarnun and then St Clether. The innkeeper/historian stood at his door to wish him luck and wave him a cheery goodbye.

'Alternonn village,' he shouted after him, pronouncing Altarnun in the Cornish way, 'is particularly famous for its impressive parish church, known as the Cathedral of the Moor, which is dedicated to the Celtic St Nonna who is believed to have been buried there. If you've time the holy well of St Nonna is well worth a visit too. The well is located only a short distance from the church, just over 300 yards above Penpont Water. The well is thought to possess curative properties especially for lunatics.'

Perhaps St Nonna's Well will cure me of my madness for Iben, Thomas speculated hopefully.

Reaching Altarnun church, he was relieved to quit the saddle and stretch his legs for a while. He tied a stomping Russel to an iron gate there. The church itself looked to have been built in the Perpendicular Style of two centuries before. He stared up to the tower which must have been all of one hundred and more dizzy feet high. Focusing back down to earth, he found a Celtic cross in the churchyard and pondered his next move. The cross looked old enough to be of the era of St Nonna herself.

The day was fine and he had no desire to go indoors. If the truth be known, after all the horrors he had witnessed on the battlefield, religion left him cold. But it would be a brave man who would admit to anyone such religious aversion after the Puritan times they had lived through.

Nonetheless, he was interested in the curative properties of St Nonna's Well. He began to explore on foot. From the old bridge he looked down into the water of the River Inny, one of the chief tributaries of the Tamar River, running through the village. This stretch of the river was known as Penpont Water where the innkeeper had told him he would find the well close by.

The well, or spring, was perched on top of a steep field. It looked out over the West Looe River and across to the wooded hillside opposite. Thomas approached the well down a flight of steep granite steps. At the bottom was a small enclosure. The outlet stream from the spring bisected the enclosure before tipping down the steep field. The water running from St Nonna's Well itself fell into a square and close walled plot.

Thomas heard footsteps behind him coming down the steps. Alarmed, was someone following him? He would be very vulnerable to attack in this place. He relaxed on seeing that his shadow must have been all of seventy years old. From his dress obviously a countryman.

'Ever hear of bowssening?' asked the countryman directly without so much as a 'how do you do? Taken aback, Thomas shook his head. 'Only the other day they made a lunatic stand on that slab of stone yers standing on. But they made that poor soul stand with his back to the pool. A sudden blow to the breast and he tumbled backwards into the cold water.' The old man pointed to the spring. 'A strong fella was waiting there to toss him alongst and athwart in the water, until the lunatic by foregoing his strength had somewhat forgot his fury. Next he was conveyed to the church, with me following on, and certain masses sung over him. If his right wits returned St Nonna had the thanks, but if there appeared to be only small amendment he was bowssened again and again while there remained in him any hope of life for recovery.'

'And did his wits return?' asked Thomas.

The old man shook his head. 'To be honest I didn't stay to see. I had had enough by then. Couldn't go through all that bowssening again.'

Thomas thought he would pass on this brutal cure of his love for Iben. Stepping off the stone he asked, 'Who was St Nonna?'

'Don't you know?' The old man was incredulous.

'I'm not from these parts.'

'St Nonna was mother to St David of Wales. She left her native Wales as one of the many Celtic missionaries passing through Cornwall on their way to Europe many centuries back. Have you been inside the church?' asked the old man. Thomas shook his head. 'Well, you've missed a treat.'

He walked back to the church where the old countryman had told him about the seventy-nine carved bench ends representing not only biblical references but also earlier superstitions and local activities. They were amazing. Thomas had never seen the like and examined each one of them carefully. They all appeared to be male: men with beards, a bagpipe player, a fiddle player like Ayla and a rather deformed court jester particularly caught his eye. There on one of the

161

oak bench ends adjacent to the square Norman font he found the name of Robert Daye. At a guess the carvings had been done early in the previous century. He had never been in such a grand church in such a small village. The villagers here must be very devout if nothing else.

No one seemed to be in the church until he noticed a black cowled figure crouched in one of the back pews obscured by the font. Maybe this man was in prayer, maybe his was a reformed lunatic or a monk come to give penitence. Whatever, the man did not seem to want to be seen or disturbed so let him be.

That night Thomas put up at the Kings Head at Five Lanes just outside Altarnun. Not as old as The Old Inn at St Breward, it was nevertheless very comfortable and he was tired after his long rides. After a dish of eel stew and potatoes he made for bed to settle down for the night.

Alas if *wishes were horses, pure [poor] men wald ride.*

Everything about him was green, thick green foliage, olive green water. He felt the thud in his chest and then falling back helplessly into the abyss. Hard water hit him first and then the cold, then the humiliation. He was being manhandled like a puppet. His eyes stung and closed as he was pushed deeper, submerged into the olive green. A pair of hands was pressing him down, holding him down, there was no pity for his spluttering surfacing. Again and again he was dunked until his lungs felt as if they were exploding. The occasional glimpse of grey sky through blurred eyes made him shiver. He felt so cold. He was so disorientated he wasn't sure which was worse to be dragged to the surface or be submerged. He began to feel death would be a welcomed blessing.

Thomas could not breathe. He woke up in a cold sweat as crushing giant hands suddenly turned softer. Their touch was lighter, caressing almost. They were hands he thought he knew – Iben's large hands? Hands that looked so dependable but perhaps were not. Despite their gentleness he could not eradicate the memory of thrashing about all night in the freezing water of St Nonna's Well. Like the crazy people who had gone before him, he had been subjected to the cruelties of bowssening. Thomas felt more troubled than rested with the lack of a night's fulfilling sleep.

Over a breakfast of meat, bread and cheese, the King's Head landlord struggled with conversation with his latest rather morose guest.

'Do you know Ansell Manor?' Thomas asked him.

'Of course,' said guardedly.

'Then you might be kind enough to give me directions there.'

'Not the best lanes to Clether, sir.'

'Nevertheless that is where I am bound for.'

'You are acquainted with the Ansell family?'

'I am.'

With no further information forthcoming an uncomfortable silence ensued until the landlord went off to present Thomas with a jug of his own brew. He carefully placed mug and jug on the table and watched Thomas attentively as he took his first mouthful of ale.

'What do you think?' he asked.

'Refreshing,' was Thomas' pronouncement. Actually the beer was customary – weak and bitter – but he could not have wished for anything better with the day he had to come. 'Tell me, is it true that lunatics are immersed to the point of drowning in the water of St Nonna's Well in the belief that such treatment will cure their insanity?'

'Aye, that's right enough.'

Since seeing men breaking down under battle distress, Thomas had developed an interest in melancholia or black bile as it was commonly known. He did not feel that lunacy was anything to be fearful or ashamed of, nor did he believe that it was the work of the supernatural, a curse or the possession of the Devil or even due to astronomical events. He knew of families, back in his own village, who hid sufferers away from the world or sought out cruel solutions to the problem like Nonna's Well.

Treatments ranged from herbal drinks to incarceration and very often much more robust practices such as bloodletting were tried. Thomas wasn't happy administering any of these. Then again, most ordinary folk couldn't afford a physician like him. They would resort to cunning herbalists like Iben, or soothsayers like the old crone who lived on the edge of his estate, or in a few cases the church for help.

Thomas had grown to believe that if enough anxiety and hardship is given to certain individuals, particularly those who are ill-equipped to cope, then breakdown and madness could follow.

'Mind how you go,' shouted the landlord after him as he left the King's Head. 'We have had some trouble with highwaymen and footpads of late. Mainly highwaymen come down the road from Devon.'

Thomas turned in the saddle. 'Thank you for the warning and your hospitality last night.'

The hedgerows were edged by creamy-white hawthorn shrubs that looked as if they were covered in snow. The only interruption in this imitation winter landscape was the occasional pinky-white of Midland hawthorn.

Despite the abundant blossoms marking out his path, he did feel exposed on the deep rutted lanes to St Clether. Whether or not it was a sixth-sense or the landlord's warning that reinforced this foreboding, he couldn't be sure. But as he went further into the wind blown countryside, his misgiving grew. Russel too began to exhibit the same disquiet he had on passing the Trippet Stone Circle.

The going was tough on what passed for a thoroughfare. However its course was not far from domesticated rolling green hills with a backcloth of distant wild moorland and tors – playground to the Celtic tribes.

He saw the beautiful River Inny valley unfolding before him again and a bridge ahead. All of a sudden a man on horseback approached him out of a small coppice on the right, totally taking him unawares.

'Stand and deliver,' bellowed the man in a West Country accent, a pistol in hand.

Thomas thought he half-recognised him as was the same cowled figure from St Nonna's Church.

'Have you been stalking me?' he demanded.

The man did not answer but smiled. Thomas thought he was joking at first, a manifestation of his own conjured up fears, until he heard the click of the gun's hammer being pulled back – the hammer known as a cock because of its likeness to the bird – the hammer that was now in the fully cocked position.

'Stand and deliver, I say.' There was no doubting the highwayman's serious intention now. The slightest movement and the gun would discharge death. 'Aye, I've followed you like I would a deer,' finally admitted the man. His breath blowing the neckerchief covering his mouth in and out as he spoke. 'Throw me your purse.'

'I haven't got a purse,' said Thomas.

'What's in there then?' The highwayman pointed to his bag.

'Just extra clothing. Take a look yourself.'

The man leaned across in his saddle. Thomas saw his threadbare coat beneath the cloak. He identified it and its symbolic regimental sleeves. His assailant must have once been part of the Royalist New Cornish Tertia. How many impoverished old infantry soldiers had been forced to make a living from the roads. A smidgen of pity flashed into Thomas' mind – however Royalist camaraderie couldn't overcome this – this man was about to steal from him and possibly kill him.

'I could do with a nice new coat,' said the man. 'Be so kind as to pass it over to me.'

Thomas flung the bag hard into the man's face. The man jerked back. The gun discharged into the air. The dobbin beneath the highwayman reared. Following a hard kick in his side Russel took off.

Thomas put all his faith in the knowledge that his stallion could easily outrun the highwayman's old nag.

Sweat ran and dried across Thomas' face. His mouth burned as they galloped on. His whole body trembled with shock. So now he would be visiting Ansell Manor without fresh clothing. But that didn't matter, at least he was alive.

He kept looking over his shoulder to see if he was being pursued. Apart from the capability of Russel, he knew he had a head start on the man as the flintlock would take time to reload. Thankfully he soon saw Ansell Manor in the distance, a rather grand country house in the Palladian style. According to his late father, the manor house stood in about four hundred and fifty acres of farm and parkland if his memory served him well. Mary's own father had made his money in tin like most entrepreneurs in Cornwall, like his good friend Theodore Gillingham.

He knew he had been inside the house once in his adolescence but he couldn't remember much about it.

Once through the open iron gates, Thomas began to feel safer, although his apprehension slowly increased again as he rode down the long tree lined approach. After all this time, he had no idea of the reception he would receive from Mary but that was another risk he was about to take.

CHAPTER THIRTEEN

Far from rundown, without significant male authority, Ansell Manor looked well kempt. The door was opened by a grand servant in livery.

'Is Lady Thoresby at home?' asked Thomas.

'Is her Ladyship expecting you?'

'No, not exactly.' The frowning servant stepped forward blocking the doorway. Thomas continued quickly. 'I am an old friend,' he explained.

'Your name, sir?' The liveried man disappeared into the house with his name. He re-emerged a minute or two later. 'Follow me, sir, if you please.'

Thomas was shown into a gallery room with a stunning carved plasterwork ceiling. Three young children, two girls and a boy, were crawling on the shiny hardwood floor playing robustly with scattered toys. A young woman and older woman sat on an upholstered sofa further down the gallery watching them. The whole scene reminded Thomas of a Jacob Ochtervelt staged family portrait.

The two women rose together to greet him.

'Well I never, Thomas Huck,' said the older woman.

Thomas bowed. 'Lady Mary.'

'And don't tell me I haven't changed,' she laughed.

'Only for the better,' he said.

'Always the gallant even as a boy. This is my eldest daughter Joan, Sir Thomas, and her three children Beatrice, Madeline and little Martin.' Joan half curtsied. 'Joan's husband is away at sea,' explained Mary. 'My youngest daughter, Isabella, is unfortunately indisposed at the moment.'

'What a lovely brood you have, madam,' Thomas told Joan, patting the boy on his springy blond curls.

'I am going to be a sea captain like my father,' announced little Martin.

'So to what do we owe the pleasure after all this time?' interrupted Mary abruptly.

'I was just passing.'

'Passing? Passing us at remote St Clether?'

'You have never been remote for me, your ladyship. I have often thought of you.'

'This was my childhood betrothed,' Mary explained to Joan.

'So why...' began Joan.

'Our marriage makers were both killed in the war,' cut in Thomas. 'Before the proposal was ever drawn up.'

'But we were never real sweethearts, were we?' said Mary.

'How could we have been at such tender ages?' reasoned Thomas. He saw that from a plain child Mary had grown into a handsome woman. Indeed both were beautiful women. There was little to choose between the two. They were more like sisters than mother and daughter. Mary must have borne Joan at a young age.

Martin began to cry and Joan lifted him effortlessly onto her knee, away from his fractious older sisters. It seemed they were all pursuing the same whipping top though there were many other toys strewed around.

'Come children. Leave Mamma to speak with her friend.' Joan scooped and dragged her offspring away, leaving Mary and Thomas within a ring of uncomfortable silence.

Mary was first to speak. 'You never came back for me. You never thought to persevere with the suit.'

'We were fledglings, Mary. It was merely a contract thought up by our fathers.'

'Better that than what befell me.'

'Was your husband not good to you?'

'Gerrard was a monster.'

'I heard something of the sort.'

'Where?'

'Just locally.'

'So it is common knowledge,' sighed Mary. 'Love, I have never known a kind love, Thomas.'

'Likewise. I am not sure I have either.'

'I see you have been scarred by that ghastly war too.' Mary abruptly changed the conversation.

'Just a scratch.'

'If anything it adds intrigue to your handsome features, Thomas.'

'How sweet of you to say that.' Thomas could not stop the flush suffusing his cheeks.

'Will you stay here tonight?'

'I have no wish to impose on your good nature further.'

'Stay, will you not? You have missed *cena* but I will arrange for bread and meats to be sent to your room. Breakfast will be served at nine o'clock. Then you can meet my other daughter Isabella in the morning.'

Thomas learnt from the valet sent to escort him to his chamber that the Manor had fifty rooms including the kitchen, nurseries and servants' quarters. He was chastened to realise that Rockfoot Hall was a modest dwelling, a cottage in comparison. Obviously Sir William had known what he was doing arranging a marriage between their two households – the Hucks had an ancient title and the Ansells had tin money. The valet went on to tell him that there had been a fire some years before and only the gallery had remained untouched.

'A fire, you say. How so a fire?' Fires seemed to follow in his wake like a burning train. After the destruction of Beadall's Farm, Thomas had developed an interest in the whys and wherefores of conflagrations and how best to avoid them.

The valet visibly clamped up. 'You'd better asked the mistress about that, sir.'

'I will, I will,' Thomas reassured him.

'Is there anything more I can help you with, sir?' asked the valet beginning to bow out.

'No, I am simply looking forward to an early night after all my journeying.'

Thomas' bedchamber was filled with beautifully crafted oak furniture. The curtained four-poster bed carved likewise. Following a brief repast of bread and meats brought to him by another servant, he climbed up onto the high bed and enjoyed the best night's sleep he had had in a long time. He woke to hear a clock somewhere in the house chime out the hour. Had he missed breakfast? Panicking he tumbled down onto the floorboards below. Once washed, dressed and downstairs, he discovered he had just under the hour to spare and decided to explore the garden.

He wandered the geometric layout of the Baroque among rose bushes, sculptures, trimmed plants and trees. He rested by restful water features. It was there that he was approached by an old stooped character who introduced himself as 'Head Gardener.'

'Since Cromwell has gone,' rasped the old man, 'we are being allowed to be more adventurous.'

'In what way?' asked Thomas.

'Come, I will show you.' The old man led him to a walled garden. 'See here we've grown lilac, mock-orange, laburnum, horse-chestnut, laurel, *arbre de Judée.*'

'Tree of Judea,' translated Thomas.

'That's right.'

'And over there I see you have an avenue of native lime saplings. Apart from oak, my favourite trees.'

'In addition we are attempting to make a flower garden in that corner with flowers from foreign lands. See a plot of tulips. All colours.'

'They're beautiful.'

'I am attempting to grow grapes and pineapples in that glass shed over there with little success so far. It is the light, you see, or at least the lack of it.'

'An embryonic orangery.'

'Pardon, sir.'

'You have the makings of an orangery. A place of brightness to grow exotic fruits,' Thomas explained. 'But see, I am expected to breakfast with Lady Mary so regrettably I must leave you.'

And it was with genuine regret that he had to leave this fascinating old man, who had little education but a lot of knowledge and common sense. How often had he found this to be the case.

Mary was alone at the breakfast table.

'Did you sleep well, Thomas?' she asked.

'Marvellously.'

'I am afraid Joan and Isabella have not come down yet. You know what young people are like.'

He didn't but nodded agreement all the same.

'My grandchildren will eat in the nursery.'

'I have just had an informative conversation with your head gardener.'

'Gospatrick. He's a wonderful old man, is he not?'

Thomas nodded enthusiastic agreement.

'He used to beat me you know,' Mary suddenly blurted out.

At first Thomas thought she meant Master Gospatrick. 'Sorry, who?'

'Gerrard Thoresby. He got so drunk one night, one of many nights, he almost burnt this place down.'

'How?'

'Let his tobacco pipe fall to the carpet. Fell asleep letting it smoulder there.'

'I am so sorry.'

'I cannot tell you how relieved I was, Thomas, when he left.'

Manchet bread cakes made of milk, eggs and sugar were first to appear on the damask tablecloth. Followed to the table by bleary-eyed Joan and Isabella. If anything Isabella was more beautiful than her sister.

The French dish of eggs in snow was the pièce de résistance: bright yellow egg yolks nestled in a fluffy bed of egg whites.

'I love this dish, Mamma,' said Joan.

'That is why I have had Cook prepare it for you, my dear.'

'It is like the sun framed by billowy clouds,' tittered Isabella poetically.

Finally Thomas decided he couldn't beat around the bush any longer. 'Do any of you ladies know of an Ulli, who lives in a farmhouse just outside Altarnun?'

'Ulli, that's a strange name,' said Mary.

'I believe her distant ancestors were Norsemen.'

'Norsemen? We don't have many of those here in Cornwall.'

'No, her maternal grandfather was a journeying mason originally from the North of England who eventually settled down here and set up a tombstone making business.'

'Is this Ulli a sweetheart of yours, Thomas?' asked Mary. There was a hint of disappointment in the question.

Both her daughters were giggling now.

'Isn't she the Davidson's girl?' suggested Joan.

'I know her,' cut in Isabella, half raising a shy hand. 'She lives at Toftgate Farm just a mile or two from Altarnun. I have spoken with her a few times while out riding. She is a lovely person but too young for you, Sir Thomas.'

Thomas blushed and said he was looking for Ulli not for himself but on behalf of a friend.

'We could ride over there together after breakfast and I can introduce you to her,' suggested Isabella.

'That would be lovely,' replied Thomas, grabbing her offer as too important to make a pretence of polite vacillation.

'You will come back here and stay another night with us,' put in Mary.

'I couldn't possibly...' began Thomas, knowing already that he would capitulate for a comfortable bed and another wonderful breakfast.

An hour later Isabella and Thomas waited in front of the Manor House for the delivery of their horses. A fresh-faced groom appeared leading Russel to his left and Isabella's fine Andalusian grey to his right. He had decided not to mention his encounter with the highwayman the day before for fear of alarming the family and Isabella.

The grey mare was compliant, whereas Thomas' horse kept twitching his head restless to be off. The black Friesland obviously felt he had been stabled for too long. Still it was a fair ride back to Altarnun, plenty of time to vent his frustrations. However Thomas hadn't allowed for Isabella's local knowledge of shortcuts which cut his original outbound journey by half. In truth, during the short ride, Thomas had to admit he and Russel struggled to keep up with the younger thoroughbred mare.

The Davidson's farm was the antithesis of Lucan Beadall's farm. Neat and in place amid beautiful scenery. A young woman was throwing corn to her hens as they rode into the scrubbed yard.

'Ulli,' said Isabella.

'Lady Isabella,' acknowledged the tall young woman, a long blonde plait running down the length of her back.

'Good that we find you home.'

Ulli smiled surprise, an unspoken question on her lips.

She took Thomas' breath away. She was equally as striking as her mother if not more so. Thomas could see Iben in Ulli straight away but as to his brother Robert's input he wasn't sure. He jumped from a feeling of elation at having found her to one of sadness with the realisation that this beautiful creature could have been his child in other circumstances.

'Ulli this is Sir Thomas Huck. Thomas is a friend of Mamma's.' Isabella struggled with the introduction.

Ulli gazed up at Thomas with curiosity. Her eyes were startling in their blueness.

'Will you dismount and come in? My parents are away at market for the day.'

'We would love to,' said Isabella, looking for confirmation from Thomas who appeared to be struck dumb.

Isabella and Thomas obediently dismounted and tied their horses to the hitching post.

As expected the interior of the farmhouse was as neat as the exterior yard. Ulli gracefully handed each of them a glass of fermented Damson wine. 'Mother's specialty.'

Thomas suddenly felt confused. Mother? Which mother?

'This is lovely,' he said instead, lifting his glass and sipping the wine before asking, 'How do you fare Miss Davidson?'

'I fare well, sir. But why do you ask?'

'What do you know of your past?'

'Oh, you mean do I know I was taken in by my Ma and Pa as a baby? The fruit of some indiscretion on the part of a peasant girl.'

Indeed, some indiscretion, pondered Thomas. 'Ulli, a lovely name.'

'My birth mother named me before she gave me away. Ma and Pa liked the name so they kept it.'

Isabella was by now looking rather uncomfortable and totally lost.

'Have you come to tell me you know who my blood mother is?' Ulli asked him with sudden insight.

'That would be something for her to tell you herself.'

'What then?'

Thomas noticed for the first time that the irises of those amazing pale blue eyes were circled and flecked with gold – like his brother's eyes.

'I think there is a possibility that you could be my niece.' Thomas swallowed hard.

CHAPTER FOURTEEN

There was a summons waiting for Thomas when he got back to the Hall. Jowan Carter and the Perranzabuloe gang were to stand trial at Launceston Assizes in the autumn.

Thomas decided to see how Albert Spear was progressing with Rockfoot New Farm. He rode out at seven in the morning just to see if he could catch the Bodmin man shirking. But no, Spear, son and foreman were already on site knocking in nails and lifting heavy roof beams into place.

However Spear looked a little sheepish under his cap. 'Good morning, sir. How do you think the building is progressing?' he asked.

'Fine. Amazingly well.'

It wasn't long before Thomas saw the reason for Spear's barely disguised discomfort. He couldn't believe his eyes as out of the nearly completed bank barn swaggered Josh Haymaker carrying a hurdle.

'Sir,' said Haymaker, still holding the hurdle in one large hand and touching his cap in mock salute to Thomas with the other.

'What is he doing here?' Thomas flushed with anger turning to Spear.

'We were desperate for a labourer to do some heavy lifting so keeping the job to schedule.'

'But I told you ...'

'We were desperate, sir.'

'All right for now but if there is any trouble.'

'I've got my summons to attend Launceston Assizes. Expect you have too. For once we are on the same side, Sir Thomas. Best let bygones be bygones. How say you?' piped up Haymaker, offering his hand. From his lofty position astride Russel, Thomas looked down on the hand as if it were an insult.

'Forgive me for speaking out of turn, Sir Thomas, but those sheep hefted at Beechfield will need shearing afore it is too hot,' said Haymaker, withdrawing his hand without comment.

'I would like a private word with you, Spear, at a future date.' Thomas pulled Russel away, shaking off his incredulity without another word to the gathering.

'Josh is a good worker, Sir Thomas.' Spear's words faded after the horseman kicking on.

'Don't bother with the likes of him, Master Spear,' snarled Haymaker, his gaze firmly fixed on the disappearing cloud of dust.

'But he pays our wages.'

On his way back Thomas called at the Hartmann's cottage and left a note with Agnes for Iben. In the note he told her he had some important news to impart. He asked her to meet him on the beach by the big rock the following morning. The quiet part of the beach where nobody ever went. That same special place where they met as youngsters.

The morning was warm, indeed the July morning was getting hotter by the minute. The sky blue, the sea blue. He arrived to see Iben running towards the breakers, wearing only a lightweight shift. The undergarment as white as the foam round her feet. She dived forward through deeper waves and began to stroke out to sea. Her strokes were strong and firm. Iben was a powerful self-taught swimmer.

Very few Cornish women ever took to the water, very few men either. But Iben wasn't like any of them – as with sex so with swimming – she was a free spirit.

Flinging off his clothes he ran after her, just as he had done as a youngster. But they weren't youngsters anymore, their juxtaposition wasn't the same anymore. Nevertheless they laughed, embraced and frolicked in the sea for minutes on end as if nothing had changed. This was their relationship: perfectly in tune one moment, totally disconnected the next.

As they dashed back up the beach, Thomas could see the outline of her nakedness beneath the wet linen. Her perfectly formed buttocks pressed pink against the material. She turned and he saw her breasts, the nipples erect, and with a jolt he remembered the body he had loved. He knew her flaws, could not bear to think of her in sexual congress with others, many others, with his own brother. He could accept such flaws in others but not in someone he was deeply in love with. If only he knew the reason for it. Suddenly they fell silent and shy towelling down with their outer clothes.

He saw her blatant appraisal of his own nakedness, aware that he had a partial erection. His body had given him away – he still had desire for her. There was still a fondness between them, he was sure of it. A fondness that was denied by her. Had her terrible experience with his brother vanquished any possibility of her loving him?

'Never remembered you being so well hung,' she said. Not with a laugh, not with any innuendo, said with her usual statement of fact. He reached for his breeches. 'So what is this news you have to give that will be of any interest to me?'

There it was that 'me' again. Thomas prevaricated.

'Did you know that there is a Yorkshireman, Dr Robert Wittie, who advocates sea swimming in the coastal spa town of Scarborough for good health? He wrote a book about it. Indeed Wittie recommends bathing in seawater for a wide range of ailments.'

'That bodes well for a long life for both of us then.'

'I had the pleasure of meeting Dr Wittie, during my service for the King, when I was posted to Yorkshire for a short time.'

'My father came from Yorkshire.' She frowned. Thomas surmised it was because of grief over her father's recent death. 'You have such interesting friends, Thomas, it is amazing that you ever bothered with me at all,' she said. 'But this Dr Wittie cannot be the inspiration for the news you have to impart to me.'

'No, of course not. I have found Ulli and talked with her. She is willing to meet you if you are agreeable.'

Iben stared at him in disbelief. 'I know where Ulli is, found her myself, but I have no wish to be in contact with her and complicate her life further, and certainly not through your mediation. I deeply object to your interference.'

Thomas raised his hands defensively. Another metaphorical slap in the face, another misunderstanding.

'I was only trying to help,' he said.

'Well, you haven't.'

'Think about it,' he said. 'Don't jump at making a decision straight away.'

'Oh, I will reflect on it. And, meanwhile, promise me you will leave it alone.'

* * *

Saturday 11th July. Thomas decided to ride to the Cornish Devon border and visit his onetime tenant, Jowan Carter, in Launceston Castle. He wanted to understand why he had cheated him. He learnt later that it was on the same day that Welsh privateer Henry Morgan, with four hundred and fifty of his men, began plundering the city of Portobello on the Isthmus of Panama and Panama City. They spent fourteen days sacking and attacking before finally withdrawing. Maybe all these crimes had the same roots in greed. How can anyone say they trust their fellow man without reservations? Thomas had never met a man or woman he trusted unconditionally.

Always a gaunt man, Carter looked totally emaciated slumped against a wall on a floor of scattered straw. A few other men, unknown to Thomas, were being kept likewise, kept like beasts in a pen. The stench was sickening, forcing him to cover his nose and mouth with a kerchief.

'They don't call this place "castle terrible" for no reason, Thomas Huck,' muttered Carter. Considering himself a doomed man, he discarded the niceties of prefixing Thomas' title. His compatriots in crime watched the unfolding scene intently.

'So this is the famous Sir Thomas Huck,' piped up one of the men.

'Leave it, Martin,' snapped Carter.

'Leave it? Why leave it? This man is responsible for us being locked up in this foul dungeon with his monetary bribes and suchlike.'

'Roger Martin, I presume?' asked Thomas.

'Your presumption is correct,' sneered Martin.

'Well, Martin, I am not responsible for you finding yourself here. You alone are responsible for that. Theft and murder is laid at your door. I suggest you start making your peace with your maker.'

'We've not stood trial yet,' said Martin, skulking back into the shadows away from the single chink of light coming through the arrow slit window. His gang growled their agreement and for the first time Thomas felt really threatened in the company of these violent men.

He turned back to Carter. 'Why you, Jowan? Why did you think fit to steal my sheep?'

'That's just it. Everything is thine. Thy sheep, thy fields, thy farm, when we toil night and day to make things work on little recompense.'

There was a general murmur of agreement to this.

'But wasn't I a good and fair master?' asked Thomas.

'There you are again, master and slave. Now see how we are treated in here less than swine.'

'Aye,' sneered Roger Martin again. 'But then you will be one of the few men feeling at home here, Sir Thomas Huck, the town of Launceston has always been for the King.'

'Aye,' followed his retinue.

'Why they imprisoned George Fox himself in here some dozen years ago.'

'That's right.'

To Thomas' astonishment the retinue crossed themselves. Doubtless an instinctive reflex to protect them against persecution, more in the manner of an oath. 'Are you all members of the Society of Friends?'

'What of it,' said Martin.

'How do you equate your religious beliefs with sheep stealing and murdering a young lad?'

'Innocent until proved guilty,' said one of the men with a contemptuous smile. 'Isn't that how it goes?'

The key grated in the lock. A burly warder with a wet nose pushed his way into the cell.

'Are you all right in there?' he asked Thomas, wiping nasal mucus onto his sleeve. Thomas nodded. 'Well, keep your noise down yous lot,' he told the prisoners. Then he was gone. Thomas didn't think he really cared about his wellbeing at all. Here was just another titled bastard he was forced to make a pretence of protecting out of duty.

'George Fox languished in this place after a preaching mission in the West Country,' continued Martin. 'And do you know why? For having long hair and refusing to remove his hat in court.'

An outraged murmur from the retinue.

'They kept him prisoner for eight months. Like us he was locked up in here, one of the three holding cells in the north gatehouse. Indeed it was possibly this very one. Fox described the place as unpleasant and few came out in good health. There was no latrine, and the shit of prisoners wasn't removed from year to year, so that it was like a mire. In some places the tops of shoes were covered in water and urine. As you can see, Sir Thomas, little has changed. Fox said that some friendly town's people took pity and brought them candles and a little straw which they burnt to take away the stink. The smoke went into the room of the head gaoler and some other prisoners housed above. The head gaoler became so incensed that he took pots of filth from other prison cells and poured them though a hole upon their heads. They were so bespattered that they couldn't touch themselves or each other. Fox described how reports of this ill-treatment generated widespread sympathy and helped promote his cause. Eventually he was moved to a better cell, and allowed to exercise in the castle courtyard.'

All the time Martin was speaking Carter held his tongue.

'I don't want to die,' he told Thomas, suddenly contrite. He placed his outstretched hand across his neck as if rehearsing the noose.

'I don't want to die,' sarcastically mimicked his hardened companions.

Ignoring them, Jowan Carter asked, 'Will you speak up for me in court, Sir Thomas?'

'Do you repent taking my sheep?'

'I do, sir. And I had nothing to do with that young boy's death.'

'Then I shall think about it.'

* * *

The night was humid. Thomas got out of bed to pull up the window. He peered out. The garden was lit by the moon. To his disappointment there was no Iben lurking in the bushes. His night was uncomfortable and damp with turning between images of Iben, Jowan Carter and the hangman's noose. He did eventually get some sleep just before dawn broke, only to be awakened a little later by the incessant territorial singing of a male chaffinch.

'I swear I will take a gun to that chaffinch if it doesn't stop its noise,' he told Josiah, who was adjusting the basin stand.

'True enough those *tinks* don't know when to stop. They can keep it up all day.'

'Were you troubled by it too?'

'Indeed I was, sir. I've heard it every morning for a week.'

'You called the bird by its Cornish name of *tink*.'

'That I did, sir.'

'I believe they get their English name because they spend hours searching chaff for seeds once a field has been threshed.'

'Of course some like their singing so much they keep 'em in cages. Keep them blindfolded believing it improves their song. I've heard tell some put their eyes out with hot needles.'

Thomas shuddered. 'Is there no end to man's cruelty.'

'Nor women's,' put in Josiah.

'What's that?' Ayla arrived carrying a pitcher of warm water.

'Nothing for your ears,' muttered Josiah.

Ayla looked to be blooming.

'How's your courtship going with the new kitchen lad?' Thomas asked her.

She flushed up. 'Stephen and I would like to be wed with your permission.'

'If you love each other you don't need my permission.'

Josiah went tut-tutting away at the mention of 'love'.

'Ah,' said with sudden realisation. 'You'll need my approval for the wedding feast.' Thomas smiled to hide a pinch of jealousy. For all his lands and wealth he hadn't a wife. His cross to bear was that he'd fallen in love with a woman who did not want an honest truthful friend only an endless supply of admirers. He wished he could rip her out of his heart.

Thomas had arranged for neighbouring shearers to visit the neglected Beechfield Farm. Apart from the stolen sheep there was still a good sized flock there.

'Wool isn't in the best of condition,' one man complained to him in the shearing shed. 'Never is after the ewes have lambed.'

'The circumstances have been difficult here,' explained Thomas.

'I know, I heard,' said the man. 'We'll do our best for you.'

Beggers should be no choosers, but yet they will. That night Thomas had the most incredible dream. He must be going mad, out of his mind, after all that had happened. However superstitious Thomas was or was not, he firmly believed that dreams were telling. The next morning he rode back to Rockfoot New Farm.

Orange blossoms perfumed the lanes – a symbol of good luck and joy – Thomas hoped this was auspicious for his coming visit. Orange blossom oil was also accredited as being an aphrodisiac, well maybe he could do with taking some the way his life was working out.

'This main building is almost weathertight now, Sir Thomas,' Spear shouted down from a ladder.

'Where is Haymaker?' Thomas asked him bluntly.

'Sir Thomas, I …' Spear began his defence of Haymaker yet again.

'Where is he?' Thomas insisted.

'Working on the floor joists inside,' said reluctantly.

'Call him.'

After two or three calls, a dust covered Haymaker sauntered out. He looked taken aback and somewhat annoyed to see Thomas in the yard again.

'I followed your advice and have started shearing at Beechfield,' Thomas told him.

'Oh?' Haymaker looked surprised.

'I was wondering if you would do me a favour when they've finished.'

'Me, do you a favour?' Haymaker looked even more surprised.

'We don't know how Launceston Assizes will turn out for Jowan Carter. I think it highly unlikely that he will be returning to the farm again. Would you be willing to look in on Beechfield from time to time, Josh?'

It's Josh now, Haymaker smiled to himself.

'As temporary manager,' added Thomas, quick to eliminate any chance of a misunderstanding.

'Let me think about it.' For once Haymaker was aware he held the whip hand over Sir Thomas Huck. 'Of course I have my work here.'

'I am sure Master Spear will get a chap to replace you. Won't you, Spear?'

Spear jumped down from his ladder, nodding agreement like a rotund wooden doll.

* * *

Spear soon appointed two successors for Haymaker. A couple of local labouring lads, eager to learn the building trade, joined his band of already skilled workers. Thomas kept popping in to see how the work was progressing. The dairy was almost completed and the bank barn was well on its way to completion. The plasterers were due to start work within the farmhouse.

A few weeks elapsed before Thomas decided to visit Haymaker at Beechfield. As he rode towards the property he saw that the gate, which had been tied up with string, had been mended and rehung and he was forced to dismount. There was an eerie silence about the place. The yard looked neat enough and the holes in the barn repaired. Thomas knocked on the door but doubted anyone was at home. After a few more knocks, Haymaker surprisingly opened. He still had his cap on which he now doffed in a sincere enough fashioned on seeing Thomas. Things were looking up: Thomas had never received such a gesture of respect from the likes of Haymaker.

'Just tidying the inside of the 'ouse. A lick of paint here and there makes all the difference,' he explained. 'Will you come in, sir?'

Thomas nodded and sat down on one side of the bench at a rustic table. Haymaker stood over him, dwarfing him, as he had Iben at little Mary's funeral.

'How about sharing a jug of ale, sir?' he suggested, pushing a cup across the table to Thomas.

Again Thomas nodded.

They supped away in silence for a minute or two.

'I really appreciate you giving me this chance,' said Haymaker. 'Times are hard at the moment. You are the first person in my entire life to trust me with such a responsibility.'

'Think nothing of it.'

'But we have had our differences, sir.'

'Yes, we have.'

Haymaker suddenly regarded Thomas intently. 'I reckon mainly because of Iben Hartmann.'

Thomas said nothing.

'You were very smitten with that lass, were you not?'

Thomas said nothing.

'As indeed I was,' admitted Haymaker.

'You were?'

'Yes, no other doxy ever caught my eye like she did.'

'Doxy? Do you not think you should show Mistress Hartmann more respect?'

'Why? Because that is what she exactly is. I accept the reality of what she is. Forgive me, sir, but I think that is something you never did.'

Thomas laughed. This was nothing more than the misogyny he would have expected from Haymaker.

'Forgive me, sir, but perhaps what you never understood, along with many other donkeys, is Iben loves to be pleasured without giving pleasure. She knows only profligacy. She replaces love with hurt, love with confusion.'

'The capriciousness of moods in the turn of a hand,' acknowledged Thomas. 'I remember once kissing her beautiful skin, her body. She jumped up suddenly and said "no", that the situation was like something else. What else? What had it reminded her of?'

'Could have been anything. Any potential for love was knocked out of her at a young age.'

Thomas sighed. 'By my brother?'

'By him and by some even before him.'

'But she was only a child of thirteen when she went with my brother.'

'That's right a pretty little girl. Very desirable to certain men including her own brother.'

'Oh no! Raph, you mean?'

'Well, I don't mean poor Walter,' said Haymaker. Thomas could hardly believe what he was hearing. 'She told me about it herself. Such a state of affairs is not so unusual in our isolated villages. I suspect old Hartmann wasn't above dipping into the pot now and then either. Why my own father …' began Haymaker.

'So you both shared being victims of abuse? You had that in common.'

Haymaker nodded. 'Not of our choosing.'

It all made sense now. The resistance of her father and brother had to his match with Iben. His undelivered leaving for war letter. He thought he was going to faint.

'Lustful congress became the only way she knew to enhance her damaged esteem.'

'I never actually attained that with her.'

'Maybe that is because she really liked you. Couldn't use you in that way.'

'All you have told me explains Iben's pleasing naivety.'

'Aye, she plays the child to pull you in. And like a three year old her interest soon wanes once her straw dolly loses novelty and becomes tattered.'

'Did she use you? Fornication with you?'

'Oh yes, many times.' Haymaker smirked at the memory. Adding, 'Not anymore though, we are just good friends now. For Iben our love making was just like sitting down to a good meal. Once her appetite was satisfied ... And for you?'

'I liked her a lot. Indeed I loved her. I still love her but I cannot put up with the madness anymore.'

'Are you all right?' asked Haymaker. 'You've gone most pale, Sir Thomas. Here let me fill your cup with more ale.'

'Yet she is very intelligent.'

Haymaker looked surprised. 'Intelligent?'

'Yes, her knowledge of the curative plants around our lanes is unrivalled.'

'A word of warning, sir. Unless you are a shallow cove like me, Iben will drag you down into her well of unhappiness. There are many dolts still down there, looking up to her to be saved. Indeed she has already cast her eyes on her next quarry, the mason, Arthur Watson.'

'So is there anything that we can do to give her a more enduring happiness?'

'Why should we want to do that?'

'For the better half of her, the good Iben.'

'Just one thing I can think of.'

'And what is that?'

'Reuniting her with her true daughter, lost to her at birth.'

Thomas couldn't believe he was forming an alliance with this man whom he had regarded with contempt for most of his life. 'I recently made contact with Ulli,' he admitted.

Haymaker gaped at Thomas in astonishment. 'You did?'

'That is what you wanted me to do all along, wasn't it?'

Haymaker made no attempt at denial. He smiled broadly instead.

'I visited Iben's natural daughter on a farm over Altarnun way.'

'Did you tell her about Iben?'

'She knew she was the product of some indiscretion. I told her that I thought she could be my brother's child.'

'How did she take that? Was she welcoming?'

'Well, she reacted a lot better than Iben did. Iben forbad me to contact the girl again.'

'I can hardly believe Iben truly meant that. She is of a very changeable disposition.'

'But what can we do more?' Thomas shrugged.

'We must be patient and see if the dropped seeds take root.'

'We,' emphasised Thomas.

'Yes, we,' sighed Haymaker. 'And I am very flattered, Sir Thomas, that you followed my hint and found Ulli.'

The future can only be glimpsed from knowing the past. Thomas realised he had never really known Iben's past. What had seemed to be had never been, and he had completely misjudged this man he was now sharing ale and secrets with.

'Are you a churchgoer?' Thomas asked as Haymaker wiped his beer frothed mouth on his sleeve.

'Occasionally. Though I have never seen you attending a regular service despite it being compulsory. But then I expect you can get away with it, no one knows if you are there or not hidden away in that box pew of yours.'

'To explain my absences I tell the curate that I worship in a chapel at home.'

'And as you are lord of the manor he accepts that.'

'Have you ever wondered why?'

'Why what?'

'Why I am not a regular attender.'

'Not really. Never gave it too much thought.'

'Original sin.'

'Original sin?' slurred Haymaker vacantly.

'Yes, according to the Bible, Eve was created from Adam's rib and, having eaten the forbidden fruit, was responsible for man's expulsion from paradise. In medieval art, the responsibility of women for this "original sin" is often emphasised by giving a female head to the serpent who tempts Eve to disobey God. The story underlined the belief that women were inferior to men, and that they were morally weaker and likely to tempt men into sin.'

'Don't they?'

'No, in my experience it is men, men like us, who corrupt womenkind.'

'Never thought of it like that.' Haymaker stared into his half full glass before swilling the entire contents down his throat. 'That could be certainly true in Iben's case.'

'Iben is whom I particularly had in mind.'

'The thing is, Sir Thomas, I for one would never deliberately hurt Iben.'

Thomas decided to ignore this saying instead, 'If you do decide to take on Beechfield for the long term, Haymaker, there is to be no more thieving and gangs.'

'I left all that behind me a long time ago,' replied Haymaker.

CHAPTER FIFTEEN

A murder of crows were roosting in the trees outside Rockfoot Hall. Thomas shivered at their primitive cawing cries. He knew of the old folktale that crows would circle and gather to decide the capital fate of another crow. Then again they were regarded as an omen of imminent death in his part of the world. But for a veteran soldier they had only one connotation, they were scavengers of the dead left behind on the battlefield.

He had officially given up practising medicine after the war but, as with the plague deaths and Hartmann drownings, his medical knowledge was occasionally called upon by the community. He wouldn't refuse anybody if his services were needed. Why should he? Thankfully though there had been no more plague victims in his area since little Mary Wood, Lucan Beadall and the poor soul found deceased in the ditch, however the later untreatable lung variant had added to his losses.

Was he a good doctor? – he couldn't say. What he hoped was that he was able, still able, to alleviate a little pain in those with sickness. Many in his profession regarded medicine as a science, he regarded it as both a science and an art. In the final reckoning he was dealing with individuals with all their fears and anxieties.

Thomas looked forward to breakfast more than any meal in the day. But that morning was to be different. Josiah complained that he woke up having difficulty seeing. His speech was slurred and he appeared confused.

As he was telling Thomas this he just dropped to the ground. Plates scattered and clattered on the flagged floor, hard boiled eggs rolled under chairs and the table. Ayla screamed as Thomas went through the motions of checking for his vital signs. He appeared to have numbness or weakness in his face, arms, and legs. His face had drooped on the left side. He could not answers questions, he could not speak. With the help of a manservant, Thomas carried Josiah to his bedchamber.

Thomas swallowed his pride and sent a message to Iben. Could she think of any herbal remedies that could help poor Josiah as he believed his old retainer had been struck down by apoplexy? Iben and Josiah had never liked each other very much so he doubted she would respond. Again he was wrong. The contrary Iben was soon knocking on Rockfoot Hall's door.

She looked down on Josiah moribund on his bed. 'Poor old fellow,' she cooed while stroking his brow.

'Is anything to be done?' asked Thomas, relinquishing medical authority to palliative nursing care.

She lifted a finger to her lips. 'Careful,' she warned him. 'It might not seem so but I am sure Josiah can hear everything we are saying.'

'Can I do anything?' asked Ayla – a second victim of Josiah's misogyny.

'You might raid the kitchen for vegetables, any citrus fruits, beetroot and ginger as prescribed by the apothecaries of the ancient world.' Iben produced a small mortar and pestle out of her shoulder bag. 'I'll crush all you can lay your hands on with this.'

'I will speak to Stephen right away.'

'Meanwhile,' said Iben, 'I already have made up a potion of cardamom, fennel, nutmeg, long pepper, black pepper, lily and cloves.'

When Ayla returned from the kitchen she was greeted with grim faces. Iben shook her head. Josiah was too ill to take the original potion.

Thomas told Ayla to cancel the order with the kitchen.

Death is often a mumbling dribbling affair, and so it was with Josiah. Thomas would have chosen him a prettier death but it wasn't to be.

* * *

Josiah was soon put to rest and his wake was a modest and private affair at the Hall. Indeed when you reached his ripe old age there weren't many contemporaries left to mourn. But what was his age? Thomas had no idea. He left those arrangements in the hands of Iben, or at least with Arthur Watson as Iben seemed to have chosen to distance herself from Thomas once more.

Josiah the ever loyal faithful servant had died in harness. Thomas found he couldn't shed tears for feisty old Josiah but a shudder of grief did pass through him as he left the graveside. Again Iben had failed to appear at the service – then Iben never did hypocrisy – or if she did only on her own terms and in her own interests.

A happier event followed in August: the wedding of Ayla Nolan and Stephen Moore. Ayla cast off her Roman Catholicism to marry in the local Anglican Church. This wasn't unusual in this time of religious unrest. Law upon law was frequently passed enforcing the doctrine and attendance of the Church of England. Three years before, the Five Mile Act forbade non-Anglican ministers to come within five miles of incorporated towns, towns with a mayor and corporation. However these measures did not stop the more committed non-conformists meeting or preaching. Nor did it stop the local boy and his Irish Catholic colleen from adapting and tying the knot in the neighbourhood's parish.

Again Thomas wondered if he should tell Ayla about his meeting with her father. On the other hand, should he inform Richard Nolan of his daughter's impending marriage. When, down in London, he had suggested a reunion between father and daughter, Captain Nolan had shown no enthusiasm. And anyway he hadn't an address for the man be it care of Lord Craven's regiment. Once more he decided somethings are best left alone and unsaid.

'All gods are the same to me,' Ayla would whisper in the night to her intended. 'All of 'em eventually let you down.'

'Like your father did,' filled in Stephen knowingly. 'Do not worry, Ayla, I will always be there for you.'

The banns had been published in the church for three consecutive Sundays before *the evil deed*, which had already taken place, could take place officially. Saturday 22nd August saw the happy couple brought to be wed in the eyes of God, a God Ayla did not believe in.

'Dearly beloved, we are gathered together here in the sight of God …'

The only kinsfolk were on Stephen's side of the church. Nevertheless Thomas saw, walking Ayla down the aisle, that villagers had thoughtfully replaced and filled her family absences on the opposite benches.

The couple were dressed in their church best. Ayla in a lovely full cream skirt and tight green bodice, her auburn hair crowned with a band of interlocking daisies. Thomas thought her beautiful and was proud for her to link her arm through his. How far had she come. Ahead a waiting Stephen, standing alongside his brother, wriggled with discomfort and embarrassment in his tight fitting claret doublet.

Luckily the day was fine for the walk back to Rockfoot Hall with a gathering of relatives, merry village folk and friends processing behind. In licking lipped anticipation of the feast to come they walked through small fields, past ancient hedges reflecting the enclosure of land from surrounding moorland. The moorland itself pockmarked with surface mining for tin and copper.

The company was not disappointed for Thomas had arranged a feast fit for kings outside in the courtyard. Beef, lamb, goat, game pies, sausages; fish in season; fruit fool, syllabub, custard tarts, bread and butter pudding, Banbury cakes, cakes of every kind; cheeses; different breads and ale of course, plenty of jugs of ale were resplendent on four trestle tables.

Once the meal was underway, Thomas had arranged for pale-faced Hall staff, red-faced garden staff, ruddy estate workers and a few local farming friends of Stephen's to join in the celebration. Indeed everyone who wished to attend the feast was welcomed. And there were many beaming faces and laughter at the trestle tables late into the afternoon. Ayla and Stephen were obviously very popular.

Josh Haymaker was there having been reluctantly exonerated by Ayla for his obnoxious behaviour as the King of Misrule. She had eventually relented over his invitation as it turned out that he and Stephen were old friends. Speaking of old friends, she and Iben had made up their differences through Josiah's passing, and Iben too had been invited to the wedding.

'So sad the old man is not here to witness your happiness,' said Iben.

'No, no,' said Edith Moore, Stephen's grandmother, who had once been employed in service at the Hall and knew Josiah well.

'Why, "no"?' Ayla asked her.

'Because, my dear, Josiah had no truck with weddings, marriage and suchlike since he was rejected at the altar.'

Thomas' curiosity was piqued. 'By whom?'

'Why Widow Collette of course.'

'Ann Collette?'

'The very same. Her maiden name was Wright. She left poor Josiah waiting with the priest, his best man and half the village and never appeared. Instead she had run off with the cooper Joseph Collette.'

'No wonder he didn't like or trust women,' said Thomas, looking directly at Iben. Indeed over the meal, despite their history and differences, there had been quite a lot of intense looks passing between the two of them. Thomas regarded it as merely part of their see-saw relationship.

'Where is Master Watson?' asked Josh Haymaker out of badness, noting the interaction between Thomas and Iben.

'At work engraving Josiah's tombstone. Anyway he wasn't invited,' Iben explained.

Ayla picked up her fiddle and the party got up to dance. Thomas was left facing across from Iben.

'Would you do me the honour?' he asked her.

'Why not,' she shrugged indifference.

They joined the rest of the party whirling round the courtyard to an Irish jig. Suddenly the tempo lifted and the whole scene seemed to be spinning and jumping or was it the ale, blinked Thomas.

Iben was particularly lively. She kept her upper body rigid but her feet never stopped moving. Her pointed footing was perfect as she haughtily passed him in the dance. Her eyes sparkled, her hair broke free, she was beautiful. *Beautiful*, Thomas could not escape that fact. Nor could he pretend to be a match for her in the dance.

'You are doing well for Cornish folk,' said Ayla, lifting the fiddle from under her chin. 'Now for something a little more delicate and slow. It is called *The Moreen*, or *Móirín* in Gaelic.'

Thomas thought he had never heard anything so sad. It seemed to express all the past sorrows that existed between himself and Iben. Ayla was playing the piece beautifully. The company listened transfixed.

'Come,' Thomas said, pulling Iben gently towards him and claiming the floor. At first her body felt rigid in his arms. Eventually she seemed to relax, to succumb to the moment. They moved around the courtyard as one to the sad air, to their sad air. He could feel the warmth of her body, her breasts. Finally she rested her head on his chest there beneath the green corn moon.

Josh Haymaker muttered something suggestive, a somewhat tempered jealous crudity for him being a reformed character with responsibilities. But Thomas was too absorbed with his own feelings to take any notice, to be bothered to listen to him. They danced on. Nobody else dared venture forth to steal Iben's and the master's stage.

He sensed her womanly form moulded into his own body, his own growing hardness as they swayed as one. For all the anger and hurt that had passed between them – there was still that electrical charge. He was falling and he had no will to turn back. He took her hand and led her away. Ayla stopped playing, the wedding guests fell into an embarrassed silence, until Ayla picked up her instrument and launched into the drinking song *The Wild Rover*.

'Where are you taking me?' Iben asked.

'You'll see.'

'You do know …'

'I know,' he said wearily. 'But how will Arthur Watson react to this?'

'Arthur,' she laughed. 'Arthur is, how shall I put this, not very much that way inclined.'

They lay together in the hayloft above the cow stalls. He made a groundsheet for her with his cloak over the scratching straw. They could not stop kissing. He did not want to stop kissing her as if his whole life had led him back to this – kissing, feeling the softness of her, moving to more intimate exploration through clothing.

Her big practical hands began to travel his body and he groaned with want. Leading the way, she stripped off and they lay naked together. She looked at him with anguished impatient desire – despair almost – as he touched and kissed her again and again. She appeared to open to him both spiritually and sexually. For the first time ever he entered her. Her moans and whimpers kept him going, gentle at first then harder, faster, deeper. He could not have stopped if he had wanted to now. Her whole inner sheath suddenly clamped onto him and it was over, over just like that. They unfurled. No words – a shocked silence resting between them. Only afterwards did he wonder if Iben had taken any precautions – something like the vinegar and honey rag Ayla had talked about – he guessed not because how could she have prepared for this to happen.

'That was wonderful. You certainly have learnt how to please a woman, Thomas Huck. You do know,' she said again, her voice warm and mellow.

'I know.' Even then he believed her, that something above

fucking was possible, that love was still possible between them despite all her previous insincerity, her changes of heart.

For all their differences he had never experienced such romantic intensity with a woman, he reluctantly acknowledged as they dressed and climbed down from the byre. Sweet smelling straw still clinging to their clothing, they had no intention of going back to a sniggering wedding party.

* * *

If Thomas imagined this coupling would change his relationship with Iben, he was wrong. Nothing changed. He wrote her a loving note, a day or two later, which she failed to answer. Rather than Iben it was Haymaker who startled a bewildered Thomas with a visit. Haymaker reassured him that nothing would change after his escapade in the hayloft. Change would only take place if Iben herself changed and that was unlikely.

'Is she involved with Arthur Watson in more than a business sense?' Thomas could not stop himself asking.

Haymaker did not conceal his amusement. 'Do I detect a little jealousy here, Sir Thomas? No, I don't think Watson's got it in him. Certainly not to stay the course with Iben.'

'That's what she said but I have given up believing anything she says.'

'Alas, I can appreciate that very well.'

'But it was you who first hinted that she might be interested in the mason.'

'Did I? Maybe it was you I was testing.'

'So you were unaware of anything between them?'

'Who knows what poor soul Iben might fix on next,' shrugged Haymaker before changing the subject. 'Tell me, is

Constable Fox keeping you informed of any new information regarding the fire at Beadall's Farm?'

'I've not seen Fox in months. He is more engaged with the Perranzabuloe gang and their forthcoming murder trial at Launceston.'

'Did you know he tried to pin the fire on me?'

'Yes, I believe he did in the beginning because of the stag mask found in your barn.'

'I denied having anything to do with Lucan's death if you remember?'

'I do.'

'I pointed out that there was another mummer representing a stag.'

'You did.'

'I merely turned up dressed as a stag to disrupt the performance. Said I had no idea who the other stag was, which was true then. However some new information has reached my ears and I am not sure how to deal with it.'

'I see,' said Thomas, but he didn't really, not after all this time.

'One of the troupe got drunk the other night in the Black Bear Tavern down the village. They started blethering about the other man playing the stag on the night of the fire.'

'Who did he say it was?'

'Wood.'

'Wood the grain dealer over Truro way?'

'No, not he.' Haymaker shook and then lowered his head reluctant to tell.

'Who, then?'

'The lad who played Little Johnny Jack said it was poor wee Mary's father. Mary's father believed, along with many others, that bad air was the cause of the plague and only by fire would the community be rid of it.'

'Like London.'

'Aye, like London. Whether or not he knew Lucan was inside the building and intended to kill him is another matter.'

Thomas' thoughts returned to the cart ride he took with Wood to the carpenter on the day of his daughter's death. He remembered Wood saying that Mary often went to Beadall's Farm to play with the new lambs. Could she have got this terrible disease from there? he had asked. It was the most uncomfortable jerky ride Thomas had ever experienced. He could not make out if Wood was mishandling either the horse or cart or both due to his heightened emotional state. Then again perhaps it was merely the conveyance's lack of springs.

'So what do you intend doing with this information, Josh?' he asked.

'I was hoping you might tell me.'

'Maybe William Wood has been through enough losing his little daughter. Maybe we should simply disregard this intelligence as coming from a drunken source.'

'Yes, that's the charitable thing to do,' agreed Haymaker.

'We are of the same mind then?'

'I was proposing to do that all along.'

'So why ask my opinion?'

'Because believe it or not I value your judgement, Sir Thomas. And I was wondering …' Haymaker hesitated.

'Come on man what were you wondering?'

'Might you be good enough to call on William Wood and warn him of the rumours circling round the village about him and the fire. He'll take more notice of you than me.'

Thomas laughed at that.

'You'll not be telling the Constable any of this?' added Haymaker.

'Not one word will pass these lips.'

* * *

A day later Iben was walking down the lane towards him.

'Good morning, Iben,' he raised his tricorne in salute.

She barely gave him the time of day. Muttered something and turned away.

How could they be so close one day and then so far apart the next? His heart and hopes fell. He was back to square one. Surely now he realised that he was purely the instrument for her sexual gratification. He had given her his love but she had no real love for him only for herself and her own fulfilment. Or was it that simple: when they were together he felt he knew her emotionally inside and out and then he felt he didn't know her at all.

It was merely a game to her. She led him on only to let him go. She was a game-player who never realised that she would be the loser in the end.

Love conquers all – no, not when the loved one changes mood and her mind minute by minute, when there is nothing constant in her nature. Maybe it was this instability that fascinated him but something never quite sat right for him with Iben. He loved her but there was always a feeling that not all was as it should be. And now there it was – the underlying hardness and falsehood revealed. He finally realised he had had enough with her unpredictability and unreliability. The two opposite values were his bedrock.

There was yet another element to this: Haymaker was right, he suspected Iben derived pleasure and self-validation from hurting him and others. However, she went for quantity rather than quality. He had given her his love both spiritually, emotionally and recently physically – more especially spiritually – and she pushed it back in his face. He kicked Russel on.

Soon Thomas dismounted at the Woods' half-timbered, thatched farmhouse. After his encounter with Iben he had fire in his belly.

He breathed a sigh of relief when Wood himself opened the door. He guessed Harriet Wood would be at the local quay buying fish along with most of the other housewives. Thomas wanted no witnesses for what he was about to say.

'Sir Thomas.' Wood stared at him in disbelief.

'Can I come in?'

'Certainly, sir. Take a seat. How can I oblige you?'

'Mistress Wood not at home?'

'No, sir, 'tis Friday, the day of our Lord's crucifixion. As you know, sir, Jesus was a warm-blooded creature the same as you and me, so we abstain from eating warm blooded meats on Fridays. The wife is away to market to buy fish.'

'I see you are a pious man, Wood.'

'That I am, sir.'

'So I hope you will treat what I have to say kindly and in the manner it is intended.'

Wood looked a little concerned at this. 'What is it you wish to say?'

'Did you attend the mumming outside Lucan Beadall's farm disguised as a stag.'

'Yes, along with Josh Haymaker.'

'He is adamant that he left before you.'

'Is he?' Wood's tone had become defensive.

'It seem accusations have been awash in the Black Bear Tavern.'

'What sort of accusations?'

'That it was you, Wood, who set the fire at Beadall's Farm.'

'Would you blame me if it was? You saw her, my sweet little girl died in terrible pain with all those boil things poisoning her blood. And she got them from 'im, Beadall.'

'You cannot know that for sure.'

'I do.'

'Did you mean to burn Lucan to death? Did you mean to immolate Lucan Beadall?' repeated Thomas.

'I meant to turn that farm to ashes.'

'You did that right enough.'

'Heard he was getting better while my little lass was dead. In truth I thought he would escape his farm once he smelt the smoke.'

'My farm,' Thomas reminded him. Everyone seemed to have overlooked that fact, the cost to his own purse of building a new farm. Then to his tenants his financial resources were limitless compared with theirs.

'Too bad if Beadall was still in there,' said Wood dismissively.

'You show so little remorse that I feel obliged to tell Constable Fox what I have heard.'

'Please don't do that, sir. In truth I do suffer from bouts of guilt over Lucan's death, but I have to put it aside and work the fields to feed my family,' said Wood, suddenly changing the thrust of his argument.

'I shall have to think it over.'

CHAPTER SIXTEEN

'Now you are a married man, with responsibilities, would you be interested in replacing Josiah as head of the household?' Thomas asked Stephen Moore the next day.

Stephen looked to the floor. 'I don't know what to say, Master.'

'Say "yes".'

'Are you sure?'

'I am sure. I cannot think of anyone better than you and Ayla to run my household.'

Stephen lifted eyes sparkling with possibilities. 'Yes, oh yes, then.'

'Please be good enough to have the stable lad saddle up Russel. I have an errand to perform.'

Little Johnny Jack wasn't a little boy at all. His real name was Aaron Richardson and he lived alone in a tumbled down dwelling towards the end of the village. He was the local character, a man trapped inside a child's body. He was extremely poor because his frail body and curvature of the spine limited his ability to work long hours in the fields. He was well known to Thomas as concerned neighbours had on occasions asked him to visit Aaron.

Thomas dismounted, tying Russel to the nearest fence. He hammered against a peeling door. Eventually it slowly, so slowly opened.

'Aaron how are you?'

Aaron was about forty-seven inches small. His stunted head barely reached half way up the entrance. He was smiling as usual. Only the expression in his eyes hinted at any maturity.

He didn't answer Thomas' question as to how he was but just started laughing louder. Aaron wasn't one for words beyond asking for food and money in the mummers' play. It was strange – only during a performance did he seem able to find his voice, other than blethering malicious rumours when in drink it appeared.

Aaron stood on his threshold. He did not have the wherewithal to invite Thomas inside his home. And Thomas wasn't sure he would accept that invitation anyway.

'I understand you have had much to say in the Black Bear Tavern of an evening, Aaron.'

The edges of the wide mouth above Aaron's big lower jaw fell. He said nothing.

'Something to the effect that you knew who set fire to Lucan Beadall's farm,' continued Thomas. Aaron's large tongue lolled forward vacantly. 'So who were you saying started the fire?' Aaron began to flap his hands in distress. 'Who?' insisted Thomas, ignoring the flapping hand gestures.

'Stag,' said Aaron.

'But there were two stags.'

Aaron shook his head in confusion.

'So which stag lit the fire? Was it Josh Haymaker's stag or William Wood's?'

'Don't know,' said Aaron. 'Forgotten.'

'Then you shouldn't be making up rumours about people if you are not sure, should you?'

'Don't know,' said Aaron again.

'If you stop saying such things we can make all this go away.'

'Yes, make go away.' He lit up with happiness and laughter again.

* * *

Mistress Wood opened the door to him this time.

'Is your husband at home, Mistress?'

'No, with Lammas well behind us he is fruit picking down the bottom field.'

Without further ado Thomas rode down to where Mistress Wood was pointing. He did not dismount as he could see Wood was lathered in sweat and busy.

'I spoke to Aaron Richardson and he has promised not to repeat the rumour of you setting fire to Beadall's Farm.'

'Will he hold to his word?'

'Yes, I think he will.'

Wood sighed his relief. 'You'll not repeat the rumour to Constable Fox then?'

'I think not. Nothing is to be gained from it. Mind, watch your step from now on.'

'Please, sir, take these.' The farm labourer offered up to Thomas a wooden bowl of berries he had collected.

Thomas shook his head. 'No more, he said, turning his horse away before riding off. 'Remember no more.'

* * *

'Haymaker,' he shouted in the yard of Beechfield. No response. 'Haymaker,' he shouted again. 'Show yourself.' Looking round he was amazed at the improvements already made. The well had been freshly grouted and repaired. The barn repaired. The collecting sheep pen replaced with fresh timbers. He tried for a final time, 'Haymaker.' The name echoed off the surrounding buildings.

Haymaker finally emerged from the barn.

'Thought it was you.' He grinned without embarrassment, buttoning up his drop front breeches. It wasn't long before a blushing maid followed on adjusting her bodice.

Thomas cleared his throat. 'I see you have been busy.'

'Sir Thomas meet Emmerline, my new milkmaid.'

'But you haven't any cows.'

'I have now,' laughed Haymaker, slapping Emmerline's behind.

'Show some respect, man,' said Thomas.

Giggling Emmerline went scuttling off, judging her slapped behind an affectionate cue to leave.

'When I said I see you have been busy, Haymaker, I meant improving the farm not wenching.'

'I prefer it when you call me Josh, Sir Thomas.'

'Josh then,' sighed Thomas rather scathingly, he hated to see women used so. He would never regard Haymaker as a friend but he had a sneaking admiration for his undisguised freedom of spirit. 'I have just talked to Aaron Richardson and then William Wood. I think the problem of the Beadall fire is at rest.'

'Heard something else that might be of interest to you, *Thomas*,' dared Haymaker. 'From a lass who was friendly with Jowan Carter.'

'Was it the girl who was just here?'

Haymaker smirked. 'The girl came with the farm.'

'You really are disgusting, Haymaker.'

'That be as it may. Do you want to hear this or not?' Thomas nodded. 'Emmerline said Jowan told her it wasn't him that killed the shepherd boy but one of the Martin brothers. Jowan wasn't even there although he did admit to being involved in the plan to steal the sheep.'

'Are you sure you are not just spreading this tale out of mean spite?'

'Spite, how spite?'

'Why, because there is history between you and Roger Martin in particular. It is well known in the county that there is no love lost between you and him.'

'No, Thomas, I swear it is what the girl told me.'

'I have been thinking of your plan to reunite Iben with her daughter,' said Thomas, eager to move the subject on.

'And does the idea appeal to you?'

'I will give the matter further attention once the Summer Assizes are over at the end of the month.'

* * *

A large earthquake had struck Northern Anatolia, Thomas was to learn a few days later. Many thousands had perished. It seemed such a long way from the small troubles of Cornwall where only five men were to stand on trial for their lives. But then not if you were one of those men.

That will set the Ottomans back a little, Seymour Glover gleefully wrote to him. Seymour's interests were always on the bigger political picture particularly if it could further his career, noted Thomas.

The next to meet her maker was Granny Pace who occasionally helped out Cook in the kitchen. She was a neighbour of Ann Collette. Ann and Granny Pace were friends as much as grouchy old ladies are ever friends – more a love and hate relationship was the way of it.

'Too many funerals,' Thomas complained to Ayla. 'I don't think I can bear to attend another one.' But he did.

He always felt slightly embarrassed taking his place alone in the family pew, while the more devout villagers took their seats on the benches behind. Though far from devout, he saw that Iben was there on one of the benches behind him and next to her was Arthur Watson. On the other side of Iben, Ann Collette sat weeping uncontrollably.

The solemn voice of the priest echoed round the church. 'Lord, thou hast been our refuge from one generation to another. Before the mountains were brought forth, or ever the earth and the world were made, thou art God from everlasting, and world without end.'

Thomas was thankful that he hadn't to endure hours of the old mass. At least the new religion was more succinct and genial to his basic needs.

Soon they processed behind the rented coffin out to the graveside. Soon the coffin was emptied of its occupant.

'Man that is born of woman hath but a short time to live, and is full of misery. He cometh up, and is cut down, like a flower; he fleeth as it were a shadow, and never continueth in one stay.' The priest and clerks sang as pallbearers lowered Granny Pace, wrapped in a woollen winding cloth in accordance with the law, into her final resting place.

Thomas could see Iben working seductively on Arthur Watson even at the graveside. Poor Ann Collette was forgotten until Agnes Hartmann put a supportive arm round her. To Agnes' right her daughter clung to Watson occasionally smiling lovingly into his face.

Haymaker winked across at Thomas from the far side. So much for his assessment that Watson hadn't got it in him. He had enough to arrest Iben's attention for the here and now.

Thomas couldn't concentrate on the graveside service for watching Iben. She removed her arm from Watson's and took his hand instead, stroking it all the while.

She gave one quick furtive glance in Thomas' direction and then another across to Haymaker. *Look, see what I've got – a mature worldly man for once.*

Thomas looked down into the occupied grave and felt as if he might tumble in there too. He felt dizzy and sick. Iben was shamelessly flirting like this at poor Granny Pace's funeral. She had caught Watson right enough, he looked bewitched by her. Maybe bewitched was the right word. Iben was a witch.

Thomas immediately regretted he had used that word. Witch hysteria had been rife during the Civil War. Hundreds of women, most over fifty years of age, were executed during that time. Many had been forced to confess to having sexual congress with the Devil.

Long after the church grounds were emptied, long after late summer darkness came in, something sinister was hidden beneath the table stone over Granny Pace's grave. A devout Anglican, Margaret Pace had insisted her grave be covered by one of the new fashionable flat stones. Indeed the stone must have taken all her savings, reckoned Thomas, but then Granny had no kith or kin left to leave money to. However, like so many village folk here and hereabouts there would not have been enough left over to pay for a coffin.

So who was responsible for placing the mystery object first observed by the churchwarden making his rounds?

It was a stoneware bottle colloquially known as the 'bellarmine'. The bottle was pot bellied and had a mask painted on it of a grim looking bearded man. It got its name from a cardinal called Bellarmine who published much anti-Protestant literature. This same Bellarmine was famous for his opposition to Galileo Galilei and the Copernican doctrine.

The curious churchwarden shook the stoppered bottle. He knew the witches' bottles were usually filled with rosemary, needles and pins, red wine and sometimes urine. But who could be responsible for covering such blasphemy over Granny Pace's remains? He removed the stopper and sniffed – true enough there was a sour smell of urine and asparagus.

'Smash that godless thing into pieces,' instructed the priest, coming up behind him.

The churchwarden did as he was bid. Needles, pins and liquid oozed across the paving stones. In the middle of this mess was a green sprig of rosemary. The magic protective spell was out of the bottle. The churchwarden looked down on it dubiously.

'What will happen in our community now?' he asked.

'Unless we know for certain there is a witch abroad, this could be some form of jest. You are not telling me that you believe it to be sorcery? Clean up that mess,' snapped the priest, pointing to the spillage on the paving stones before shrugging in disgust and walking away.

The priest did not want to know who was responsible for the hideous bottle lest it involved further research on his part, but the churchwarden remained curious. It must be someone empathetic to the old religion.

* * *

Thomas had tried telling himself that he did not mind Iben's dalliance with Arthur Watson – and only a dalliance he was sure it was – Iben didn't go in for anything deeper. But just when he had convinced himself that he had cast her from his mind, he knew he hadn't. He was looking forward to physically getting away for awhile.

On the cusp of summer and autumn the Perranzabuloe trial was due to take place. It would be presided over by one of the travelling justices on the Western Circuit.

Launceston looks as though it is preparing for a carnival rather than the serious business of the courts, he observed.

'Come in from Bodmin for the trial. No greater spectacle than a hanging,' one old wag shouted up to him.

'Ever heard of "innocent until proven guilty"?' Thomas snarled down on the bald head.

Launceston's timber-framed Guildhall was situated on the corner of Broad Street and High Street and from its architecture cannot have been more that twenty years old. Though the assizes did not start until the next day people were gossiping in groups outside every tavern, vendors were selling everything from cloth to fruit to bread and cheeses. There was a sense of expectation and excitement about the town. Donkeys bearing huge pannier baskets kept the vendors supplied as the animals weaved their way in and out of citizens, occasionally shitting on setts and shoes without discrimination. Supply and demand was the order of the day.

The London Inn was recommended by his childhood intended, Mary Thoresby. The inn was situated at 25/26 Church Street. He was greeted by the landlord, Julius Mann, who was standing in a proprietorial manner outside his premises watching all the comings and goings.

'Always busy during the Summer Assizes,' were his first words.

The second thing Thomas noticed about Julius was his beam – he was all jovial welcoming beam but then that must have been part of his job.

'Would you have a room for me and stabling for my horse?'

'Well, I am not sure.' The beam began to fade. Thomas was dusty from head to foot from the journey and cannot have cut a very imposing figure.

'You were recommended to me by Lady Mary Thoresby.'

'Of Ansell Manor?' Mann looked more interested and rather surprised.

'The same,' Thomas replied curtly.

'I'll have the lad collect your horse. There is stabling round to the back.'

'And a room for me?'

'And a room for you if you don't mind climbing a few steps, sir. All our best rooms are already taken as you can well imagine. While you wait, a pot of ale or glass of wine in the barroom so the lass can prepare your chamber?' suggest Julius.

Half an hour later, Thomas was struggling with his bulging overnight satchel up the newel spiral staircase. It seemed to go on and on until he reached a barrel-shaped ceiling on the top floor with Tudor doors and half-timbered walls. He had not conquered his mountain yet, not until he took the last few narrow steps to reach an austere attic summit.

He was thankful to find Julius and the maid had wasted no time and a pitcher and washing bowl filled with warm water awaited him. The ceramics laid out on the stand were decorated with delicate red flowers painted on a clean white background. Splashing the water on his face and person, he immediately felt refreshed.

Back down on the ground floor, a hungry Thomas pushed open a heavy Elizabethan oak door. The night was cool and he was delighted to see a roaring fire beneath a two-foot wide granite lintel. The inn was blessed with many such granite fireplaces. Over supper he questioned Julius about the lintels, wondering if he could incorporate granite into Rockfoot New Farm.

'A little before my time,' said Julius. 'I have wondered about them myself. Maybe a previous owner had connections with a local quarry.'

'Quite so,' said Thomas, looking down on his lamb chops and potatoes with relish.

'Are you here for the trial, sir?' asked the landlord, standing proprietorially over his table, holding out the ordered bottle of claret in one hand.

Thomas hesitated. 'I am,' he admitted 'but I prefer not to talk about it.'

'Five men in the dock, I understand.' Thomas watched Julius pour the dark red wine into his fluted glass. 'Five men for a capital offence,' his host persisted.

Thomas sighed a weary 'yes'.

'The Perranzabuloe gang have caused mayhem in our area over the years.' Julius Mann obviously wasn't one to let a subject go easily once his curiosity was piqued. 'That Roger Martin isn't even Cornish, he is a Devon man.'

CHAPTER SEVENTEEN

Thomas decided to walk the short distance from the inn to the Guildhall. Clear his head. He cleared his head right enough but nearly drowned at the same time in a deluge of rain, Cornish rain which was never far away. The County Assizes had been held in the town since 1201. But the Guildhall venue in the town centre wasn't completed until 1647. It accommodated both the nisi prius court and the crown court. It had a new feel to it. Nonetheless if it had only been a cave, Thomas would have been relieved to find shelter there. Shaking the drops from his cloak on the stone flagged floor, steaming and ready for action, he wondered what awaited him.

A true bill had been found by the Grand Jury against all five accused.

Thomas took a seat in the cramped floor of the courtroom. He blinked through a tobacco fog of pipe smoke as the five shackled defendants were marshalled past the bar which separated them from a raucous public. They were flanked by a gaoler on either side. A short stocky fellow, with the appearance of a clerk, stood next to them. He had obviously been seconded as their advocate for the day. The twelve free men jury, about to find for or against the defendants, were already wriggling their buttocks on the hard benches in discomfort and anticipation.

But Thomas knew, as the rest of the court did, the power wasn't really with the jurors or the advocates, the power was with the gloomy bewigged old gentleman who had just stepped onto his dais. His full periwig in the style of the King would not have been out of place promenading down the Mall.

'All rise.'

The public were already fractious waiting for the performance to begin. Reluctant to rise for the judge, they began jeering at the defendants. Pale Jowan Carter particularly looked alarmed and fearful, and so he should, mob justice had been ubiquitous during recent civil disorder.

The separation between public viewing and official legal business required more than just a physical barrier of the bar; in fact, courtroom order was typically maintained by the judge and bailiff and so it was in this case.

'Silence!' The judge shouted those indefatigable words. 'Silence in court!'

Sir Jonathan Mowbray was dressed for summer in a violet robe, faced with shot-pink taffeta. A black cincture bit into his girth.

'Looks like a fine old lady, don't he?' A stage whisper came from the rustic public benches accompanied by titters, applause and shuddering stamping of feet.

Thomas' attorney, Richard Chalmers, representing the plaintiffs – the dead shepherd boy's father, his mother and Thomas as the owner of the stolen sheep – got to his feet to briefly outline the case. Thomas looked on proprietorially. He was the only one able to cover Chalmer's fees which he had happily agreed to.

In response to Chalmer's lean succinct presentation, the overweight advocate for the accused struggled up saying 'all would be revealed as a lie against these five innocent men in the next few hours.'

Thomas was comforted to see one familiar individual sitting a little way off the rabble. Constable Garren Fox gave a little wave and smiled across at him. Thomas' written testimony, taken by Fox, had now to be substantiated in open court. Thomas had not been privy enough to the actual crime to be called before the local Perranzabuloe magistrate, Ronald Gatsby, nor before the Grand Jury as most of his testimony was hearsay. But Fox thought it best that he attend court as he was the actual owner of the sheep.

The Firths, the shepherd boy's parents, sat huddled and distraught in a corner.

'Robert Firth Smyth, call Robert Firth Smyth.'

The tall thin anaemic looking youth's hands shook on the holy book as he stuttered his way through the oath. 'The ev… ev…evidence…I sh…sh…shall give.'

'Sh…sh…shall give,' mimicked some drunks, who arriving late somehow had barged their way into the courtroom.

'Kindly remove those men,' Mowbray instructed the bailiff.

'We're bloody not going anywhere, ninny lobcock,' the drunks shouted back at him. 'Sycophant valet, slubberdegullion,' they jeered, swearing and swinging a flagon of ale between them. 'You've had our friends and kindred, standing over there before you, locked up in that bloody awful castle for months, them being guiltless men.'

The judge's face turned puce framed in his cream wig. 'I'll not have drink or disorderly conduct in my court. You three men leave immediately.'

Uproar. The bailiff approached the ruffians cautiously. He was at a loss, totally out numbered and muscled. At first he tried to reason with them. They pushed him, he pushed back. It wasn't until Fox and Thomas got up and weighed into the fray that they were able to propel the men out through the courtroom door. Securing it from the inside with an upturned table, they blocked any chance of their return.

'Goodness gracious,' said the judge. 'Any more disorderly behaviour in my court and I will clear the entire room for good. This case can be heard in another town, a more civilised town far away from here.'

Chalmers turned and whispered to Thomas, 'And a good thing too.'

Robert Firth Smyth began his evidence. He said he was a cousin of the victim, Harry Firth. At the behest of Joseph Crenshaw they agreed to herd sheep across to Beechfield Farm for a small fee. On leaving the Parish of Kenwyn the lane had narrowed through a wooded area. It was there that they were set upon and badly beaten up with cudgels by three masked men.

'Do you see those men in court today?' asked Mowbray.

Firth Smyth looked fearfully round the room and then up to the judge. Shaking his head he said, 'They wore m…m… masks. We… we…we didn't stand a chance, me lord. Not ev… ev…even the chance of running away.' No one was laughing at his stuttering now.

'Any questions, Troy?' Mowbray asked the defendant's advocate who, Thomas learned later, had until recently been clerk to his own advocate. An incestuous profession the legal one.

'No questions, my lord.' Troy shook his head vigorously. Roger Martin notably regarded him with disappointment.

'Did you see me there?' Martin shouted across to Firth Smyth.

'No, sir, can… cannot say I did.'

There would come a time when questions could only be asked through the conduit of counsel – that time had not yet come – Mowbray's court personified more a free for all.

One by one witnesses from the countryside stood to take the oath, squeaking in their boots and high leather gaiters. The public found its voice again, jeering them on all the way. Mowbray, losing control, repeatedly asked for silence. Once the evidence had started to be given, it would be near impossible to find another venue.

Thomas nodded to Joseph Crenshaw as he stood to speak.

'They were my sheep originally that were sent to Jowan Carter's place, on instruction from Sir Thomas Huck who bought the sheep and actually owned Carter's farm.'

'Did anyone else know of the movement of these sheep?' asked Chalmers.

'Michael Martin. Earlier in the day he had been interested in the sheep that Sir Thomas bought.'

'Michael Martin? Do you see Martin in this courtroom?' Chalmers sought clarification.

'Aye, Roger Martin's brother. He's stood over there along with the rest. When I told him the sheep and rams had been sold, he didn't like it one bit and asked me where they were bound for.'

Thomas, who had been lolling in his seat, sprang to his feet in indignation.

'Sir Thomas?' Mowbray appraised him with raised eyebrows.

'If it pleases your lordship, I would like to ask a question of this witness.'

'Please go ahead, Sir Thomas, for if you can shed any light on this case it is welcome.'

'Crenshaw, you told me nobody knew where the flock was going and now you tell the court this.'

'Michael Martin's interest in the sheep only came back to me when Constable Fox questioned me about the sale,' explained Crenshaw defensively.

Shaking his head in disbelief, Thomas flounced back into his seat.

'So, doubtless Michael told his brother over there about the transaction,' suggested Chalmers. Silence finally fell on the court, deadly silence: this was the connection, this was corroboration, this was incontrovertible evidence.

'Troy?' sighed Mowbray.

'I have little to say but that Farmer Crenshaw's statement points to coincidence rather than confirmation.'

This wasn't so for Thomas. He now realised that the plot to rob the flock was hatched in Truro market by the Martin brothers. Whereas he had wrongly suspected that Jowan Carter had been key in its conception.

Three of the men on trial, including Michael Martin, refused to give a defence. Certainly their inept clerk attorney did not offer one on their behalf. However a defiant Roger Martin chose to stand his ground.

'You have nothing to connect me to this offence. Nothing.'

'How about a bill of sale between you and Richard Nancarrow, a farmer on Bodmin Moor?' Chalmers shook the bill in the air.

'Never heard of him.'

'This bill is for two pens of Devon Longwool ewes and three rams. Exactly the same tally as those stolen.'

'Know nothing about them.'

'And you've never heard of Richard Nancarrow?'

'No.'

'Your sister-in-law's husband?'

The court let out a collective groan.

'Try as you might, you've no proof,' continued Martin defiantly. 'And certainly no evidence that I was with the men who beat up those two boys.'

'Maybe not but you know who they are. Indeed I understand you are something of a leader,' suggested Chalmers.

'Must be them over there.' Martin pointed in the direction of his terrified brother and the three accomplices.

'What about Jowan Carter?'

'He wasn't there.'

'How do you know Carter wasn't there?'

'Heard,' said Martin.

'You do realise that sheep theft is a capital offence in itself,' cut in Mowbray.

'You cannot hold me responsible for any of this, me lord. I am an innocent man with a wife and children to support. I've never done anyone harm. Never, never, knowingly harm.' His words splattered on the floor of the court like dung from a cow's backside. And from the distasteful expressions on his co-defendants' faces his betrayal smelt like dung to them too.

A woeful expression on his face, Jowan Carter, who looked near to fainting, took a step or two forward separating himself from the others. He told the court that Roger, the older Martin brother, had threatened him if he didn't fall in with the sheep theft and deception.

'"Do you want to finish down a mine shaft?" Roger Martin asked me,' said Carter.

'Did you play any part in the physical act of sheep theft?' asked Mowbray, straight to the point and disregarding any excuse of coercion.

'No, sir,' mumbled a glowering Carter, his eyes fixed to the floor. Superficially his despondency could have been taken as sulkiness rather than shame.

'Do you know who struck the fatal blow against young Harry Firth?' asked Chalmers.

'I wasn't there so I only know what I have been told.'

'And what were you told.'

'That Michael Martin took a lead in the murder.'

Mistress Firth began to weep loudly. At this stage of affairs, Thomas passed a note to Chalmers.

'Forgive me, my lord, Sir Thomas Huck would like to address the court again.'

Carter lifted his face to Thomas with the frightened pleading eyes of a bloodhound that has lost the trail.

'Proceed.' Mowbray nodded across to Thomas.

Thomas cleared his throat. 'Jowan Carter was one of my tenant farmers. Indeed the Carters have been tenants of my family for generations. He was always an excellent worker as indeed all the Carters were. But alas Jowan did not marry and the rest of his kinfolk died out. He was left to run the farm on his own. In light of information given to this court, I feel he must have been under terrible duress to comply with the Martin gang.'

'In fear for his life no less,' piped up the unlikely source of Troy. Having given up on defending the Martin gang as a whole, perhaps he finally saw that here was a glimmer of hope for success.

'I do not see him as a thief or murderer but more as a man pressed into doing something totally against his will,' said Thomas. 'The fact that his farm and livelihood have gone surely is punishment enough.'

'Forgive me, Sir Thomas, but that is for the court to decide,' said Mowbray.

And you are the court, thought Thomas. He passed another note to Chalmers, this time asking for a list of the Perranzabuloe gang members standing accused. One Robert Shaw stood out on the list as a possibility. He looked younger, delicate, less seasoned in criminality than the others.

'May it please you, my lord, my client would like to question Robert Shaw,' said Chalmers.

'Sir Thomas?' The judgely raised eyebrows again.

'You are Robert Shaw and you reside in Perranzabuloe?' asked Thomas. Shaw nodded. 'And you with other men stole the sheep bound for Beechfield Farm, isn't that so?' Shaw looked to the floor. 'Isn't that so?' Thomas persisted. 'Was Jowan Carter with you that day?' Shaw shook his head.

'Yes or no,' insisted Mowbray, thrusting his wig this way and that as if it were a living thing. Then again it quite well could have been.

'No, sir,' replied Shaw.

'My lord,' corrected Chalmers.

'I did not see Jowan until much later, me lord,' said Shaw.

'So Jowan Carter took no part in the actual stealing of the sheep or the murder of young Harry Firth as already stated by him to this court?' asked Thomas.

'No, sir, he didn't.' Shaw's humiliation sought the ground again.

'Did you strike either of the shepherd boys?'

'No, sir, I didn't. One of the lads fell unconscious almost immediately after the first blow. 'Twas Michael Martin what finished the other off.'

'How did you know it was Michael Martin when you were all masked?'

'As soon as we were away he took his mask off. It was covered in the lad's blood.'

Mistress Firth swooned as her elderly husband struggled to revive her with salts.

'Thank you, my lord.' Thomas resumed his seat.

The court fell into absolute silence as it absorbed Shaw's evidence.

'My lord, a surprise witness has just come forward having been delayed on the highway,' said Chalmers.

'I hope he wasn't detained by brigands,' smirked Mowbray. 'Too much of this sort of thing going on nowadays.'

Constable Fox's eyes fluttered prior-knowledge across to Thomas as the rest of the court looked askance at the recently opened doorway. A scrubbed Josh Haymaker stood there, a lead actor waiting in the wings, before striding into court wearing green breeches with gold buttons, a matching coat and fashionable squared off shoes.

'You are Joshua Haymaker now of Beechfield Farm, are you not?' asked Chalmers.

'I am that, sir.'

'And did you accompany one of the defendants to a farm on Bodmin Moor a little while ago.'

'I did, sir.'

'Who was that person?'

'Jowan Carter.'

'And whose farm was it on Bodmin Moor?'

'Richard Nancarrow's.'

'Why did Carter take you to Nancarrow's farm?'

'As part of an initial approach to the farmer there and see if he would be interested in taking on extra sheep.'

'And was he?'

'Yes, very much so. Jowan asked me if I would help him move the sheep up to Bodmin Moor.'

'And how did you reply?'

'I asked whose sheep they were.'

'And how did he answer?'

'He told me they were Sir Thomas Huck's sheep stolen by the Perranzabuloe gang.'

'And what was your response?'

'I told him I didn't want anything to do with it, with Sir Thomas' sheep nor with the Perranzabuloe gang. Jowan said he felt the same but was pressed into it by Roger Martin who he owed a gambling debt to. Likewise he said he felt uncomfortable with the whole affair.'

Chalmers bowed and resumed his seat.

'Any more questions, Troy?' asked Mowbray. The advocate shook his head. Mowbray outlined the essential facts of the trial before addressing the jury. 'Gentlemen of the jury you have heard all the evidence now be good enough to retire and return your verdict on these five men.'

During the jury's absence Chalmers and Thomas engaged in a quiet if heated discussion before Chalmers approached the judge. More whispering ensued up to the judge's dais.

'My lord, Sir Thomas Huck is very impressed in the fair way you have conducted this trial,' smarmed Chalmers. 'However he feels it would be a miscarriage of justice for Jowan Carter to suffer the same fate as the Martin brothers and their like. Carter obviously acted under terrific coercion as did, Sir Thomas suspects, the young lad Shaw. The young lad was so honest in his testimony. If you think it fit, Sir Thomas would like to make a small donation of fifty guineas to you and the court towards clemency on behalf of Shaw and Carter.'

Mowbray reddened, blew out his cheeks, Chalmers was fearful this could go horribly wrong.

'We will see when the jury returns,' said Mowbray.

The jury did return in under an hour wearing contrite expressions.

'We cannot reach a verdict on all of the men,' said the foreman.

'Well,' said Mowbray, 'you will remain here without fire, food or drink until you do.'

'But your lordship,' objected the foreman.

'Off with you.' Mowbray waved a dismissive hand.

With bowed heads the jurors exited the courtroom like whipped schoolboys to deliberate more.

Another hour or two must have passed before they returned.

'Well?' Mowbray impatiently asked the foreman. The judge had already had to leave the court twice to relieve himself. Old man's bladder, Chalmers had quipped to Thomas.

'We find all the Perranzabuloe men guilty of sheep theft, and Michael Martin guilty of murder with the rest aiding and abetting him. But we would like to put in a request for leniency regarding Robert Shaw owing to his youth and remorse.'

'And Jowan Carter?' asked Mowbray.

'The same. He was not actually present in person for the thieving or for the murder.'

'Roger Martin, Michael Martin, and Stephen Tremethyk step forward.' Mowbray reached for the black cloth which had rested ominously on his table. The courtroom sighed as he placed the cloth on top of his bewigged, flea infested head.

'The law is that thou shalt return to the place whence thou camest and from thence to a place of execution where thou shalt hang by the neck till the body be dead. Dead. Dead. And the Lord have mercy upon thy soul.'

The two Martin brothers and Tremethyk were led away by the gaolers. They looked empty of all emotion. But then Thomas felt they had been resigned to their fate for a long time. Because scowling Roger Martin was a fighter, he could not give up without a fight, he would go down fighting. Thomas hoped for his sake he would relax and not fight the rope.

'It is late,' said Mowbray. 'I will pass sentence on Shaw and Carter tomorrow. I will see Richard Chalmers and Sir Thomas Huck in my chambers at nine o'clock in the morning.'

Chalmers and Thomas looked at each other with misgivings.

CHAPTER EIGHTEEN

Despite their reservations about the morning interview with Mowbray, Thomas enjoyed a lovely pheasant dinner and a good bottle of red wine with Richard Chalmers at the London Inn. It was a quiet night and Julius Mann took the opportunity of joining them to share a glass at their table. He was very interested to know how the trial had gone. Both Thomas and Chalmers were reticent regarding the landlord's probing, but, as is often the case, the interrogator can reveal more than he gains.

'How did you find the judge?' asked Julius.

'Fair-minded,' said Thomas.

'Not everyone would agree with you there.'

'How do you mean exactly?' asked Chalmers.

'It is said Sir Jonathan isn't immune to ...' Julius rubbed his thumb and fingers together.

'Really?' said Thomas and Chalmers together.

'Aye, I've heard if it is a hanging offence he pays the hangman a little extra on behalf of the condemned man and his relatives to make it quick and easy. Out of that he retains a small consideration for himself.'

'Really?' said his two companions again.

'Good this pheasant,' said Thomas.

'Good this claret,' said Chalmers.

After a rather turbulent night of tossing, turning and tied-up bedsheets, morning came and Thomas made his way to the Guildhall.

'Good morning, gentlemen.' Mowbray greeted him and Chalmers in what felt more like a lair than chambers.

'Good morning, my lord.' The two men nervously echoed each other.

'As you know I have yet to sentence Shaw and Carter. I understand that you, Sir Thomas, have an interest in these two men's welfare.'

'Yes, particularly my tenant Jowan Carter, my lord.'

'Hum! I see, I see.' Mowbray seemed to be running over in his mind the significance of Thomas' relationship with Carter. His eyes narrowed with a private computation. 'I understood from Chalmers here that you are willing to pay a small fee towards both of those felons avoiding the death sentence.'

'That is correct, my lord.'

'Hum! Fifty guineas,' said Mowbray.

'Fifty guineas?' queried Thomas.

'Yes, fifty guineas should see them right,' affirmed Mowbray.

The tension back in court was palpable. Shaw and Carter were almost dragged before the judge, their weakened legs clanging in chains, their faces drained of blood. They had had an extra sleepless night to contemplate their fate.

'Robert Shaw, Jowan Carter step forward. After careful consideration I feel neither of you were principals in this appalling crime. However you were both involved with sheep stealing. You, Shaw, owing to your lack of years and experience knew no better. You, Carter, acted under extreme intimidation from the Perranzabuloe gang. I sentence you both to be transported to the Americas for life.'

Shaw crumpled. Carter's legs finally buckled totally beneath him too. Whether from shock or deliverance Thomas wasn't certain. A beaming Troy congratulated both men.

'Not a bad outcome in the circumstances,' said Chalmers, turning round to Thomas. 'Not bad at all.'

'The captain of the *Cumberland* bound for Virginia wants an extra five guineas,' Mowbray told them back in his chambers.

'But Sir Thomas has already offered a generous fifty guineas,' objected Chalmers.

Thomas put a restraining hand on his arm. 'It doesn't matter, let it go. Shaw and Carter will not hang that is all that matters.'

On the pavement outside the Guildhall the Firths, clinging to each other, passed without a word.

Two straws in life's cruel storm, thought Thomas.

Constable Fox shook his head, 'Poor creatures, 'twas their only son. Will you be returning for the hanging?' he asked Thomas.

'A spectacle not to my taste,' came the reply. 'Saw too much of the same while in service for the King.'

'I really think you should attend, Thomas,' chipped in Richard Chalmers. 'You were a plaintiff in this case.'

* * *

Thomas was amazed at the almost finished Rockfoot New Farm. A historical story of the region's stones, mainly granite and slate. With the addition of colour staining of different natural minerals – a chronicle patchwork quilt – each stone telling its own geological tale.

'You only see it when you takes the time to look closely,' said that master of stone, Albert Spear. 'How did the trial go?' said in the next breath.

'Three of the five men will hang.'

'Jowan Carter?' asked Spear.

'Transportation for life to the Americas.'

'And the young lad that was with them?'

'Robert Shaw, the same.'

'Are you going to the hangings, sir?'

Thomas shook his head. 'I'm not sure yet.'

* * *

A scaffold for three had been quickly erected on Castle Green outside Launceston Gaol.

The gallows bell rang out two days later, the crowd was disappointed hoping for five hangings rather than three. Nevertheless, they flocked to Castle Green in a jovial mood. With people rushing to get the best spot close to the gallows, these public spectacles were known irreverently as the 'hanging fair', 'stretching', or 'collar day.' The event had a carnival-like atmosphere. Young children sat on their fathers' shoulders to get a better view. Boys and girls laughed into the faces of their lovers in anticipation. Old men and women licked their lips that someone else would be dying today before they departed.

Constable Garren Fox had saved Thomas a seat, in the front of one of the stands, on the off chance he would attend. It hadn't just been three people who had asked if he would be going to the hanging, even Ayla and her husband, Stephen Moore, had chipped in. It became apparent to Thomas that, if not a spectacle to gloat over, it was his duty as a plaintiff of the case to witness the Martin brothers' and Stephen Tremethyk's demise.

Homes near the execution sites had rent out their balconies. Seats in the stands and on the balconies were very expensive, the prices were raised based on the infamy of the criminals and the crimes.

Thomas passed Fox a crown for his trouble.

'No, no, it is my pleasure, sir,' said Fox, passing the coin back and shaking his head. 'Well, not strictly a pleasure is it?' he muttered on reflection.

Vendors had shown up early and set up their food and wares stalls. They would make good money out of the event, selling food, drinks, and relics related to the hangings. On his way to the site, a man had already stuck a pornographic paper into Thomas' face. He pushed the licentious rascal with bad breath and more gum than teeth roughly aside.

Pamphlets were being distributed, at a cost, to the crowds claiming to have printed inside them the dying speeches of those about to be hanged. Known as the 'Last Dying Speech', the quotes were usually fake, but they were selling well nonetheless. These broadsheets had the same woodcut print image of a hanging that was reused at each event, and also gave apparent information about the condemned individuals, and sometimes even poems or songs said to have been written by them and found in their cells. Occasionally it was something else more personal, like a letter written from the condemned person to a family member or loved one. Much of what was written was often entirely fictional.

'Sensational muck,' said Fox, pointing to the broadsheets some of which had escaped fluttering across the green.

But where were Roger Martin, Michael Martin, and Stephen Tremethyk. The condemned were allowed a stop at the local church, as well as local pubs where the criminals were given drinks before taking their place on the gallows. The two Martin brothers remained obdurate and chose the Bell Inn for their final drink. Tremethyk chose to ask for forgiveness for his sins at Saint Mary's Church near by. Crowds lining the street waited patiently for the procession to begin.

The three men were driven in a horse drawn cart, sitting on the coffins they would be buried in. Their hands were tied in front so that they could pray. Soon, too soon, they mounted the stage, mounted the boxes, as the hangman adjusted the ropes round their necks without further ado.

The clergyman asked if they wished to make a final address to the crowd. At first they all shook their heads in unison. The Martin brothers looked out into the crowd. Tremethyk kept his eyes fixed to the ground.

Then Roger Martin began to moan that it was all a mistake. His eyes welled with tears of drunken self pity. His brother looked startled as the crowd began to throw rotten vegetables at them. The mob – for that is what they were – despised the elder Martin for showing fear and weakness, for begging for mercy. The hangman quickly blindfolded each man but Roger Martin refused his. Michael Martin's legs were shaking and appeared to be giving way. Only Tremethyk seemed to be treating his imminent death with dignity and a firmly planted stance.

'See,' someone in the crowd shouted pointing to Roger Martin. 'He is pissing his breeches.'

'Worse will follow,' replied his seasoned companion.

Thomas shuddered as the mob began to laugh and jeer. Fearing a riot, it was time for the authorities to signal the hanging to take place.

The boxes were kicked away from beneath them and Tremethyk and the Martin brothers began their death dance at the end of the rope. It wasn't a quick process. Since it was a short fall, necks often would not break, they would strangle to death instead which could take ten to twenty minutes.

Thomas felt impotent and sick. He had, in the recent past, to witness the quick beheading of noblemen and the slower hanging, drawing and quartering of knights accused of treason against the King. He was not new to such terrible scenes of civic vengeance whether warranted or not.

'Is there nothing we can do to shorten these men's suffering?' he asked Fox.

'Why, sir, you've gone quite green.' Fox looked genuinely concerned.

'I have seen one too many of these gruesome scenes in the war. This brings every one of them back to mind.'

'Sometimes the families of the dying are asked to pull down on the legs of their loved one to help speed the process along. But there doesn't seem to be anybody abroad for these poor souls.'

'Go ahead, Fox, at least help Tremethyk on his way.'

Fox pushed forward onto the stage and began climbing up the ladder to a chorus of boos. People grabbed at him attempting to pull him back. Perhaps they knew he was a constable, perhaps they thought he was a relative of the condemned men. By the time he reached Tremethyk, Tremethyk had gone. Michael Martin's bulging staring eyes were fixed to one side of his slumped head. Roger Martin alone kept dancing until Fox seized his legs and lent his enormous bulk to transport him into the next world.

The crowd rushed forward to the stage to try to get a souvenir from the bodies. Hangmen were known to take possession of bodies in order to cut off pieces of clothing to hawk out. Ropes could also be cut up and sold, the cost based on the crime and fame of the hanged. Thomas had seen these macabre souvenirs displayed above fireplaces in comfortable rural cottages.

He patted the constable on the back. 'Well done, Fox. Such a disgusting business.'

'You are a doctor, Sir Thomas, so tell me what are the mechanics involved in hanging?'

'I think a longer drop would be kinder but not so much fun for the fiends here on Castle Green. Compression of the air passage, closure of the blood vessels around the neck, finally a slow death unless they have a friend like you.'

'Not a nice way to go,' grunted Fox.

'Nothing is a nice way to go, but there are nicer ways than this,' said Thomas, nodding up to the three swinging inanimate puppets being pulled this way and that by the crowd hoping to secure a trophy.

CHAPTER NINETEEN

Arriving back home to the village, Thomas found the place was fizzing with word of Catholic conspiracies and witches, specifically the witches' bottle on Granny Pace's grave. Indeed the local community was more taken up with that mystery than the outcome of the trial and the Launceston hangings.

''Tis the sprig of rosemary added to the bottle that is the giveaway,' Thomas heard a woman shouting across to her neighbour as he rode past.

'Aye, 'tis that right enough,' agreed the neighbour.

Rumours and counter rumours travelled the highways and byways, in and out of folks' cottages, until they could no longer be ignored. 'We'll have to send for the witch chaser at this rate.'

James IV of Scotland, later James I of England, sanctioned witch trials after an alarming confession in 1591 from an accused tortured witch, Agnes Sampson. It was revealed that 200 witches – some from Denmark – had sailed in sieves to the church off the coastal town of North Berwick on Halloween night in 1590. James held them responsible for his previous treacherous crossing of the Northern Ocean while attempting to rescue his Danish bride-to-be held up in Norway. 'Mikle foull wather of a stormie winter,' had nearly cost him his life. This misogynist king's pursuit of any poor females suspected of witchcraft was vicious and relentless. But then this might be expected of a man who was believed to prefer fornicating with other men rather than women.

England was a country torn between the occult and religious beliefs, and when in 1605 Robert Catesby and his fellow Catholic conspirators had attempted to blow up the Houses of Parliament, it further cemented division and religious intolerance.

Ayla cornered Thomas one day, a worried expression on her face. 'Master, they are saying that Iben Hartmann is responsible for the witches' bottle left by Granny Pace's grave. Such talk is dangerous and growing.'

'Why? Merely because she is a herbalist?'

'Not sure, Master.'

'Why such concern on your part? I thought you didn't like Iben very much.'

'She is a woman, therefore a sister, and much put upon.'

'Send word to her that I would like to see her.'

* * *

'Was it you? Did you do this?' he asked Iben.

'Did I do what?'

'The bottle business on Mistress Pace's grave.'

'I don't believe in God so I am hardly going to believe in such superstitious nonsense,' she responded. I can imagine who did do it but I will not say.'

'Not even to me?' he asked.

'Especially not to you,' she replied coldly.

'So, if not by your hand where did the sprig of rosemary come from?' he asked. Iben shrugged, that mute shrug. Thomas felt his anger mounting. 'You are aware of the Witchcraft Act that defined witchcraft as a crime punishable by death? I cannot help you if you will not tell.'

'I will not tell.' She was obdurate.

'Josiah once told me Ann Collette never joined in the annual 5th of November celebrations for England's delivery from the gunpowder plotters.'

'If you are saying she failed to attend the thanksgiving church service, and refused to stand next to one of the fires lit to burn an effigy of the pope, added to which she never threw a single fire cracker with others in that loutish congregation, because if that is what you are saying, Thomas, you can judge me the same.'

'Josiah believed Ann Collette adhered to the old religion.'

'Well, so he might. He had his own miserly reasons for saying that.'

'As she is just about your only friend in this village, I would expect nothing else than a stout defence from you.'

'If she did, and is a Catholic by heart, and I am not saying she is, she will have meant no evil by placing the Bartmann bottle there as an aid for Margaret Pace into the next world. The bottle would be a precaution to protect her friend against witchcraft.' Iben smiled at the ambiguity. She was well aware that Margaret Pace was not of Ann's religious persuasion, they argued about it all the time.

'But the bottle is smashed, the spell broken,' pointed out Thomas.

'I know and Ann is distraught because her friend will no longer have protection against the witches' evil in heaven,' Iben admitted.

'Neither will you,' pointed out Thomas. 'So you were privy to this ungodly meddling.'

'Ungodly, I like that coming from you and your family.'

'My brother is not me,' objected Thomas. Iben winced, paled but said nothing. 'Do you know what torment they put poor women through whom they suspect of witchcraft?'

241

'Don't worry about me. Haven't you noticed that it is usually some old crone over fifty who they accuse? – past childbearing, past attractive fornication – a dispensable scapegoat for a community's ills. I heard that one hapless soul was put to the ducking stool for the same offence recently over Barnstable way. Because she didn't drown they hanged her anyway.'

It was Thomas' turn to flinch. He knew the ordeal of 'swimming' was endorsed by King James at the end of the previous century. James stated in his *Daemonologie* (1597) 'that God hath appointed ... that the water shall refuse to receive them in her bosome, that have shaken off them the sacred Water of Baptisme, and wilfully refused the benefite thereof.'

'I am just warning you Iben, as a friend.'

'Pah, a friend is it?'

Thomas ignored her contempt. 'Please go carefully about your business,' he told her. The story of bowsenning lunatics in St Nonna's Well was still fresh in his mind.

He was surprised to hear again from Iben sooner than he expected. A little urchin arrived at his door with an urgent message from her to call at Hetty Chenoweth's cottage along High Street.

Hetty had something of a reputation for the lowlife in the village. Iben stood in the doorway of her cottage nursing a newborn.

'He is so unwell, so unwell, so small, so very small,' she sang like an incantation.

'Let me see.' Thomas gently lifted the flopping child from her. Wrapped naked in a white cloth, the baby looked like a skinned rabbit. The child rested limp and drained of all colour in the crook of his arm. Thomas lifted his ear against the tiny chest.

'I could hardly get him to breathe at first,' complained Iben. 'He didn't cry, not once.'

'The child is not breathing now, Iben. He is dead. Too premature to live.' He placed the child on the earthen floor. Iben looked devastated, perhaps remembering her own experience of birth and eventually loss though through different circumstances. 'Where is Hetty?' he asked her.

'Back there,' Iben pointed to a straw crib in the darkened room. 'She is not good either and the afterbirth has not come away yet for a good hour.'

'Have you given her anything?' asked Thomas.

'Only caudle for comfort.'

'I've not been with a man, not ever,' moaned Hetty, doing her best to absolve herself. She seemed more intent on this than the state of her baby's health. ''Twas the Devil's work.'

'Do not distress yourself, Hetty love,' Iben told her, massaging Hetty's lower stomach, her womb, to enable the final stage of birthing.

Then a cry. Then the blood came, gushing like a pail of crimson liquid from between Hetty's legs and over the straw.

Iben looked to Thomas in terror.

'I must try to clamp the placenta by hand,' he told her, shaking his head. This was outside his usual battlefield experience but he knew enough to know that to do nothing would result in Hetty bleeding to death.

He worked his fist up the birth canal and compressed her womb with his other hand as Iben had done. Hetty screamed. 'If this does not work I will have to try and remove the placenta by hand.'

'Have you done that before?' whispered Iben.

'Just the once on a camp follower.'

'And?'

Thomas could not meet her eyes and she knew. 'The poor lass was only fifteen and very narrow. It was excruciating for her and hopeless,' he admitted; his fist still inside Hetty who looked to be swooning into unconsciousness. He decided to risk a withdrawal.

He and Iben slumped back with relief. Just as the haemorrhaging had begun it stopped. Hetty regained consciousness, let out a deep sigh, and slumped further into the crib.

After a few minutes, Thomas gently pulled on the umbilical cord and the afterbirth slithered out like a plate of liver into the bed pan held out by Iben. It smelt warm, meaty and bloody. Iben turned up her nose. Although she had experienced birth herself as a child, this was far from her administering of sweet smelling healing potions.

Not once did Hetty enquire about the child.

'Maybe she knows,' said Iben. 'What shall we do with the child?'

'Hetty,' said Thomas, 'your child has passed into God's hands. Do you wish to see him?' Exhausted Hetty could barely shake her head.

''Tis not called labour for nothing,' muttered Iben to herself.

Again Thomas and Iben were forced to collude in a pact. They decided to cover up Hetty's social indiscretion, and get rid of the dead baby quietly. At least Hetty would be saved from the stigma and humiliation of paying penance in church for giving birth to a base child. Whether the child had lived or not it didn't matter – Hetty would be an outcast from her community for the rest of her life.

Dawn was blinking on the horizon. The tide was in at Chapel Porth. Thomas and Iben each took a corner of the sack, took joint responsibility, and flung it with its contents of infant, afterbirth and stones from the cliff top into the water below. They watched in silence as their small gift to the sea was washed away by foaming waves. Weighed with additional stones, they hoped it would soon sink into oblivion.

'And the father gets away with all this scot-free,' said Thomas.

''Tis always the way of it,' said Iben. He could not read her expression, only guess at her cynicism.

* * *

Alas, that was not an end of it. What had happened to Hetty's swollen belly? Gossip prattled about the village. Not only talk from the womenfolk but from one or two curious men. No baby, no sin for Hetty to answer for but where had it gone. False pregnancy had been known since Hippocrates. It was generally known that Mary Tudor suffered from the condition later to be called pseudocyesis. Maybe, just maybe, this was how it had been with Hetty.

Hetty said nothing and in truth she knew nothing. She had never laid eyes on the dead child. She had no wish to because of the shame that came with it. A stout woman, her pregnancy had been well concealed though there was no doubting she had developed a bump in the latter stages.

'Maybe she had something like sheep bloat,' suggested a farmer's wife.

'Sheep bloat, my arse.' Her old husband in leggings spat on the ground. 'Why old Hetty has opened her legs for half the village. Wonder is she hasn't been caught afore.'

And so the speculation continued, but with nothing to see there was nothing to prove, until someone suggested a curse might have been put on Hetty for her lewdness. Yes, a curse. Wasn't a witch's bottle found recently on Granny Pace's grave as well? Was the village being cursed?

The church was summoned. The Reverend Angrove arrived like an avenging knight to question Hetty. With his cassock flying behind him; his cassock totally covering his trusty steed like a caparison; his arrival would have been comical if the possible consequences weren't so serious.

'Hee haw! Hee haw!' Alerted by his donkey's braying one of Hetty's neighbours appeared in her doorway to see Angrove struggling to dismount the animal. She tried to stifle her amusement but failed miserably.

'Didn't our good lord himself ride into Jerusalem on an ass,' he yelled across to her, patting the donkey with indifference.

Yes, thought the woman to herself, but you are certainly not our good lord and this is not Jerusalem.

Angrove came from a religious family going back over a century. Indeed his great-great-grandfather had adhered to the old religion in the time of Queen Mary but, fearing degradation because of a liaison with a married woman, he had buried his passion deep into the ground. Once the old queen had passed on, Angrove's great-great-grandfather had abruptly embraced Anglicanism and married the recently annulled wife and love of his life. So Rupert Angrove came from a dynasty of staunch Anglicans – stalwarts of the new religion in line with the newly converted.

Hetty naively repeated those fateful words to him, ''Twas the Devil's work.'

'How do you mean, Hetty?' asked Angrove.

''Twas the Devil that put the child inside me, and 'twas the Devil that took it away.'

'Are you admitting to having congress with the Devil?' Angrove's stern face never flinched apart from a growing expression of horror round the eyes. 'Are you saying our village is damned?'

'I am.' Hetty began to laugh maniacally.

'Those are the words of witchcraft,' pronounced Angrove. 'I will convey this conversation to the Bishop, but first I must question Sir Thomas Huck and Iben Hartmann who were seen visiting you.'

'Thems know nothing. Thems thought I had the gripes that's all.'

'Nevertheless.' Angrove was persistent if nothing else.

Iben was collecting parsley, coriander and rosemary in her family garden, when she saw the priest's ridiculous arrival on that ass of his. One ass on top of another, was her malicious thought.

'Good morning, Reverend,' she said instead, as Angrove stumbled before her on his dismount.

'Good morning, Mistress Hartmann. I wonder if you could help me with a little problem.' Angrove sounded out of breath.

'And what might that be, Reverend?'

'Hetty Chenoweth.'

'Ah, Hetty. I hope nothing is amiss with her again.'

'Again?'

'Yes, she had a bad case of the colic recently. So worried was I, I asked Sir Thomas Huck to take a look at her.' Iben laughed at her unintentional rhyme. Angrove's haughty expression remained fixed as it had done through this whole process. But he was becoming more frustrated and angry within.

'Well, I best have a word with him then.'

'Do that,' shrugged Iben. 'I am sure he will be happy to see you.'

'Hetty Chenoweth, Sir Thomas.'

'What about Hetty Chenoweth?'

'I understand you visited her at the behest of Mistress Hartmann.'

'That is so.'

'May I ask why?'

'You may ask but I will not tell you. I don't discuss patients' complaints with other persons.'

Angrove looked taken aback. 'Not even with a man of the cloth?'

'Not even with him.'

'Mistress Hartmann said Hetty was suffering from colic.'

'So you already know. So why come here bothering me? If Mistress Hartmann divulged that Mistress Chenoweth was suffering from colic why doubt her word? But I will personally neither confirm nor deny it.'

Angrove knew he was going nowhere with this. He suspected that Iben Hartmann's and Sir Thomas' story was well-schooled. They were in league, and he was growing more suspicious.

Thomas did think of suggesting that if Angrove was unhappy about this affair, why didn't he ask Constable Fox to investigate. Then again he thought better of it. He had no desire to push his luck any further in regard to Hetty Chenoweth. Unfortunately, Angrove was formulating his own plan to solve the situation. Malicious rumours began to circulate once more round the neighbourhood. Some of them started by this upstanding man of the church himself. Why should he involve the Bishop? No, he would find a solution himself to this slur of witchcraft on the parish.

* * *

'Master come quick, the villagers are threatening to swim poor Hetty Chenoweth believing her to be a witch,' announced Ayla. 'They have been baying at the poor woman's door since dawn.'

'Baying as in hounds?'

'Aye, baying like hounds sensing blood. Iben, I mean Mistress Hartmann, has just told me.'

'Iben?' Thomas' ears pricked up. 'Is Iben here?'

'No, Master, I met her down in the village.'

'I thought you weren't friends.'

'As I think I have already explained to you, Master, we weren't at first but now we are. We found we had something in common.' Her smile was suggestive but indeterminate. 'Mistress Hartmann says the Reverend Angrove is leading the mob against Hetty.'

'Angrove?' spluttered Thomas. 'Swim her where?'

Ayla raised her hands in helplessness.

Minutes later, knocking and further chaos followed at Rockfoot Hall as Albert Spear, with Stephen behind him, broke into the comfortable, civilised withdrawing room. Spear stood blinking at the peat burning hearth in disbelief to the news he was about to impart.

'Come on, man, what's wrong?' Thomas pressed him impatiently.

'They are dragging poor Hetty Chenoweth towards Locken Pond and threatening Iben Hartmann with the same.'

'How did you come by this information?'

'By chance. I needed locks for the farm and decided to visit the locksmith whose workshop is close to the pond.'

'Stephen, get my cloak and have Russel saddled.'

Thomas had warned Iben about this ritualistic torture but as usual she hadn't paid it any heed, especially coming from his lips.

Swimming was like the ducking stool but if anything worse. As advocated by King James, it was believed that water rejected servants of the Devil and that if a suspected person floated and refused to sink it was proof of guilt, if they sank they usually drowned innocent. Hadn't he just read about it in *Daemonologie*? Hadn't he just warned Iben of the same?

There were about fifty people gathered round Locken Pond. Thomas pushed his way through to the water's edge. Using his crop on one individual who refused to give way.

'I've done nothing, she has done nothing.' Her wrists bound, Iben stood over the poor naked form of Hetty Chenoweth pleading both their innocence. Thomas had never seen Iben look so afraid.

'Careful mistress or you will finish the like. A nice piece of flesh to dunk instead of this,' leered the local butcher, pointing down on Hetty who was snared in ropes. Though she had endured great hardships, Thomas guessed Hetty to be only in her forties. He had never seen such a pitiful sight: her body emptied of child, her stomach and breasts sagging, her pubic hair spare like those of a much older woman, stripped of all dignity sprawled out there on the grass.

'Let me be, let me be,' cried simpleminded Hetty, looking up in bewilderment.

Only tiny Aaron Richardson was crying, living up to his role of Little Johnny Jack.

'What finds you here, Sir Thomas?' asked Reverend Angrove, feigning surprise.

'I came to stop this cruelty. And you can unbind Mistress Hartmann straight away.'

'Well, since 'tis All Hallows' Eve we can afford to be a little merciful.' Angrove instructed the butcher to cut Iben free. A gesture he was willing to make having bigger fish to swim in the form of poor Hetty. 'This really has nothing to do with you, Sir Thomas,' insisted Angrove, nodding to two men holding the ropes on either side of his victim. With another line they bound Hetty's right thumb to her left big toe, and she was dragged upright as best they could. With a blood-curdling scream she was pushed into the water before anyone could react.

'No,' shrieked Iben.

'See, she floats. She is guilty,' someone said gleefully.

'No she don't,' said someone else as they watched poor Hetty spluttering, taking in water before sinking.

The two handlers pulled on the ropes attempting to lift her to the surface – attempting to prolong the entertainment – but to no avail.

'See, she is drowning. She is an innocent woman,' shouted Thomas, flinging off his coat. The coldness of the water hit him as soon as he dived for Hetty.

The pond was deeper than he thought. He could not see Hetty through the muddy water but located her body with his hands along one of the taut ropes still held by a tormentor, the other having let his end go. Dragging the rope from the man's grasp, Thomas pulled Hetty out onto the bank. She did not move, she did not appear to be breathing, her distorted prone body appeared to be lifeless.

Both Ayla's and Iben's dexterous fingers began to untie the knots that had bound Hetty to her terrible ordeal.

'Blow smoke up her arse,' suggested the local butcher offering up his smoking pipe. 'I've heard that works.'

Thomas ignored him. *Splodge*! Turning stout Hetty from prone to supine, he began to pummel her chest. Nothing and then, without warning, she began choking, coughing. He turned her onto her side and she vomited into the grass.

'You've interfered with the Lord's justice,' whimpered Angrove. 'You must be in league with the Devil like her, tools of Satan like Hetty.'

It was then that Thomas hit him, hit him hard. Angrove collapsed over his bloody nose sobbing, leaving a choice of sides between the man of the cloth and the lord of the manor. Nobody stepped forward to assist Angrove to his feet.

'Call yourself a Christian. See how you have humiliated this poor woman,' Thomas screamed down on him.

Ayla retrieved Thomas' long coat and covered Hetty's nakedness with it.

'Playing the big hero now, Sir Thomas, along with your tally-woman,' sneered Iben in a theatrical whisper.

The mask had dropped. He turned from her, hardly crediting her malevolence even in these circumstances.

'But that is just what he is,' said Ayla. 'He has a consideration and kindness beyond the understanding of your self-centred soul.'

By his warm hearth that evening, Thomas was to reflect on the day's events. Just like hanging, swimming the witch was merely mob violence, cruelty and hysteria. Led by an irrational man of the cloth, the rational becomes primitive too. He reflected on Iben as well – the two Ibens – one a warm sensual creature, the other cold, petulant, and totally selfish.

CHAPTER TWENTY

While Isaac Newton tried to catch light from the sky at his farm at Woolsthorpe-by-Colsterworth in Lincolnshire with his recently developed reflecting telescope, Thomas was intending to visit his own latest developed farm. Newton built the telescope because he believed it would prove that white light was made up of a spectrum of colours – Thomas felt as transparent and empty as that white light without the rainbow of colours Iben added to his own life. She so reviled him that she couldn't even given him credit for saving Hetty's life. Never mind, she would not stop him creating the farm of the future. He was determined to leave his mark, his legacy on the hereafter.

Albert Spear had kept to his promise and had all but completed Rockfoot New Farm before the winter months set in. It was a splendid place, so much so Thomas could have seen himself living there.

There was a letter waiting for him on the side table by the door when he rode back to the Hall. It was addressed to him in open flourishing strokes. Isabella Thoresby's hand was like her personality – wide and generous. She wrote that she had spoken to Ulli. Ulli was keen to meet her natural mother and hear the story of her illegitimate birth from Iben's own lips. Isabella suggested she and Ulli could ride over to Rockfoot Hall at a time convenient to him.

Anytime was convenient to Thomas but what about Iben. Would Iben agree to the plan or panic and baulk at the fulfilment of her deepest desire?

He sent word via Ayla to the mason's yard. To his surprise Iben's reply came back by return. Yes, she agreed to the plan and suggested Saturday week.

On the given day, Thomas heard a horse and rumbling wheels approaching down the driveway. He was startled at first and made for the door – a one man reception party for the small carriage. Few carriages of any sort were ever seen around St. Agnes, few people could afford such a vehicle in the countryside. So Isabella and Ulli had decided not to come on horseback after all. A bigger surprise awaited as Mary Thoresby, who had been squashed between the two girls for the journey, emerged from the carriage assisted by the coachman. She wore a hat festooned with ostrich feathers which quivered as she alighted. Though a little rumpled she looked as if she had come to conquer which rather subdued Thomas' own response. He kissed Mary coolly on both cheeks in the French manner and bowed to the two younger women. Isabella and Ulli burst with a physical warmth and abundance that made him wary. As an older man their exuberant beauty made him feel both excited and uncomfortable.

Iben was late. Thomas could see Ulli's nervous frustration growing by the minute. He heard her whisper to Isabella if she thought she was doing the right thing. The same question Josh Haymaker had asked him, 'Was he really sure he wanted this?'

'Yes,' replied Isabella. 'What have you to lose?'

'Yes,' Thomas had replied to Haymaker. What had he to lose when he had already lost Iben, indeed never really possessed her.

Ayla attempted to relieve the monotony of waiting for Iben with tea and Cornish hevva cakes in the great hall.

Mary Thoresby never took her eyes off Thomas as she sunk her teeth into the light spongy cake.

'There is a real tradition to hevva cakes,' explained Thomas.

'Really,' said Mary.

'Yes, see that criss-cross pattern, it is a reference to fishing nets. Pilchard fishermen employed clifftop lookouts known as *huers* to watch for shoals near the coast. If they spotted one they cried *hevva*, sending the men to their boats – *hevva* meaning there is a shoal here. The cry also alerted the fishermen's wives to start baking the *hevva* cakes.'

'Interesting history,' said Mary.

'Delicious,' said Isabella, tucking into her piece.

Meanwhile Ulli did not seem so interested in talking or eating but quietly sipped at her tea, her hands shaking.

'How do they make them?' asked Mary.

Thomas called the young girl back. 'Ayla, be good enough to explain to Lady Mary how Cook made these cakes.'

'They are simple and frugal, cooked with no eggs or spices just with flour, fat, sugar and currants.'

'An unleavened recipe then,' said Mary. Ayla nodded, curtsied and left.

'However it is made, can I have another piece?' asked Isabella.

'Bella, you will never get into your wedding dress.'

'You are to be married?' Thomas' eyebrows raised in surprise.

'No, mother jests. I haven't found a suitable husband yet.'

'I cannot decide whether it is a cake or shortbread,' announced Mary. 'May I take another piece too?'

Thomas looked out of the window. Fearing this constrained talk of cookery and dresses was beginning to pall, it was with some relief that he saw Iben walking up the drive with all her usual flowing freedom, only as she neared the door was there a momentary hesitancy in her long stride.

He rang his hand bell for one of the servants to let Iben in. Ulli turned white.

Sometimes there is love at first sight, sometimes there is immediate dislike in a friendship that could flower later or not. Thomas could see Mary regarding Iben with the latter as soon as she stepped into the room. Nevertheless, he went ahead with the introductions. Iben's gaze was only focused one way. She had no interest in anything or anyone else other than her daughter.

'Why?' asked Ulli straightaway.

'Because I had no choice,' replied Iben. 'You were stolen from me. Our future together was stolen from us.'

'But it is not. We have found each other,' said Ulli, reaching for her mother's hand.

The tears began to flow from both women. Thomas finally saw it clearly now. Either intentionally or by accident, Ulli was the only serious investment Iben had ever made towards her tomorrow. She had never received the love and support that she craved from her own mother. His brother had let her down. Even her own brother, and possibly her father, had taken advantage of her. From that time on she viewed the rest of her relationships as impossible. They were to her just dalliances, vicarious pleasure – living in the now. He saw there was no place for him in the two women's embrace. They were like two halves walking the earth and now they had come together.

How could Iben trust or love anyone who was not directly part of her blood after being deceived from childhood? Regrettably, Thomas realised his love was never truly reciprocated by Iben – not enough anyway – but then maybe love was never part of her nature. She loved herself so much that only her bloodline stood a chance. She just was never there for him. With him, as with other lovers, her pattern of behaviour was idolisation, devaluation and finally rejection.

'Shall we leave these two ladies together for a little while and retreat to the parlour?' he suggested.

Mary Thoresby, who was still fixed on Thomas throughout most of Iben's and Ulli's reunion, nodded to him enthusiastically.

Thomas realised he had restored Iben's linchpin and he was happy about that. His father always told him that if some things went unanswered, and were a mystery, always look to the next chapter – family and Ulli were Iben's next chapter and there was nothing he could do about that.

But what waited on the next page for him, let alone the next chapter? There was one thing he was sure of, it wouldn't be Mary Thoresby with the nodding feathers and light conversation.

* * *

'Are you happy now?' asked Josh Haymaker, limping across to him over Beechfield yard. He carried two frothing milk pails on a yoke over his broad shoulders.

'Your leg.'

'My foot,' corrected Haymaker.

'How did that happen?'

'Some wench objected to me kissing her and stamped on it,' admitted Haymaker sheepishly.

'Good for her.'

'It was just a little kiss. I think she's broken my big toe. That's women for you. Heard about Iben getting back with Ulli,' said Haymaker. Thomas smiled unwilling to give too much away. 'Have you ever wondered why Iben was only with child the once, that one time with Ulli, after all the fellas she has been with?'

'I supposed she used some sort of protection.'

'No, she never really liked protection.'

'You sound as if you knew her well.' There it was again – the hint of jealousy seeping out, a jealousy that burned deep within, a jealousy that Thomas could never leave behind.

'I can tell you this, Thomas, she would never have been able to give you an heir.'

'How so?'

'I slipped up once or twice.'

'And?'

'And nothing. She didn't seem able. I wouldn't have minded having a bairn with her. She always blamed it on the fever she had soon after Ulli's birth. That's what first sparked her interest in herbs and suchlike.'

Female infertility was a subject Thomas had little knowledge of along with most of his military colleagues. He had read books on it of course. An early work, in the previous century, by the Italian Vesalius immediately came to mind. His assistant anatomist, Gabriele Falloppio, provided a detailed description of the fallopian tubes. Vesalius thought their anatomy resembled trumpets, tubes in Italian, which was misunderstood and became the English tube. Thomas wondered vaguely if it was Iben's tubes that might have become blocked by infection, or indeed the womb itself. At this point in time there was no knowing for certain.

'Anyway, are you truly over your obsession with her now?' asked Haymaker.

Thomas nodded. 'I am to be married.'

* * *

The beginning of another year, rent day, Thomas' least pleasing day. His bailiff stood at his side noting who didn't attend. Josh Haymaker had been at Beechfield Farm less than a year, so he wasn't expected. Rather grudgingly William Wood turned up but then he had to, Thomas had too much information on him. With Lucan Beadall dead and Jowan Carter transported to the Americas, Thomas' tenants had dwindled to half a dozen. And a sorry line it was after war and pestilence had taken their toll. Taking pity, Thomas agreed to take part payment for half a year rather than a full payment that nobody could or would be able to fulfil.

At the end of the line stood Henry Winter, apprehensively wiping aside his forelock.

'Henry,' respectfully acknowledged the bailiff as Winter took out his purse. Winter had never any problem meeting his yearly obligation, not in Thomas' time anyway.

'How goes it, Henry?' asked Thomas.

'Times are tough but manageable,' said Winter, not wanting to appear boastful in front of his less fortunate neighbours.

Perhaps less fortunate or is it less industrious, wondered Thomas. It was then that the idea struck him.

'Henry, are you free tomorrow as I have something I'd like your opinion on?'

The next morning Henry Winter stood before Rockfoot New Farm open-mouthed. Spear remained on the periphery looking like a proud grandfather about to have his beautiful grandchild appraised.

'Now tell me honestly, do you like it, Henry?' Thomas asked him.

'Do I like it! It's magnificent.'

'There's the dairy, the bank barn and even a brew house should one wish to use it. See there at the bottom of the vegetable plot is a dovecote.'

'A long and traditional Cornish farm but with all the latest amenities,' muttered Winter more to himself.

'Built in the finest stone,' emphasised Thomas. 'No Atlantic winds will breach those walls.'

'It is out of this world,' said Winter.

Spear spoke for the first time judging things were going well. 'Would you like to see inside? The building's frame is of sweet chestnut, the beams of oak.'

'How many bedchambers?' asked Winter, blinking at the roaring fire in the inglenook fireplace.

'Three chambers upstairs,' Spear told him. 'Would you like to see them?'

Winter nodded enthusiastically but there was a hint of sadness there too, sadness at this all being well beyond his means. Looking out of an upper floor mullioned window across meadows towards the sea, he could not help fantasising how his wife, Nancy, and their two boys would react to Rockfoot New Farm. There was even a fireplace in the main bedchamber.

'The meadows are waiting to be grazed,' was all he could think of saying. Overwhelmed, the words had dried up.

'Do you think you could run this farm, Winter, with the help of your wife and two lads?' asked Thomas.

CHAPTER TWENTY-ONE

Yet another year passed before bells rang out. Spring flowers adorned every corner of Thomas' small village church. Their sweet scent nullifying the mustiness of age. Though not as grand as Altarnun church it was a plain and homely building. And, thank goodness, after the attempted drowning of Hetty Chenoweth the Reverend Angrove was no more. Perhaps he had been excommunicated or called to some obscure parish by the bishop for his own safety – the church had a habit of moving unpopular priests around – whatever, Angrove was gone, replaced by the popular portly Reverend Curnow.

Thomas looked back down the nave to see a forest of white ostrich feathers – obviously a favourite with the Thoresbys – waving like exotic grasses above the pews.

Ayla beamed at him next to her husband Stephen. Constable Fox likewise. Albert Spear was there. Disappointingly Josh Haymaker was not there. He had declined to come. A position Thomas fully accepted.

'Dearly beloved we are gathered here in the sight of God, and in the face of this congregation, to join together this man and this woman …' began Curnow melodiously from the new, eight year old version of the Book of Common Prayer.

'Never thought I would see this day,' murmured Seymour Glover into Thomas' ear. 'You a confirmed bachelor.'

Glover stood on Thomas' right, his betrothed on his left, her nervous uncle hovered somewhere in the background.

'Who giveth this woman to be married to this man?' asked Curnow. The uncle stepped forward and gave Isabella Thoresby's hand to the priest who in turn gave it to Thomas.

Like a country bride Isabella's hair was dressed with wildflowers, myrtle and miniature sheaves of wheat. In hands perfectly still, she held a bouquet again of myrtle and orange blossom. Her garments adorned with jewels, gold and silver thread. She looked magnificent.

Once the promises, prayers and obligations of marriage were out of the way, Thomas gently placed a gold ring on his bride's fourth finger. 'With this ring I thee wed, with my body I thee worship, and with all my worldly goods I thee endow.'

Isabella's uncle nodded satisfaction as Thomas placed a purse of two hundred guineas on Curnow's prayer book. Isabella, in contrast, looked down on the symbol of her and Thomas' love and affection – the gold ring – depicting a love flowing in a circle and continuing forever.

Soon the solemnisation was over and Thomas and Isabella walked back down the aisle as man and wife.

Mary Thoresby, who had been seated in a front pew stood as they passed. She nodded bravely, her smile tight, her eyes were full of give away regret.

Iben with Ulli were in the pew behind Mary. Iben glanced up and caught Thomas' eye.

'Marriage was never for me,' she whispered to Ulli. 'It is all too like passing the parcel.'

'I feel the same,' agreed Ulli. 'I hope Isabella wasn't too offended when I declined to be a bridesmaid. There is too much history there between you, me and Thomas' family.'

'I am sure she will have understood.' There – a note of remorse in Iben's voice – a note hardly ever heard before. She should never have led a sincere person like Thomas on. She should never have punished him for his brother's actions, for all the abuse she had suffered at the hands of other men.

Though Thomas had wanted a private ceremony with only his close friends and Isabella's family, the High Street was packed with well wishers as the wedding party walked back to Rockfoot Hall.

Wheat, for fertility, was thrown in handfuls by the villagers on Isabella's head as she gaily laughed back.

Out of the bystanders a plump figure suddenly wobbled into Thomas' path.

'This is the first opportunity I have had to thank you for saving my life, sir. You are a good man, a just man, the best of his kind,' said Hetty Chenoweth. Those neighbours about her applauded their agreement.

'She's right,' said Isabella, possessively pressing harder into his side. 'You are a good man.'

Ulli, arm in arm with Iben, overheard. 'They are right, Thomas Huck is indeed a fine man. Why, he helped me to find you,' she whispered in her mother's ear.

Yes, he did, accepted Iben sadly to herself. 'Just be thankful that something went well for once,' she told her daughter.

A COMMEMORATION OF THE PRINCIPALS
WHO INHABITED THESE PAGES

One day Iben's personality type would be given a name, Thomas was sure of it. Then again perhaps there was no name or cause for Iben's behaviour – nurture or nature – Iben was Iben. With Arthur Watson she successfully ran her late father's tombstone business until Ulli eventually took over. The tombstone maker's daughter lived for her family – her family of two – Ulli and Walter. None of them ever married. With Thomas' marriage to the fecund Isabella, Iben gave up all thoughts that Ulli would ever inherit anything from the Rockfoot Estate. In the end we all make decisions that we have to live with, Iben had made hers.

Ayla and Stephen Moore lived in a cottage in the grounds of Rockfoot Hall. They had many children. Though devoted to Isabella and Thomas up in the big house, they always preferred to spend Christmas with their children in the cottage. With Cromwell and the Puritans no longer in power and their ban on all Christmas festivities a distant memory, Ayla and Stephen would throw themselves into the mid-winter celebration with gusto. The Moores always had one regular guest though. Cook would arrive at their door on Christmas Day flushed from the walk and with a beaming smile, carrying in her basket a goose and plenty of mince pies. With six small excited children clinging to her skirts all the while, she did her best to produce a feast suitable for King Charles himself.

Josh Haymaker proved to be a fine yeoman farmer in his own right. He shared the hundred pound reward with Albert Spear for information given to Constable Fox regarding the sheep stealing and murder, and eventually bought the land surrounding Beechfield Farm off the estate. He never married.

Agnes Hartmann outlived her rival Ann Collette by a few days. Although she would never admit it, Agnes was extremely jealous of the esteem her daughter held Ann in. Agnes died happy in the knowledge of her victory of longevity over Ann.

Hetty Chenoweth did not suffer any ill effects after her near drowning. However one night she went missing, simply disappeared into the darkness. It was believed that witch hunters must have come and spirited her away. Poor Hetty was never seen again.

Albert Spear's business prospered after building Rockfoot New Farm. For years to come folk arrived from far and wide to view this pioneering concept, occasionally to the annoyance of Henry Winter and family. But, hey, they couldn't complain. Albert passed his thriving building business onto his son.

As for Seymour Glover, there would be no more visiting the whorehouses for him: against all expectations, his wife Matilda gave him a son and heir despite her maturity.

In her final years Thomas' London landlady, Damaris Page, became close to her sister Margaret to whom she left money in her will. On 9th October 1669, during incarceration in the Marshalsea prison, Damaris fell sick and died. She was buried the following day at St George the Martyr, Southwark. Though deserted by the great and the good, she had amassed a considerable fortune by the time of her death.

For many years nothing was heard of Jowan Carter and Robert Shaw transported to the Americas. Then word began to seep out that they had gained their freedom, eventually setting up a small tobacco farm together in Virginia. Good grade tobacco became popular in England and Europe and their farm and wealth grew and grew with each crop.

Constable Garren Fox became a good friend of Isabella and Thomas. Sadly he died of apoplexy five years after the Launceston trial.

And then there were the Hucks themselves... Isabella's mother, Mary, her sister Joan and Joan's children regularly visited Rockfoot Hall. They watched out for their kin like protective shepherds over the flock, wanting no repetition of a circling wolf in man form. Fear not, Thomas reassured them that he was no Gerrard Thoresby. Thomas was never quite sure that they were really convinced but they laughed anyway. He never had the pleasure of meeting Joan's husband, his absent brother-in-law, who seemed to be perpetually away at sea. His love for Isabella was uncomplicated and trouble-free, she was an easy person. Whereas his feelings for Iben remained strong if troubled, their love would have been beautiful if only Iben would have allowed it. They had shared the best of times and the worst of times – passion and misunderstandings; civil war, survival, plague and deaths. Alas, it was always the misunderstandings that came to the fore between them. Yet he would never forget the love he had for Iben, while acknowledging it had been misplaced. She was for him sand, sky and wild sea. In the spring of 1671, a new chapter began for Rockfoot Hall, Isabella gave birth to a son and heir, William. Mary, in the role of sole grandmother, soon got over her disappointment at not being the chosen bride.

Years later Thomas learned something incredible about Iben's favourite artist Artemisia Gentileschi who painted *Mary*

Magdalene as Melancholy. In 1611 her father, Orazio, had been hired to decorate the Palazzo Pallavicini-Rospigliosi in Rome, alongside another painter, Agostino Tassi. Hoping to help the 17-year-old Artemisia to refine her painting technique, Orazio hired Tassi to tutor her. This gave Tassi a one-to-one access to Artemisia and during one of their tutoring sessions, he raped her. She later described the ordeal, 'He threw me on to the edge of the bed, pushing me with a hand on my breast, and he put a knee between my thighs to prevent me from closing them. Lifting my clothes, he placed a hand with a handkerchief on my mouth to keep me from screaming.' After the rape, Artemisia started a relationship with Tassi, believing that they were going to be married, but Tassi, later, refused to wed her. Regarding this as a family dishonour, her father took the unusual decision to press charges against him for rape and the subsequent trial went on for seven months. This hinged on the fact that Artemisia had been a virgin before Tassi had raped her. The trial revealed various other scandalous details, including accusations that Tassi had murdered his wife. As part of the court proceedings, Artemisia had to undergo a gynaecological examination to prove her claim that she had been a virgin, and she was tortured with thumbscrews in order to test the truthfulness of her testimony. For an artist, this form of torture could have been devastating, but Artemisia fortunately avoided permanent damage to her fingers. Her impassioned testimony, where she claims she might have killed Tassi after the rape, gives an indication about her character and her determination. After a seven month trial, Tassi was imprisoned for two years. His verdict was later annulled and he was pardoned by the Grand Duke of Tuscany.

A story to haunt Thomas to the end of his days. Had Iben experienced a similar assault and injustice in her youth? Haymaker alleged that Thomas' own brother, Robert, raped her and then refused to marry her. So many questions remained unanswered. But this went someway to explaining her identifying so strongly with Gentileschi's art, this would explain Iben's difficulty in trusting relationships ever again particularly with the Huck family.

OTHER TITLES BY THE SAME AUTHOR

ARAM

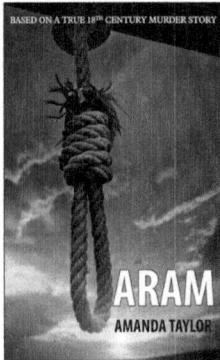

ARAM is a true story of class and religious bigotry, incest and murder. The story unfolds through the investigative eyes of Felix Kendle.

R v Houseman, Aram and Terry was the sensational cause célèbre of eighteenth century England. After his co-defendants had turned King's evidence, Eugene – a brilliant linguistic scholar – conducted his own defence, attacking the doctrine of circumstantial evidence and so making legal history. The nineteenth century saw Thomas Hood's poem, The Dream of Eugene Aram, in print and Lord Lytton produced an imaginative work based on the same subject. In the early twentieth century, Aram was the subject of three melodramatic silent films.

What exactly did happen when a young shoemaker, and a historically ignored travelling Jewish servant-boy, simply vanished on that snowy night back in 1745? With the help of extensive research and a lot of luck, the writer has done her best to solve a cracking mystery that has intrigued generations.

Brilliant book, fantastic read.

A readers review

This award-nominated Dales author hopes not only to entertain but solve a real-life murder mystery from the 18th century.

Graham Chalmers,
Weekend Editor of the Harrogate Advertiser

THE FALCON WITH A VIRGIN'S FACE

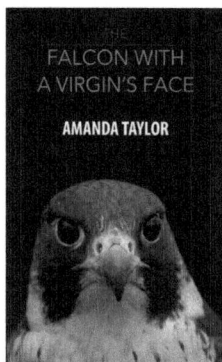

Fifteenth century England is in turmoil with the noble houses of York and Lancaster vying for the throne. Following one of the bloodiest battles in history, an oxcart travels east from Skipton Castle. It carries a farmer, his wife and a seven year old boy. The boy is Henry, Lord Clifford, son of the man who has recently slain the new king's favourite younger brother. Henry is fleeing for his life and will be pursued for the next twenty-four years by Edward IV and Richard III. This is the stuff of legend.

I read this book in just two days; it is impossible to put down, especially for someone so familiar with the places central to the story - Barden Tower, Bolton Priory and Skipton Castle. This is a fascinating imagining of a very turbulent time in our history and I finished the story wanting more.

The Duke of Devonshire

ABSURD PETUNIAS

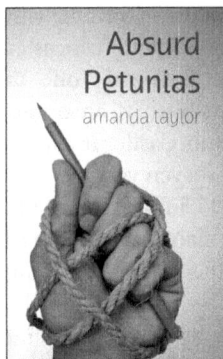

This is a love story, a spy story and a story of resolution. It is appropriate that this novel opens with a quote from Anna Politkovskaya, a Russian who died in pursuit of press freedom.

Fastidious old Etonian and newspaper office Lothario, Erik Jordan, is less than happy having a gauche Lancastrian, Celia Grey, foisted on him as a travelling companion. Sent to the Greek island of Paxos to investigate the blowing up of a London based Russian oligarch's luxury yacht, slowly Erik comes to realise there is a lot more to his 'Bridget Jones' companion.

The two become entangled in the complex risky world of Balkan and Middle Eastern politics and espionage. Far from leaving any personal threat behind in Greece, it follows them back to England. Unlike the Duke of Wellington's retort of 'publish and be damned', for Jordan and Grey it becomes a question of 'publish and possibly die'.

www.amandataylorauthor.com